Extinction Protocol

Arlo Quinn

Chapter 1.

Arizona desert.

Hunter opens his eyes. His focus clears. He gazes up at the clear sky. The baking Arizona sun is high, the air stagnant. The previous night's events were hazy, but Hunter knew who was responsible for dumping him in the desert.

"God damn it, not again," he yells at the desert sky. He sits up and takes off his cowboy boots and pours the sand from them. He takes a well-worn handkerchief from his pocket, he polishes his boots. They are his pride and joy, tailor-made by one of the finest boot makers down in Texas. Hunter designed the image himself on the blood-red leather. No-one else on earth had the same boots, and they stood out among the cowboy boot-wearing folk of the Southern states.

Hunter gathers himself together, scrambling to his feet. His head is groggy and his mouth dry. He looks around, he can see sand and rocks for miles. He can make out the outline of the town wavering in the rising heat from the sand. That is where he needs to head. His cell phone rings. He pats himself down to find the phone, finding it in his pants back pocket.

"Hello?"

"So, Hunter, you're still alive."

"You, you shape-shifting son of a bitch!" Hunter yells. "When I catch up with you, I'm gonna tear you a new one. Where is she, you bastard?"

"Calm down Hunter, save your energy, you have a long walk ahead of you! When you are calmer, I will contact you again. We have much to discuss. It is of the most importance. Please believe me. I am here to help. You have nothing to fear from me."

The caller hangs up. Hunter is furious. He storms off into the desert, heading for a town in the far distance, mumbling and swearing to himself. He calls his pal Brennan, to pick him up on the Highway to the south and take him back to town. Hunter is on a mission. Find his truck, get some lunch, find the culprit, interrogate him, maybe even kill him!

Brennan pulls onto the side of the highway, followed by a cloud of dust. Hunter looks down at his now dusty boots.

"Really?" he says, still looking at his boots.

"Get in," demands Brennan. "Let's get you something to eat and drink, you look like crap."

"Thanks, man, that's what I need to hear, you're a good friend," replies Hunter. The pair drive towards the town in Brennan's sedan.

"So, what happened to you, dude?" asks Brennan.

"That son of a bitch Jaii, again. Every time I get close to catching him, I wake up in the damn desert. I've got no idea how. I just end up in the dirt."

"I got some intel from a colleague that might be useful," explains Brennan. "Do you remember Riley Walton, he was there when you worked in data analysis, runs the records department now, nervous little guy, weird accent, British, I think?"

"Sure, I remember him. What intel?"

"Well, strictly in confidence, off the record…"

"Sure, no problem, who am I going to tell?"

"Well," Brennan continues, "There was an incident up at Flagstaff airbase last night. All hush-hush, of course. The military is denying everything, as you would expect. It seems the air traffic tower picked up some unidentified air movement. USAF scrambled a couple of F-35 fighters to intercept. Seems they couldn't even keep speed with the damn thing. Then the craft, whatever it was, buzzed the tower. It literally flew right up to it, hovered above it for a minute, then took off at a speed so fast it was gone in the blink of an eye. The guys in the control tower hit the floor when it shot towards them. They were shitting it, man. Unbelievable."

Hunter stares out the window as they drive along the dusty highway, processing the information, analyzing it in his head. What was it searching for, or rather who was it searching for? Why let itself be seen? These crafts can probably move around unseen. And why now? Brennan was still talking in the background.

"And another thing. According to Walton, they picked up a signal at the same time, a series of binary digits, transmitted over our radio signal."

"Hang on," Hunter interrupts. "They got a signal transmission? Has this ever happened before?"

"Not that I know of," replies Brennan.

"This is huge dude," Hunter says. "Seeing craft is one thing, but tapping into a signal. This is unheard of. Are they communicating with us? I know that shape-shifting bastard Jaii is one of them, I just can't get the proof."

"Are you still convinced he's responsible for Laura's disappearance?" asks Brennan.

"I'm sure of it. I saw him standing over me when I came to, laying on the highway after the crash. I wasn't fully aware of what was happening, but I saw him take her and carry her off. I passed out and woke up in a hospital bed, staring at your ugly mug."

"You were pretty beat up, Hunter. The doctors didn't think you would survive."

"Nor did he, that's why he left me there, to die. He caused the crash, I chased the lights for several miles, then something shot across the front of us and the truck rolled. Well, you know the rest. I've been chasing him ever since, I'm getting closer, it's just a matter of time. I need to get up to Flagstaff today, do some sniffing around."

They approach a sign saying Rock Springs Cafe and Bar. The pair stop to pick up Hunters pickup truck from the diner just off the freeway. This is the last place he remembered being, following a lead, before he found himself lying face up in the desert. Over lunch at the diner, they discuss the next step.

"Can you find out any more info at the base?" Hunter asks Brennan under his breath. "I need you to find out who is working on the signal they received, see if you can get hold of the data. I might be able to decrypt it. Hell, that was my job at the agency for years."

"I don't want to lose my job, Hunter. I've told you about the incident in confidence, against every ethical code I have ever signed. I told you because I want to help you find your daughter. I can't risk being hung out to dry by the agency like you were."

"I wouldn't ask if it wasn't important. I don't want you to risk your job, just do a little digging around, see if you can get even the slightest look at the data. Anything that will give me a clue to looking in the right places," pleads Hunter.

"I'll see what I can do, but I can't promise anything. What's your plan for today?"

"I'm gonna take a ride up to Flagstaff and talk to the locals, try to scope out what went on last night."

"Take it easy, man, I'll call you if I get any info at the base." Brennan leaves and Hunter sits in the diner booth, staring out the window. He watches Brennan drive away in a dust cloud.

Hunter is thinking about how he came to know Brennan. They started at the agency together, working in several departments. Although they were both data analysts, Brennan specialized in long-range weapons deployment and Hunter worked in code analysis and signals. He was responsible for code-cracking and listening to signals sent through satellites, to monitor the enemy, whoever they might be. He also wrote computing code for the military, training others how to program remote artillery stations. When Hunter reported unusual activity in the skies over US nuclear facilities, they shut him down and told him to stop tracking. This made him suspicious, so he carried on. He wanted to figure out what was going on. There were reports of increased UFO activity over crop farms, nuclear silos, water reservoirs, Texas oil fields and gas platforms in the Gulf. There was a pattern like they were observing human resources, planning something big on the horizon. Before he knew it, they reduced his security clearance. He was told to keep his mouth shut or they would shut it for him. The agency didn't mess around and they would carry out any threat they made if they had to. He still got contract work with the government, but on a much lower security clearance. But he had to find his daughter. He needed to know the truth. He had to keep digging.

The diner is quiet, only a few customers. A man sat at the counter on a stool with his back to Hunter, occasionally talking to the waitress. A young couple in a booth two booths along from Hunter. They looked like newlyweds, holding hands, looking at each other with interest when the other spoke, oblivious to the rest of the diner. Hunter could see the head of the cook through the serving hatch. A man around sixty, overweight, looked sweaty. The waitress served the counter and the booths. Hunter thinks she must have worked there for a long time. She wasn't fazed by anything, taking it all in her stride, smiling and serving. A not unattractive middle-aged woman, long blonde hair tied back in a ponytail, she looked like she might have had big dreams of a career, but circumstances prevented it and she had settled for her lot in life. She approached Hunter.

"Another refill, honey?" she asked him. She stood over him with the coffeepot.

"Sure, thank you." Hunter looked at her hand as she poured. The hands of a woman who spends her time cleaning. Her hand was clean, not manicured, but well maintained. Fingernails short, pink nail polish, some bits chipped.

"Do you remember me being in here last night?" he asked her.

"Sure, sweety, you were over at the bar around the corner there," she nods in the direction of the end of the diner counter, where the room turns around to the left.

"Was I alone?"

"No, I'm sure you were with another guy, tall chap, looked foreign, can't say I paid much attention. My shift ended around ten. Think you were still here. Too much to drink, was it," she enquires with a knowing smile.

"Yeah, something like that," Hunter lies. The waitress leaves the booth to serve another customer with coffee. Hunter notices her legs. He thought she might have been a dancer once. Maybe she had danced down in Vegas, but now works twelve hours a day here, in a dust bowl diner in the desert. Hunter is looking out the window when a large black sedan with blacked-out windows turns into the parking lot. He watches as the automobile drives slowly past his truck. It stops just beyond it, sitting motionless with the engine running. He can't see anyone inside. The license plate is blacked out. He watches it for a few minutes, then the vehicle slowly drives out of the parking lot and turns right onto the southbound freeway. He thinks no more about it. He finishes his coffee, leaves a generous tip. He walks out into the hot afternoon sun. His truck is sitting almost alone in the sparse parking lot. He climbs in, starts it up with a plumb of gas fumes and sets off onto the freeway heading Northeast.

Chapter 2.

Ranger's station,
Navajo reservation, Arizona.
Jo is sitting at her desk, looking at the untidy pile of papers and used coffee cups scattered around on top of it. She was always meaning to get on top of the paperwork, sort it out, file it or at the very least, put it in a drawer. The desk across the office is her colleagues. Jeff keeps his desk immaculate, everything in its place, neat and tidy. She hates Jeff. The door swings open and three old men step inside. They are the elders of the reservation, the high council. They are tribal chiefs, and they are looking for Jo.

"Gentlemen, good morning," she says as she stands up and walks around her desk to meet them.

"What can I do for you today?" Jo asks. One of the elders speaks. He looks like the elder of the group, weathered face like leather, a slight hunch on his back, still tall for his age, but has probably shrunk two inches with age. His voice quivers in his throat, sounding like sandpaper.

"We have been informed by one of the young men who tends to his cattle up near the mountains, that he has seen lights in the sky at night over the mountains, coming and going at great speed. He believes the visitors are based at the foot of Great Mountain."

"Ok, I will go and have a look around. Did he see any vehicles coming and going on the reservation roads? It could be prospectors or tourists who haven't registered their presence." Jo takes a small notebook from her hip pocket and searches the desk for a pencil. She makes notes in the book.

"I don't think prospectors or tourists would have the ability or means to fly in or out," replies one of the elders.

"Perhaps it's a military training operation, but they haven't informed the Rangers," Jo replies.

"Nor us," the third elder speaks. "We have granted no permission for military to be on our land. The mountains are sacred, they are the heart of our land, they are also the resting place of our ancestors. They must not be disturbed."

"Leave it with me, gentlemen. I will let you know if I find anything of interest," Jo says, reassuring the men of her concern. They file out of the office, leaving Jo alone in the Rangers station. She goes to the wall and looks at a map of the reservation. The mountain range sits to the far end of the reservation, to the northeast. She knows the land well, having worked there many times. It is remote, accessible on foot, or by horse, but she can only go as far as the ranger's outpost by truck. The outpost is a small overnight cabin for Rangers to bed down when working up in the region. She puts some items in a backpack, torch, coffee, dehydrated food packs, water, a compass, a satellite phone, a GPS tracker and a book. If she has to spend the night there, she might as well have a good book to read. Jo slings the backpack over her shoulder, grabs a set of keys off the wall hooks and writes in a journal on the desk which vehicle she is taking, the time and where she is going. This was procedure. Just in case someone doesn't return when out on duty, the other Rangers can track them down using the GPS tracker. She leaves the office and climbs into a red pickup truck and leaves a small cloud of red dust as she heads off northeast towards Great Mountain.

#

Jaii ends the call to Hunter. He walks along the line of fighter craft the Anunnaki pilots were preparing. They stretch far into the mountain tunnel they had constructed, cut with lasers to create a huge cavern filled with fighter craft, supply vessels, maintenance ships, offices and living quarters for the crew. The

Anunnaki had been on Earth for many years and had visited for thousands of years, secretly providing guidance and technology for humans to evolve further and develop into a strong, peaceful race. This hadn't always worked, and with human nature as it was, they used much of the help for warfare and greed. Perhaps that warfare would come in useful now, Jaii thought.

They had encountered the Nezulli fleet before, with a huge number of casualties. The Anunnaki were no match for the Nezulli, in either numbers or technology. Jaii's pilots are dedicated and skilled and they would follow his leadership to the death, of that he was sure. They each lost some or all of their loved ones when the Nezulli destroyed their planet. Some were from other planets, who succumbed to the same fate and who joined the Anunnaki to fight against the Nezulli, to help save others. They were all good beings and loyal. Getting help from Hunter would weigh up the odds better for the Anunnaki, give them a fighting chance. But Hunter was a stubborn man. Jaii had tried many times to make contact, to gain his trust, but without success. Hunter had the skills and knowledge he needed to counteract the Nezulli. Jaii needed to take a new approach, come at Hunter from a different angle. Jaii would have to enlist the help of another human, even if they were not aware they were helping. He had set up base on the Indian reservation, knowing they were a spiritual people. If they noticed their presence, they would accept it as a spiritual happening, as something from the spirit world. This would give Jaii and his team some protection from outsiders. The Navajo would protect their land and any visitor on it, whether from Earth or beyond. Jaii would use them to draw Hunter in, as Hunter was part Navajo. These were his people. They could communicate with him, steer him, guide him in the right direction. Hunter would respect the elders on the reservation. He would do as they asked, Jaii hoped. He formulated a plan.

#

Jo asks to meet with the elders on her return from Great

Mountain. It had been two days and arrives back late afternoon. The elders meet her in the community center where they spend most of their days discussing politics, young people, the diluting of their culture, and socializing with each other. The three men are seated on old sofas in the main community hall. Jo is tired and still dusty from her trip, but she is eager to report her findings. She walks in and waits for them to ask her to be seated. One of them indicates to sit on the sofa opposite them. Jo sits, then explains what she has found. She isn't sure how they will take it, whether they might not believe her or think she may have misunderstood her findings.

"There is a cave in Great Mountain. But this cave is new, it is man-made, well, at least it's not a natural cave, designed by nature." The cave is perfectly symmetrical and the walls are like glass. It's like no cave I have ever seen." The elders look at each other and close in tight to discuss it.

"Did you witness anything coming or going from the cave?" one elder asks.

"I saw lights from my cabin at night, far in the distance, and it looked like they were in that general area."

"Did you go into the cave?" another elder asks.

"I only stepped inside a few feet. It looks like it goes on for miles. I didn't deem it safe to enter alone, I will need someone with me for safety, if I revisit it."

"Quite right," the third elder says, "best to be safe. Did you see any markings or drawings that looked familiar?"

"No, nothing. This has not been made by our people. If it's military, they would have it fenced off with warning signs everywhere. I don't think it's military either, it's the weirdest thing I've ever seen," Jo replies. The elders have a short discussion among themselves.

"We believe this may be our ancient visitors, the Star People," explains the first elder. "If so, they have been here many times before, to warn us of danger and to help guide our people. This is something which will require someone with special skills to help you, someone with knowledge of such things. It must be someone from the nation, a Navajo."

"No outsiders are to go near the cave, you must not talk to anyone about this," the second elder says. "We will contact a man who knows of these things, he grew up on the reservation, north of here. He has worked with the government, but we think he can be trusted, I knew his father. He will help. His name is Hunter. We will bring him here."

Chapter 3.

Anunnaki Earth Base, Great Mountain
Navajo Reservation, Arizona.
Jaii inspects his fleet of aircraft, as his crew work on readying the craft for action. Jaii is from a distant planet called Quanzar B, long since destroyed by the Nezulli invaders. He and all his crew had lost their loved ones when the Nezulli struck, when Jaii and his team were out on an exploration mission. They destroyed the planet, the Anunnaki enslaved, then killed when of no more use. Jaii often thought of his partner, Shii and his children Rooq and Huyli. Shii was a wonderful mother to their children, and he remembered going on walks together, strolling among the Yaki trees, watching their planet's two suns setting in unison, casting a red light across her face. He missed her so much. Jaii had been a loving partner and his role in society had been as a scientist and doctor. They lived, like many, in a living pod in a complex attached to the science labs where he worked. This was common on Quanzar B. Most Anunnaki lived and worked in the same place. Travel created pollution, so it became a prerequisite you lived where you worked, to maintain a cleaner planet. He had dedicated his life to helping heal others and finding new cures or methods of healing beyond the physical. He had developed extrasensory healing, healing patients remotely using thought transfer and stimulation protocols.

When he returned to his planet and found the devastation, he stopped healing. Jaii felt they damaged his heart beyond hope, and he could not provide the treatment his patients required. He stopped practicing and became a fleet commander to track down and eliminate the Nezulli. He felt he had let his family down, by not continuing to heal, but his mission to destroy the Nezulli was a greater calling. Jaii was avenging his family's deaths. He didn't like to admit it, and he didn't feel good about it, but he couldn't help feeling this way. He had a selfish motive for destroying the Nezulli.

Chapter 4.

Flagstaff was a town well known to Hunter. He stayed there many times in the same small motel across from the airbase. Sales reps frequented it, on the road for work and drifters searching for a purpose. But most of its customers were airmen, on assignment to the airbase or staying a night or two, while their base accommodation was prepared. The motel has a small bar and diner next to the reception and the rooms were small, basic, cheap. A double bed, shower and toilet with well-worn furnishings. Beige colored walls with wipe-clean paint for low maintenance. Hunter books in and settles on the bed, hands behind his head, staring at the slowly revolving ceiling fan. He is thinking, who can he call to find out about the recent airbase incident? How could he get into the base without clearance? Why does the fan even bother turning, it doesn't give out any noticeable cooling air, is it to keep the flies from landing on the bulb? The motion of the fan sends him to sleep.

Hunter wakes with a jump, like he is falling. He looks towards the window; it is mid-afternoon, the bedside clock, chained to the bedside cabinet, chained to the wall, shows 15.36 pm. Hunter hasn't brushed his teeth in two days. He goes to the reception and buys supplies, toothpaste, shower gel, shaving foam, a razor. In his motel room, he sets about cleaning himself up, washing socks and underwear, polishing his beloved boots, dusting off his jeans. He watches the local news network on the television. There was no news about the UFO sighting, not from the air force, nor the public. Someone must have seen it. The base skirts the edge of town. There are residential roads close to it. But he knows it isn't beyond the reach of the military to hush people and the press with thinly veiled threats. He had experienced it himself; he knew what they were capable of. Hunter's cell phone rings.

"Hi, Hunter," he answers.

"Mr. Hunter, I am Asama, an elder of the Navajo reservation. We would very much like to talk to you about some unusual activity up here. Would you be interested in talking with us?"

"Sure, yes, I'm in the area, I can meet you later today. Let me know where." The elder gives Hunter the information and hangs up. This was the best lead he could have wished for. Someone with concrete information and willing to talk about it. Hunter is excited about the news.

The Navajo reservation is about an hour's drive from Flagstaff. Hunter thought speaking with the elders might bring some insight. As a boy and young man growing up on the reservation, the old chiefs would often tell the young about the 'Star People'. They described them as Gods from the skies who visited the Navajo many times over the centuries. They claimed they brought wisdom and knowledge. Hunter had often thought the stories were just traditional tales used to tell the kids of danger or embellished to keep traditions alive. He also suspected the stories resulted from the Navajo's frequent use of Peyote, a hallucinogenic plant. But now he was sure the stories were true. He had witnessed a visit himself in his youth. He had mocked the other kids for believing, now he believed without a doubt. These Star People were openly talked about on the reservation, but not with outsiders. They would often discuss sightings within the community, but they clammed up if questioned by outsiders, especially the government. Hunter was part Navajo, he could talk with them. He was no longer a government employee, they should open up to him if they have seen anything.

Before dusk, Hunter drives out of town, northeast towards the reservation territory. Driving into the reservation, much of it looks as it did in his youth. There is no sign of wealth here, just a few rundown homes, some abandoned homes, left to fall into disrepair. There is no oil money here, no gambling license fortunes, no mineral mining fees. The Navajo are a proud people, they prefer traditional living over fortune. They farm crops and breed horses, sheep, and cattle. There are a few who have made their way in the world beyond the reservation. Many of them pump money back into their heritage. Hunter thinks of how he had 'escaped' the limited life of traditional Navajo. He had won a scholarship to study, to get a college education. It led him to a career with the government. He didn't make much money. He wasn't able to pump money back to his people. When he joined the government, they had turned their backs on him. It was seen as working for the enemy, their repressor. Hunter's view on it was different. He felt education was the best way forward for the Navajo. Become captains of industry, leaders in politics, high ranking officials. Then change the laws to benefit your people, not sit around talking about traditions and how the white man has suppressed your culture. Do something about it, or shut up. That was Hunter's viewpoint. Now they wanted his help.

The journey through the territory is rough, the road is a dirt track, unfinished, unkempt. The buildings along the roadside are sparse, the occasional small store and gas station. Everything looks like it is caught in a time lock, unable to move forward. Hunter looks out across the desert to his left. Now he saw improvements. Cell towers are visible in the distance. He sees the remains of cable laying, workmen have dug ditches, huge rolls of fiber cables are by the roadside, waiting their turn to be laid into the long ditches. Perhaps, he thought, they were catching up with the world. Progress would be the only thing to save the Navajo. He knew it, they knew it, but traditions were strong among the elders.

The road continues, just a series of potholes held together with small patches of tarmac and dirt. After what seems an age, Hunter arrives at the community center. A small wooden building, in a semi-circle with a few other wooden buildings. There is a surgery for traditional medicine, a reservation rangers' station, manned entirely by Navajo officers. The state police had no jurisdiction here, matters are dealt with by local reservation rangers. There is a dental surgery, a new building, recently added. The schoolhouse is set back from the other buildings, larger, recently painted. The school is the hub of the community. A reservation community center is used mostly for court proceedings, but the school is the main building for events, community meetings, weddings, funerals. Hunter pulls his truck up in front of the community center. There are a few people milling around, curious to see who has driven up the eight-mile dirt track to visit them. Two kids are wheeling around on bikes, kicking up dirt, two teenage girls leaning up against the community center wall, whispering to each other, giggling. They watch this tall, slim figure climb out of his truck. He squints in the evening sun, looking for some guidance as to who he should speak to. The air is still and silent, other than the giggling teens and the dirt rumble of kids bikes. A figure appears in the community center doorway and beckons Hunter in with a hand gesture. The figure is a female, native American, a little younger than Hunter, with traditional long black Navajo hair, silky swarthy skin, dark eyes, very attractive, he thought. The figure waits patiently as Hunter walks towards the building, checking his boots, which are now dust-covered again. He glances at the young native girls by the wall, pretty, pretending to be shy, but checking the stranger out. As he passes them he speaks.

"Ladies," he greets them. They burst into a fit of giggles and hurry away in a tight whisper, arm in arm.

"Welcome," the figure greets Hunter. She moves aside to allow Hunter to enter the building. He brushes past her, looking at her as he passes. She is shorter than Hunter and she gives him a warm smile as he passes. Inside, to the left is a serving counter, with a kitchen behind it. Closed. Close by are three sofas, tan leather, well worn, almost ready for the bonfire, but still in use. They look like they will probably outlast the people sat on them, Hunter thought. The sofas are in a circle, on the hardwood floor, with markings for what looks like a basketball court. On one of the sofas, there are three old timers reservation chiefs. On the sofa to the left are two younger men, still probably in their sixties. Hunter assumes they must be part of the reservation council, who will inevitably progress to elder status. The figure that showed Hunter in is younger again. She is behind Hunter when she first speaks.

"Please take a seat." Hunter sits on the third sofa to one side, leaving space for the young woman to sit. She remains standing. There are a few seconds of silence, each waiting for the other to speak first. It was polite custom to listen and let the elders speak. But today, they seemed reluctant, waiting for Hunter to talk. Asking questions was seen as rude in young Navajo, they were taught to listen and observe. With patience, they would find the answers. It felt like Hunter was back in an old schoolhouse. Not the newer one next to the building he was in, but an old wooden shack they used years back for small group schooling. He didn't recognize anyone in the room, this was not an older group of friends meeting up. These were elders from a different part of the nation he knew little about. But he got the impression they knew more about him than he did about them. The silence seemed unending. Finally, the young woman standing, speaks.

"The elders have been told you know about the Star People?" she asked in a question.

"That's correct," Hunter replies. He does not elaborate. He leaves it hanging, testing to see if they would bite. He didn't ask a question, he simply replied. This is a sign of respect, he hopes. The old men in front of him sit silent, staring straight at him, through him, barely blinking. The game is on. One of the older men glances at the young woman standing, no words, but a signal to prompt the conversation. So, it was code. This is Hunters specialty.

Chapter 5.

Hunter sits analyzing each movement of the eye or twitch of a finger. The young woman speaks again.

"You are Isaac, the son of Atsa, of Hunters Point?" Again, it was a question disguised as a statement. She was trying, Hunter thought, but losing this game.

"I am," he replied. The elders sit stone-faced. Silent. Then one of the elders sits forward and puts his hand out, palm upwards. It is a sign for Hunter to place his hand on top. He knew this sign. They would slide hands up to grab each other's wrist. He has won their respect, shown them he remained traditional, he hasn't forsaken his culture. Hunter slides his hand across the elders and grabs his wrist, allowing the elder to grab second, another sign of respect. Hunter gives a powerful tug of the elder's arm, locked in the embrace. The chief releases first and they both sit back in the comfy old tan sofas, both relieved, both satisfied they have upheld their side of the traditions. Hunter chooses to speak first.

"The Star People. I've heard of a sighting, close to here. What can you tell me about them?" he directs at the elder who had taken his arm. It had to be a question, Hunter had no choice. The old men look at each other, leaning in together, mumbling in Dine language. After about half a minute, they sit back. The elder the question was focused towards speaks.

"For many generations, the Star People have visited our people. It is believed that we are they, and they us. They bring wisdom, truth, and knowledge to our people. They return not for gain, but to provide." Hunter sits silently for a few seconds. He wants to see if the old man will continue, elaborate further. He doesn't. The young woman standing remains silent.

"Provide what?" Hunter asks.

"The future," replies the old man. Hunter sits and thinks. He looks across at the old men, not really looking, thinking, but holding their gaze. He has many questions, but the answers are a series of riddles. They give away nothing more than they need to, protecting the Navajo and the reservation.

"If they and we are the same, do you mean we are descended from aliens?" Hunter had to ask bluntly. The elders sit quietly, staring at Hunter. No reply, just a slight knowing smile. People of the nation had spoken about Star People visiting, it was passed down in folklore for thousands of years. Hunter knew how these things worked. Often it was just a story or a dream, translated into a verbal story, told to the younger members of a tribe. Over the years the stories grew big, bolder, wilder, more ridiculous. This was human nature, expand on the truth for effect. Now he was told he and they were descended from aliens. This one was a step beyond belief. Hunter had seen the visitants himself, but he could not imagine they were his cousins. He smiles gently, nodding as he heard the information. He hopes his eyes don't give away the fact that he thought it was nonsense. He doesn't want to offend the elderly tribesmen. The middle elder gestures with his raised hand.

"This young woman is Johona, she is a Ranger on the reservation. I have asked Johona to take you deep into the mountains. She will show you something that we believe will help you understand." Hunter looks up at the young woman standing by the sofa. She smiles and walks towards the exit.

"Follow me, Hunter," she says. The meeting is over. Short and sweet. Hunter stands, gives a nod of thanks to the elderly council, and follows the young woman to the door.

Outside, the sun is low on the horizon. Hunter watches the young woman, Johona, as she walks down the path. She is slim, very attractive, wearing slim fit denim jeans, a loose blouse, white, which allows him to make out her figure when the light catches it just right. It becomes almost see-through. Her hair is in a long black ponytail, tied up with a thin red ribbon. Her footwear is practical. Tan hiking boots with low heels. Perhaps, he thinks, these are part of her Ranger outfit. She doesn't look much like a Ranger. They are often big, tough, outdoor types. Johona is petite by Ranger standards, but Hunter knows to become a reservation Ranger, she would have had to have passed a series of rigorous tests, both physical and mental, so she must be much stronger than her frame would suggest. Navajo women were strong, physically and mentally, they had to be to cope with life on a reservation. Hunter thought back to his own mother, working hard to keep the kids clean, the house clean, working in the fields to provide food for Hunter and his sister, Miri. His mother was full blood Navajo, but his father wasn't. His father was part Navajo and part Irish. Hunter's great, great grandfather had emigrated to the United States from Ireland to escape the famine. He met and fell in love with a Navajo girl. Usually, this would mean they would be expelled from the tribe, but his Irish ancestor was a skilled storyteller and a fierce fighter, which the elders liked. They accepted him as a member of the Navajo tribe, he became close to the elders and they looked on him as one of their own.

"It's Jo," she tells him, "I prefer Jo." She looks down at his footwear.

"Nice boots."

"Thanks," he replies.

"What should I call you?" she asks.

"Hunter's fine, just call me Hunter."

"We'll take my truck," Jo announces. He walks over to a red Chevy pickup, a little worse for wear, a few scratches in the paintwork, a dent in the front passengers' side wing. It has huge tires, perfect for the dirt tracks and desert, not so good on slick, tarmac freeways. Again, Hunter thinks, practical, like its driver. The pair get into the truck, the engine roars and they set off in a plumb of dust. They head Northeast. Hunter has the window down with his elbow resting on the frame.

"Where are we heading to?" Hunter asks. He looks across to Jo, she is concentrating on driving. He can see on her face she is deciding whether she should tell him or leave him in ignorance. Hunter feels she would be informative, she seems friendly. She was helping him, she had no reason not to tell him.

"There's a place way up in the mountains. Where the elders used to go to die, to pass over to the next world. That's where we are heading." She smiles at Hunter. When she smiles, her eyes smile too. He liked that. They drive for some distance, well over two hours, sitting in silence mostly. Hunter reckoned their average speed on the dirt tracks was about forty or fifty miles per hour. He guessed they must have covered some eighty or ninety miles or more. Eventually, Jo started the conversation.

"So, Hunter, what are you really doing here? You're not a journalist, or a researcher, what's the angle, why did the elders bring you here?"

Hunter sits for a while, thinking of a lie he can tell her. He has nothing. He likes Jo, not being truthful with her doesn't sit right with him. What harm can it do to tell her the truth?

"It's my daughter. I'm searching for her." The statement takes Jo by surprise.

"What happened to her," she asks. Before he can answer, she announced they are here.

"Here, where?" asks Hunter, looking around at the dark empty desert.

"This is as far as we can go in the truck," replies Jo. "There's a small cabin just up ahead." Jo pulls the truck up to the front of it.

"This is the Rangers' cabin. We use it from time to time when working up in the mountains. We'll bed down here for the night and continue on foot in the morning, at first light." Hunter is fine with this. He is tired and dusty and will be glad to have a bed for the night. They climb out of the truck, Jo grabs an overnight bag from the back and they go into the cabin. It is a small, one-room wooden shack, pitched roof made from corrugated tin sheets, rusting, a stone-built fireplace with a skillet hanging over the remains of a fire. The room has a small window on either side of the door, there is a cot bed in one corner near the fireplace and a rolled-up camp mattress in another corner. Two worn armchairs are in front of the fireplace, old, tatty, but they looked comfortable. A wooden bench acted as a kitchen, with some pots hanging up above it from butcher's hooks. No sink, no toilet, no luxuries.

"What about the bathroom? Where is it?" asks Hunter.

"There's a shack out back with a composting toilet, that's it," comes the reply. Hunter grunts. It isn't ideal, but he had been in worse places. Jo rummages for some kindling for the fire. She places some wood on it from a pile by the fireside. Using her lighter, she gets the fire started, gentling adding small wooden shards, ever-increasing the size until the fire is in full bloom and she can add logs onto it. Hunter sits in one of the chairs and watches her as she skilfully arranges the fire. The chair is as comfortable as he had assumed. He stares into the fire in silence, thoughts racing through his head. What is Jo going to show him in the mountains, where could his daughter be, will this trip lead him any closer to finding her? He is tired.

"Are you hungry, Hunter?" asks Jo. He is, but he doesn't feel like eating.

"I can heat something up, we have some canned food in the cupboard, I think."

"No, thanks, Jo, but I appreciate the offer," he replies.

"What about coffee?" she says.

"Sure, I'd love a coffee," replies Hunter. Jo sets about heating some water over the fire to make a pot of coffee for them both. Jo feels Hunter is relaxed enough to bring the subject of his daughter up again.

"You said about your daughter, back there in the truck. You said you were looking for her?" Jo's face, lit by the fire and a small lamp on the fireplace, looks deep with concern. Hunter feels she was asking out of a want or need to help him. He needs to off-load some of his feelings, but this is not something he did often, or easily. Not since long before his divorce. Here he was, with a beautiful woman, who seemed to have a genuine interest in his life. He had missed that.

"You don't have to tell me if you would prefer not to," Jo tells him, as she can see his reluctance. She is giving him an out, an escape route from emotional involvement. He hesitates for a few seconds. Jo pours coffee into tin mugs. Hunter takes a sip. It is strong, dark, hot. And it tastes great. He hadn't had a coffee since lunchtime, at the diner with Brennan. But this one tasted better, raw, edgy, just better. Hunter cups the mug with his right hand, Jo sits in the other chair, turning partway to face Hunter. She holds her mug with both hands, warming them as the night air turns chilly. The fire sparks and crackles. Jo sits patiently. She feels Hunter will tell her when he is ready, when he has it straight in his head. She doesn't push any harder.

"What about you, what's your story?" Hunter asks.

"Me, nothing really, just a girl from the reservation making her way in the world, you know," Jo tells him.

"What made you become a Ranger?"

"It was the only thing I wanted to do, from a small child. My dad was a Ranger, so I guess it was natural to follow in his footsteps," she explains.

"Sure," Hunter continues, "but it's mostly men who become Rangers. I've never known a female from any tribe who became a Ranger."

"Well now you do," Jo replies sharply, "why shouldn't a female do a man's job? They do in other lines of work, even do it better in some," she replies, sounding irritated.

"Sorry, I know, I didn't mean to sound sexist, just, I mean, it's unusual, that's all," Hunter explains.

"I've been told you were a government agent, FBI, was it?" Jo asks.

"Yeah, sort of. An agency within an agency, within an agency, kind of thing."

"It all sounds very intriguing," replies Jo.

"No, not really, mainly analyzing files, lots of paperwork and admin, that type of thing," Hunter tells her, dismissing it as unimportant.

"So, tell me Jo, what is it in the mountains you need to show me?"

"Patience, Hunter, you'll see soon enough. Let's get some shut-eye and get an early start. You're on the floor over there,"

Jo points to the bedroll on the floor. She loads the last of the woodpile into the fire.

Chapter 6.

The cabin was cold in the night. The fire had gone out at some point and Hunter could feel the damp air in his lungs. The light streamed through the windows. Hunter climbs out of his sleeping bag and curls it around his shoulders. He had remained dressed, except for his boots. He slips these on and looks across at Jo's bed. She is gone. He walks out into the morning haze, a light mist just beginning to lift as the sun slowly raises its head above the mountains. Hunter looks around for Jo. She appears from behind her pickup truck with two rucksacks.

"Got our supplies ready for the journey, you ready to go?" she asks him.

"Sure, more or less," he replies, "any coffee on the go?"

"Sorry, no. Maybe when we get up there, we can brew a pot, got some in your backpack." She throws one rucksack to Hunter. He rolls his sleeping bag and straps it on top and slings the bag over his shoulder. They set off towards the mountain range, Jo a few steps in front, taking charge of the expedition.

Now Hunter could see the landscape in the morning light, in its full splendor. The vast open desert to the north, lined along the western edge with a huge mountain range. This is where they are heading, at least three, maybe four miles in the distance. The terrain is a mix of smooth sand and rocky passages. They wind their way through crevices and gaps formed millions of years before. It doesn't look like many people had passed through this way for many years, Hunter thought. There is little sign of human activity. He watches Jo navigate the rocky outcrop with ease, experienced.

The sun is soon casting shadows as the pair continue in their pursuit. Other than brief stops for drinks from their canteens, they maintain a steady pace to the mountain range. Soon, they were looking up at the high ridges of the red mountains. Hunter follows Jo as she seeks a path she had used before. The climb becomes steeper and more strenuous. Hunter feels the pain. He is not as fit and agile as Jo, slowing his pace, struggling to keep up with her.

"Come on, Hunter, nearly there!"

"Where?" he replies, "Nearly where?"

They make it to a wide ledge some four or five hundred meters up. Hunter is exhausted, but Jo is bouncing with energy.

"Wait, wait," he says, "Let me get my breath back," as he doubles over with his hands on his thighs.

"You are so unfit, Hunter. Work out more, go to the gym, play a sport, take up jogging," Jo teases.

"I'll have you know," he replies between gasps, "I was a Navy SEAL in my younger days. Well, I did the basic training at least, maybe didn't make it into the SEALs."

"Long, long time ago, by the look of things," Jo replies with a cheeky smile. "Let's go, just around this ridge, then we are there."

They continue on for a few minutes, walking the ridge as it meanders with the contour of the mountain. As they wind around it, they face the side of another, even larger mountain.

"This is it," Jo announces, as she stands near the edge of the ridge. Hunter looks at the mountain and shrugs.

"What?" he asks.

Jo points down to the wide valley between the two mountains. Hunter steps closer to the edge to look over. He sees what she is pointing to.

"Wow," is all he can say, as he stands in amazement. In front of him, lower down the side of the second mountain, is a huge tunnel. Not just a cave mouth. He can see it is a perfectly cut circular tunnel, heading, from what he can see, deep into the mountain.

"How could someone get all the gear up here to cut that in the mountain?" he asks. "I mean, you would need some sophisticated mining gear to make that. The opening must be, what, maybe eighty to a hundred meters in diameter at least. It looks like a laser has melted the rocks," he tells her, looking at the smooth, almost glass-like finish to the tunnel.

"I know," Jo replies. She is looking at Hunter, still with his mouth-open, his eyes wide with excitement.

"It's weird, no-one has been up here with any cutting equipment, there is nothing," she tells him. "I have looked around, there is nothing, not even a dropped shovel or a broken pick axe."

"Can we get down there to have a closer look," he asks.

"Sure, follow me." She sets off down the side of the mountain, following the least gradient path, weaving her way down towards the sandy valley, with Hunter in tow. They reach the mouth of the enormous cave. Hunter reaches out to touch the cave wall.

"It's as smooth as glass," he says, "and perfectly spherical. I mean, to get a smooth finish like this, it must have been some powerful equipment." Jo and Hunter gaze at the cave, Hunter still touching the wall as he walks in.

"Let's go in," he says. "Have you been in at all?" he asks her.

"Hell no. I've been this far, not any further. Who knows what lies inside, or even how far into the ground it goes. One farmer said he spent some time near here, across the plains, over on the lower ridges. He saw lights at night, coming from this area and flying up into the night sky in an instance. In the blink of an eye, in his words. So, something strange has been happening here for some time. No one dared enter, for fear of upsetting the spirits of the dead."

Hunter smiles at Jo and walks further into the cave, still looking back at Jo, hoping she will follow.

"Come on Hunter, don't go in there. Let's go."

Hunter ignores her and pulls a flashlight from his rucksack and continues inward.

"God damn it Hunter!" Jo says exasperated by him. She takes out her flashlight and reluctantly follows him into the cave. They walk into the darkness, shining their flashlights ahead, staying close to the right-hand side of the tunnel.

"It must go on for miles, I can't see anything ahead," Hunter says. The tunnel gradient begins slight, then becomes steeper the further they go. Soon, they are walking downwards as the tunnel continues. After about twenty minutes of walking, the tunnel expands into a large cavernous space.

"You could probably get the Yankee Stadium in this space," Hunter says, looking around the huge space with its dark glass-like walls, his voice reverberating around the space. Without warning, a flash of light comes right up to them at lightning speed. The pair hit the ground as it almost hits them.

"What the hell is that?" Jo yells, as the light halts abruptly. She holds her breath with fear. She can see a gray shimmering object, glowing, pulsating light, hovering in mid-air. Hunter gets to his feet slowly. As he stands, the craft silently moves over Jo towards him. Jo watches from her position on the floor, her heart pounding is the only thing she can hear. The craft slowly circles Hunter, as if to scan him. His training in the government kicks in. He analyzes the object, making mental notes. Color – gray, shimmering lights, almost translucent, size – maybe ten meters across, shape – triangular with a domed upper, movement – high speed, maybe Mach 5 to a sudden stop, no sonic boom, silent, propulsion – unknown, no fuel smell, no displaced air draught. Hunter stands in amazement. He has seen one similar before, way back. He reaches out to touch the object. As his fingertips touch it, he sees a brief glimpse of binary code in front of him, as if a back-projected glass had appeared. On touching the craft, it shoots off down the tunnel as fast as it had appeared.

"What the hell was that?" Jo breaks the silence.

"That is the key to all of this. That is what I've been looking for, for a long time," Hunter tells her.

"Let's get out of here Hunter, I don't want to be here if that thing comes back," Jo replies.

"No, Jo. You go back if you want, but I'm going on, I'm going down the tunnel. This might be my only chance to find my daughter." Hunter turns away and walks further into the tunnel. Jo watches for a few seconds, thinking. Should she help him, should she go in with him, should she go get help? But she had brought Hunter to this place, she was responsible. She knew she had no choice. She turns and follows Hunter deeper into the tunnel.

They walk for some time. On looking back, Jo can't see the light from the entrance anymore. They are about two miles into the tunnel, under the red desert and hills above. As they continue, a small shard of light appears ahead. They cautiously make their way forward, in silence, as the light grows larger. They are getting close to something, some type of base. They don't know what lies ahead, but Hunter is determined to find out.

The pair approach the lit area of the tunnel, a vast cavern. They can see craft similar to the one that approached them, all lined up in rows.

"There must be a hundred, maybe more," Jo comments.

"This must be a military base or something like that," Hunter replies.

"Not one of ours," Jo tells him. They get closer to the area, keeping close to the tunnel wall nearest their right side. Hunter feels they are being watched. At that moment, he turns to look behind him, only to see Jaii standing behind them.

"Welcome Hunter, I knew you would get here eventually," he says.

"Jaii, you bastard," replies Hunter, swinging a miss aimed punch at the guy. Jaii just leans back, hands by his sides, allowing the blow to pass without making contact. Jo watches, not sure who the stranger is. He looks and sounds like a normal human. She is confused. Hunter composes himself.

"Jo, this is Jaii, one of the alien shape-shift scumbags I've been trying to catch up with. Don't believe anything he says or does. I knew you were one of them," Hunter tells Jaii, "you might fool everyone else, but I knew."

"Quite," replies Jaii, "but all is not what you think. Some of those you trust are not trustworthy. We, my people, as you say, are not here to harm you. We are here to aid you. We have done so for many thousands of your years. I have been trying to talk to you for some time, but each time we meet, your anger is too much, I cannot talk to you in such a state. Come, you have much to learn, my friend."

"I'm not your friend, let's get that clear," Hunter replies in anger, "and each time we meet you knock me out and leave me in the bloody desert." Jaii smiles and holds out his arm to guide them forward.

"Nice boots," Jaii says, looking down at Hunters boots as he walks past him. Hunter ignores him. They walk along the lines of craft. They see lots of human-like people dressed in gray uniforms, working, moving stuff, repairing craft. It looks like any other airbase, except for the fact that it is a couple of miles down a tunnel, Hunter thinks, as he makes mental notes on how many crew and craft he can see. Jaii beckons them to a small room off the main cavern, also cut smooth. They enter through a metal door. The lights in the tunnel are bright, daylight color temperature, Hunter notes. He has not seen or heard any generators.

"What's your power source down here?" he asks Jaii. Jaii walks to a desk and sits in a chair behind it. He motions for the pair to sit in the seats opposite. The room is gray shiny stone walls, the furniture is dark gray, metal, no books or phone or anything like a human office, just the desk, chairs and next to the wall on their left is a console with screens and various blinking lights and what looks like touchpads, no buttons. Hunter studies it for a few seconds, hoping to recognize something from his previous work, but he doesn't know what it is.

"You said you are not here to harm us, but you took my daughter, where is she?" Hunter demands.

"Your daughter is safe. She was taken for her own safety. The incident was unfortunate, but she and you were both in grave danger, we had to act fast and decide to separate her from you. I hope you will understand later when things become clearer, but please believe me, she is safe and well."

"I need to see her," Hunter replies.

"You will, but not yet. We have a lot of information for you to process and not much time," Jaii tells Hunter. Jo sits in silence, trying to comprehend what is happening. Earlier that day, she was in the mountains, going about her business, showing someone a strange tunnel, next she is in an alien lair, watching a man she has only known for less than two days, have a conversation with an alien, as if it was the most normal thing in the world. She lets out a suppressed giggle, as she thinks about it. Hunter and Jaii both stop and look at her.

"Sorry," she says, trying not to burst into laughter.

"You okay?" Hunter asks her. She just nods, suppressing more giggles. Hunter and Jaii carry on.

"My race is called the Anunnaki. We are from another universe, not unlike yours. We have been here many times, returning to observe mankind's progress. But mankind is in grave danger. Not only from yourselves and how you are treating your planet, that is questionable, but from another visitor, a dangerous race known as the Nezulli, led by a war-mongering entity called Vok. You, Hunter, were on the right path. You were following the clues. Your government knows more than you think, that is why they stopped you."

"Why should I believe anything that comes out of your fucking alien face?"

"The sooner you get over your hate for me, the sooner we can work together," Jaii tells him.

"Wait," Jo interrupts. "What do you need Hunter for? He isn't in the government anymore."

"This is so," Jaii replies, "but Hunter has skills which would benefit us in stopping the Nezulli." Hunter stands up and walks around the room behind Jo, thinking, analyzing the situation.

"Right, let's pretend, for argument's sake, that I believe your cock and bull story. You haven't told us why the Nezulli are a danger, what they want from us, when they are likely to come to Earth and what skills I have that you could need. Look around you, Jaii, you guys built this. It’s way beyond the capabilities of our technology. So, if you guys are so far advanced, why can’t you kick the Nezulli’s ass yourselves?"

"You can get access to the government files we need. Whilst we can attack your systems and retrieve the information we need, this would highlight our being here and our knowledge of an imminent attack by the Nezulli. Your government has sources within that are in collusion with the Nezulli."

"Hold up for a second," Hunter replies, “you’re telling me that the government is working with an alien race?"

"Yes, they have been for many years. Ever since the crash in the New Mexico desert. That was a Nezulli reconnaissance craft." Jaii tells him.

"God damn it," Hunter replies, "I worked on hacking the code from a computer unit from that craft. They had tried for years, I found a way in and manipulated the code, sort of, before they shut me down."

"Therefore we need you, Hunter. You can gain access to the base and help us. This pen drive has all the info you need to access." Jaii hands a pen drive to Hunter.

"I don’t get it," Jo interjects. "What exactly are these other aliens after and why would our government be working with them? It makes little sense." Jaii looks at Jo and replies.

"There are resources on this planet which the Nezulli requires to continue their journey through the multiverse. Energy is the real currency of any universe. They will mine various minerals to create their power source. This is not the first planet they will destroy, they have done so before and will do so again."

"But what’s in it for our government, what do they get out of it," Jo asks.

"Your government has a rogue element within its structure. They want the Nezulli to wipe out certain third world and progressive countries, to enable your government to establish world dominance. In return, they will provide the Nezulli with the resources they need to move on. But the Nezulli cannot be trusted. They will not leave until they have created total destruction of the human race."

"But surely the government must see that?" Hunter adds, "They must know that if the Nezulli has the power to create such destruction, they don't need the US government, they could just wipe us out and take what they want."

"This is the case. But why do the work yourself, when you can enslave humans to do the work for you, speed up the process, then wipe them out?" Jaii tells them.

"So, let me get this straight in my head," Hunter repeats, "the Nezulli work with our government to get access to the resources. In return, they wipe out their enemies. But then they turn on the government, enslave the healthy as miners, extract all our resources, kill everyone left alive, then just fuck off into the cosmos?"

"That's not quite how I would put it, but yes, that's the plan as we believe it to be. It is what they have done before," Jaii explains.

"Wow," Jo pipes up, "this is some crazy science fiction shit."

"Quite," replies Jaii. Hunter sits down again, thinking about the conversation.

"You said it is the plan how you believe it to be," Hunter asks Jaii, "how do you know, how sure are you?"

"I know this to be the case. This is how they destroyed my planet. We were advanced in our technology, so some of us survived, we could move across galaxies to save ourselves, but almost all of our race met an end like the one your people will endure. Attempts have been made to destroy your human race before, by the Nezulli."

"We would have known if aliens had attacked us," Hunter replies.

"Not so. They used viruses, some airborne, some in your water supply, some in your agricultural produce. Are you familiar with a plague that wiped out many in your Roman Empire, around 541AD? Over thirty million humans died. This was the work of the Nezulli. There was the Black Death in around 1346 in which up to two hundred million humans lost the lives and in China and India in 1855, over twenty million deaths. More recently, the Spanish Flu pandemic in Europe caused the deaths of up to one hundred million humans. These were not natural disasters. These were strategic attacks on humanity. The Nezulli have become more effective and efficient since those attempts. We were here to help stop the spread of the diseases, but we have limited resources and abilities to prevent such attacks. The next one could be the final one." Jaii explains.

"This would explain my results showing increased UFO activity over farms, water supplies, power sources, and mines." Hunter replies, "that's why the government didn't want me digging any deeper, it's a cover-up."

"There is one more thing that's important to know," Jaii pauses. "The Nezulli are not of mortal DNA as you and I are. They are not organic. They once were, but they developed artificial intelligent beings to fight their wars. Unfortunately, these artificially intelligent entities developed themselves further. They destroyed their creators, the mortal Nezulli race. These entities are self-learning, self-building, destructive machines. They are also powered by the resources they seek. Destroying them is not an easy task. This is where your skills will be needed, Hunter."

"Me, what can I do? How can I fight robots? Not in my skills set, I'm afraid," Hunter replies.

"Wait Hunter, this is serious stuff," Jo adds, "I believe this guy. As far-fetched as it sounds, what if it is true and we do nothing? Everything we know and love could be taken away, the world would be a dark place if we even survived. I mean, yesterday, my only worry was whether I should get new tires on my truck. Today, it's whether or not there will be a tomorrow. We need to do something, we can't just walk away from this."

Hunter gets up and paces the room, looking for answers. Jaii watches from behind the desk, waiting for the severity of the situation to sink in. He knew Hunter was a man of great resolve, resourceful, skilled and dedicated. He had watched him from afar when he worked for the government. He knew what he was capable of, his analytical mind, his coding knowledge. These were skills he needed. He knew he had the right man.

"You're thinking of that night, the night of the accident in which you were hurt," Jaii directs to Hunter. "You and your daughter were in grave danger. It was the Nezulli. They too knew of your work in the government. The government sent them to remove you. You were a liability to their plans, you had to be silenced. They were about to kill you and your loved one. That is when we intervened. We shot down the Nezulli craft to save you. Unfortunately, your vehicle got hit in the attack and you were injured. I am very sorry for this, but the situation was severe. I hope you can forgive me." Hunter looks at Jaii.

"I should punch you square in the face," he replies.

"Please, do so if it will make you feel better. I have no feeling in this face anyway, I have many more besides," Jaii replies. Hunter looks at Jo. She is shaken by the whole event, but she is strong, she will fight for what is right, Hunter can see her restraint. He knows she's right, they must do something.

"Okay, what do you need from me," Hunter asks Jaii.

"I need you to get back into the base where you worked, I will give you some access codes and a gate pass. You must use the mainframe computer to retrieve the information we require. You must also retrieve the computer components you worked on from the crashed Nezulli craft. They are stored on the same level as the mainframe. They may hold the key to destroying the Nezulli." Hunter ponders the mission. Getting into the base should be easy enough, getting into the server room, easy, but accessing the mainframe, that will pose a challenge. The computer files are encrypted.

"These AI entities, what can you tell me about them. It would help to know what to look for to destroy them. Do you know what system they are using for computing?" Hunter asks Jaii. Jaii hesitates.

"The system was designed by our race. It was designed as artificial intelligence to work on medical procedures. The AI could diagnose and treat a patient much faster and more accurately than a mortal doctor. They discovered our system, took it and developed it for warfare. They are more advanced than ourselves in some areas, codes and systems being one of those areas."

"So, you guys developed this," Hunter replies, "so you would have detailed information on the system, code structure, power, how it learns and recreates, that kind of thing?"

"To some extent, yes, but it has been redeveloped far beyond our knowledge base. If you can find a way into the system, then we should be able to stop them from regenerating themselves. But unfortunately, I cannot help you with how you do this, this is why I have enlisted your help," Jaii tells Hunter.

"How soon before the Nezulli arrive?" asks Jo.

"We are unsure of this, but they are mustering their craft in your orbit. Once they are assembled, they will attack with viruses. Nation after nation will get sick and it will spread fast. When Earth is vulnerable, then they will strike. Perhaps you have two, maybe three earth days before they begin."

"Okay," Hunter adds, "let's get to work. Jo, can you come with me, I may need your help?"

"Sure, what else would I do?" she replies.

"I will transport you back to your vehicle," Jaii concludes, "if you need me, just hit *3 on your cell phone, I will know you need my help. Please follow me, I have a craft waiting." Hunter and Jo follow Jaii out of the room. They walk across to a triangular craft, much bigger than the one that approached them less than an hour before. The steps are down. Jo looks around at the aliens working in and around the parked craft.

"Jaii," she asks, "you and everyone else here look so much like us. Why is that?"

"You are we and we are you," he replies. "Although we can change our appearance into many shapes, and speak many languages, we share a common DNA. Not by accident. Our involvement in your evolution goes back hundreds of thousands of years. It was our ancestors who help mankind to develop and prosper, to learn and nurture. We sent one of our watchers some two thousand earth years past, to live among you, to show you a new way forward."

"Whoa," Jo stops on the spot. "Are you saying what I think you are saying?" Jo and Jaii's conversation is interrupted by Hunter.

"Come on, Jo, let's get going," he shouts from the bottom of the steps to the craft. Jo leaves Jaii and jogs over to Hunter.

"You won't believe what Jaii just told me," she begins.

"It'll have to wait, let's see what's inside this thing," he replies as he climbs the steps. Jo follows, excited, but nervous. They enter the craft and the entry hatch closes behind them. It is sparse. Two seats emerge from the gray floor, like liquid forming a shape. Hunter touches one, it is solid metal.

"How the hell did they do that?" he asks. The walls are dark gray, with panels similar to the one in the room they were in with Jaii. They both sit in the chairs next to each other. A strap comes across both their laps.

"I guess we're going to take off," Hunter says. The craft silently takes off and leaves the cave and heads towards the Rangers cabin. About ten seconds later, they feel the craft landing. With that, the straps descend back into the seats. The hatch opens and the steps appear. They get up and climb back down the steps. They are shocked to find themselves back at the cabin so quickly. They step out into the bright desert sun, squinting with the brightness. The craft takes off in an instant and is gone.

"Wow," is all Jo can say.

"Wow indeed," adds Hunter.

The pair climb into Jo's truck and head back to the reservation where Hunter left his truck. They drive in silence for some time, processing everything they have learned. Finally, Jo speaks.

"This is all bizarre, how are you so calm?" she asks.

"I've been working within a department; whose primary aim was to track and record UFO sightings. When I saw an alien craft for myself many years ago, I knew it was real. Today has just reaffirmed what I already knew."

"Do you think you have the skills to help Jaii defeat these robot things?" she asks Hunter. He looks at her and smiles. It's a reassuring smile, but inside, he has no idea if he can do the job or not. They drive on along the red dusty roads, finally reaching Hunters truck. He gets out and thanks Jo for the ride.

"I need you to go over to Flagstaff, ask around, see if anyone has any information on a UFO a few days ago, Monday. It was seen by the airbase staff. Maybe someone there will talk. Tell them you’re a Ranger, maybe say you're after cattle rustlers or something." Hunter explains.

"Sure, I’ll have a nose around," Jo tells him.

"This is my cell phone number, call me when you have any info." Hunter writes his number on a scrap of paper and hands it to Jo.

"Do you have a plan then, for when you get to the base?" Jo asks.

"Nope. But I will have by the time I get there," he replies, "it gives me about two hours to figure one out."

Chapter 7.

Hunter climbs into his truck and sets off southwest, heading out of the reservation towards the Nevada desert. Jo watches him drive away in a cloud of red dust. She puts the paper in her pocket, climbs into her truck and heads off towards Flagstaff. The journey is dusty, the dry arid land wide open before her. She re-tunes her radio to try to catch some news. She tunes in to a local radio news channel, but there is no mention of UFO's or aliens or viruses. Perhaps it's all a hoax, she thinks, some kind of government mind game. She re-tunes the radio and picks up some Nashville country music. She settles for the pleasant, placid country tones of Willie Nelson, singing Blue Eyes Crying in The Rain.

Hunter picks up speed when he reaches the freeway. After a long rambling bumpy journey along the dirt tracks of the reservation, the smooth tarmac is a relief. Traffic is light, and he makes his destination in good time. Hunter pulls off the freeway onto a dirt track and parks up. He gets out and climbs a small hill. He peers over the top, looking down onto the base. He knows the base well. Making his way to the server room would be easy, although he had never been inside it, so he was unsure what to expect.

Hunter jumps into his truck and heads down to the base. He calls his pal Brennan on the way.

"Hey buddy, are on the base today?" he asks.

"Sure, I'm working today, what's up?" he replies.

"Could you call gate security, tell them I'm visiting you, be there shortly. Thanks, buddy."

"Sure, no problem, let me know when you get here. Is anything wrong?" Hunter hangs up. He would explain to Brennan in person, phone calls around the base were usually monitored. He knew this from his own work. Hunter drives up to the gate security office. A military guard comes to the side of the truck. Hunter tells him he is visiting Brennan. They check his government identity card and a pass Jaii supplied, then raise the barrier to allow him to proceed. Hunter knows the base well. He heads over towards the office building he used to work in, or actually under. All the office buildings are a front, the actual offices are deep under the desert floor. He parks up and grabs his rucksack, slings it over his shoulder. Brennan appears from the building to greet him.

"Hey, dude, what's up? How did you get on with finding info on that UFO at Flagstaff? Any luck?" he asks Hunter.

"No, but some real heavy shit is going down, Brennan. Have you seen or heard any intel? Anything out of the ordinary?" Hunter asks.

"Hell, this is a high-security military base, everything here is out of the ordinary, that's what we do," Brennan replies.

"Anything on top of the usual unusual weird shit that goes on?"

"No, nothing. Why? Are you onto something big?" Brennan asks.

"Could be, I'll keep you posted," he tells Brennan. "Gotta go run an errand, catch you in a bit." Hunter leaves Brennan by the truck and runs off towards the mainframe lift. Brennan watches him go. Hunter catches sight of Brennan's reflection as he passes a window. Brennan is talking into his body comms. This startles Hunter. Who would he be talking to? Why? He knows Hunter is there unofficially? Surely his oldest friend wouldn't betray him? He turns a corner and reaches the outer doors of the lift building. He swipes the pass Jaii gave him. The door buzzes open. Hunter steps inside. There is no one around.

There is a panel to the right of the lift doors. He opens it, it is a service entrance to the lift shaft. He climbs in. Looking down, he realizes just how deep the shaft goes. He climbs onto the metal ladder that runs down the length of the shaft and begins his descent. The lift is lower down on his right side, moving up and down between lower floors. The cables creek and move up and down, carrying the weight of the lift. The shaft is dark, only lit by occasional service lamps at intervals, every second floor. Hunter continues down. He reaches floor twelve. He exists through another service hatch, peering out to see if it is clear. It is. He quickly makes his way to the mainframe server room, gaining entry with the code from Jaii. Inside, it is cool, with a chilly airflow from the cooling ducts keeping the temperature stable for the servers. The room is lined with racks of servers, blinking and humming. Hunter heads to the main terminal. He uses a login Jaii provided. He looks through the file structure. He can't see any of the files on the list from Jaii. There must be another hidden drive. He searches deeper into the computer system and finds a classified folder marked Vok. Hunter tries to recall his meeting with Jaii. He recalls the name Vok. This must be it. He opens the folder, puts the pen drive in and copies the encrypted folder. The files begin to copy. He hears footsteps outside the server room. Someone is trying doors, walking towards the room. The files are slowly copying to the pen drive. The progress bar continues 38%, 40%, 43%. Hunter waits, his heart pounding. 57%, 59%. There are voices outside the door. 68% 70%. Hunter looks for another way out. The entrance is the only door, the walls are lined with computer racks, no other exit. The voices are getting closer. He is sure it is security. Perhaps Brennan did give him away, telling them he was an intruder. Hunter thinks back. Maybe he shouldn't have told Brennan he was onto something big. 84%, 87%. The footsteps and voices are closer. He can hear them trying door handles and swiping cards on doors. 93%, 95%. Hunter looks around for somewhere to hide. 97%, 98%. The door handle is squeezed. 99%. He hears an access card being swiped and the buzz of access granted. 99%. The door opens and two military security guards enter, armed with assault rifles. 100%. They look around. Nothing looks to be out of place. No one in the room. Everything looks normal. The security guards leave and close the door behind them. The room remains silent for a moment. Then Hunter crashes to the ground from a cooling duct above the mainframe. He is shivering and covered in frost. He just made it into the duct in time, with the fully downloaded files on the pen drive. Next task, get the computer from the crashed Nezulli craft.

Hunter slowly opens the door, peers out left and right, all clear, he steps out and carefully closes the door behind him. The corridor leads back to the lifts on the right, and to the left, more doors on one side, then the corridor turns right. This is where he needs to go. He moves along the corridor, glancing back to make sure security is not behind him. He peeks around the corner at the end of the corridor, empty. He proceeds along the passage, looking for the artifacts store. Hunter finds it halfway along the corridor. He swipes the card and goes straight in. The room is a large square space, with industrial racking in lines running the length of the room with an assortment of cardboard boxes on the shelves. Hunter walks up and down the rack aisles, reading the labels of each artifact. His only clue will be the date. 1947. After about fifteen minutes of searching, Hunter spots a date that matches. He reads the label. Art. 2323-0054-Roswell-1947-FTD. He opens the box, he recognizes the item as the same one he had worked on some years before, a computer part with a nanochip. It was some sort of quantum supercomputer, far in advance of anything he had seen before. He had some success in accessing the code, but the agency had shut him down, moved him to another task and gave the job to someone else. Hunter figured that person failed, and the item was stored ever since. The agency didn't want him getting too close to the truth. Now he knew what the truth was, they were working with aliens to obtain world power. Hunter grabs the item and puts it in his rucksack. He leaves the room and heads back towards the lift shaft. He climbs back up the shaft to the ground floor. He leaves the building the same way he entered, walks to his truck. Hunter dumps the computer part and pen drive in his toolbox in the back of his truck, covering them up with old tools and rags. He climbs in and drives to the gates. The security guards give his truck a brief look over, one opens the toolbox, closes it, then gives the nod to open the barriers. Hunter drives away from the base. He breathes a sigh of relief.

"Well, that was easy," he says to himself. "Good old government security, as bad as ever."

#

Jo drives into Flagstaff. She pulls up into a parking space at an angle to the road, opposite a local diner on the main street into the center of town. It is a busy mid-terraced diner, a long counter heading away from front to back, a few booths along the wall on the right, smells of coffee. Jo enters and takes a seat at the counter. There are three others at the counter, two older ladies and an older gentleman. The waitress puts a cup in front of Jo.

"Coffee?" she asks, holding up a clear pot half-filled with dark, black coffee.

"Sure, thanks," Jo replies. The waitress pours the coffee. Jo looks at the old man next to her. His face is a map of creases and his hands are as weathered as his face. He looks like a farmer or some sort of job outdoors, she thinks as she watches him read the local paper.

"You local to here?" she asks him, striking up a conversation.

"Eh, yeah, sure, I'm local, been here man and boy, near on eighty years now," he replies, setting the newspaper on the counter, glad of the conversation.

"I guess you know everything about this town, then?" she asks.

"Sure do. Ain't much happens in Flagstaff that Charlie Gates don't know about." He sips his coffee, holding the mug with both hands. Jo notices his hands shaking.

"Well, I'm sure there must be stuff goes on out at the airbase you don't get to hear about, what with their secrets and all," she teases.

"Well now, young lady, my eldest boy works out there. Let me tell you, he can tell you some stories, all manner of crazy stuff they do out there."

"Did he say anything strange happened on Monday night?" She tries to extract more information from the old man.

"Reckons he did say something, some kinda commotion, all manner of crazy, can't recall, though. You a reporter or something?" he asks.

"No, I'm a Ranger on the Indian reservation over to the East, just trying to track down some cattle rustlers. You heard anything about that, Charlie Gates?" she asks him.

"Can't says I have. No, nothing about no cattle, just some strange lights in the skies over that ways, that's what Clyde says. Over the reservation way, all manner of crazy goin' on over there."

"Who's Clyde?" she asks.

"Clyde? He's my eldest, works over at the airbase there." Charlie points over his shoulder to the street. "Been there for years."

"What sort of lights, did he say? Colored, moving, what did he say?"

"All's I know is they was hovering over the desert, then again over the airbase. Clyde and his guys watched them, shot off over the reservation, up towards the mountains, he said. He'd never seen anything move so fast. Not one of ours, he would know. He watches the planes come in and take off, he knows them. Not one of ours. All manner of crazy, that's for sure. Don't think they'd be rustling cattle, though, do you?" he asks Jo.

"No, I guess not. Well, thank you Charlie Gates, it's been lovely to talk to you." Jo throws a couple of dollars on the counter for the coffee and gets up to leave.

"You take care now missy, whatever you are looking for, might be something else indeed, that's for sure." Charlie turns back to his coffee and newspaper. Jo smiles at him and leaves the diner. She knew there was something going on at the airbase. It must be the Nezulli. They could have already started their attack. She calls Hunter. He pulls his truck onto the roadside. He answers.

"Hi Hunter. Been talking to an old guy in Flagstaff. He says his son told him about strange lights over the airbase and reservation. Do you think that's what Jaii was talking about?"

"Sure sounds like it. I hope we're not too late," he replies.

"Yeah, that's what I was thinking," Jo answers. "How did you get on?" she asks. Jo is walking to her truck. Just as she gets to the door, a black panel van screeches to a halt, blocking her in. The side door slides open. Two men, dressed in black suits, jump out and grab Jo, one throws a black sack over her head and they drag her into the van, as she kicks out at them. She drops her cell phone, kicking it under her truck in the commotion.

"Wait, no, you've got the wrong person," she yells, "I'm a Ranger, you've made a mistake." They bundle her into the back of the van, climb in with her, slam the side door shut and the van speeds away.

"Jo, Jo, answer me, Jo, what's going on," Hunter is still on the phone.

"God damn it," he shouts at the phone. Hunter is fuming. He now knows the government is on to them. He takes out his cell phone and hits *3. He waits.

Chapter 8.

They pull the bag up off Jo's head. She squints as the light hurts her eyes. Her vision adjusts, and she looks around, trying to gauge her situation. Her hands are handcuffed behind her back and to the back of the chair they have placed her on. Two men in dark suits are standing across the room to her right, whispering to each other. She can see the space more clearly as her eyes adjust. It looks like an interview room the police would use. The walls are gray, there is a table in front of her with a chair on the opposite side. The lights are fluorescent tubes, set into the ceiling. There is one door in and out and a glass window facing Jo. She looks at her reflection, sure it is a two-way mirror and she is probably being watched from the other side.

"Where am I, what's this all about?" she directs at the two men. They look at her, then turn back to their conversation. The door opens, and a woman walks in. Jo watches her as she walks around the table and sits in the empty chair, placing a folder on the table in front of her. She puts on reading glasses. She smiles at Jo. Jo studies her. She reckons she is around fifty years old, dyed blonde hair, slim, keeps fit. Her suit is dark, very business-like. Her face looks tired, like she has struggled to get to her position but has to continue to battle for a place at the table in a male environment. Jo hoped this woman might be more forthcoming with information than the two men.

"Why am I here?" Jo asks her. "Can you please undo the handcuffs. My arms are sore?" The woman signals for one of the men to undo the handcuffs. He steps over and releases Jo's arms.

"Thank you," Jo directs to the woman. The woman doesn't look at Jo. She looks down at the folder, opens it and spends a few seconds studying the contents.

"My name's Peterson. Why were you in Flagstaff, Miss… Yazzie is it?" Peterson asks Jo.

"Yes, it's Jo Yazzie. Who are you and why do you want to know?" Jo replies. Peterson looks up over the top of her glasses without raising her head.

"You're not in a position to ask questions, Miss Yazzie. Please answer my question." Jo folds her arms.

"No comment," she replies, "I want a lawyer," she tells the woman.

"That is not an option, Miss Yazzie. We have information from Homeland Security, they believe you to be a risk to national security. You don't get a lawyer until we say you can. This is not the local police station, you have not been brought here for a traffic violation. What is your relationship with Hunter?" Peterson asks.

"Who?" replies Jo.

"Please don't underestimate us, Miss Yazzie. We know you have been working with Hunter."

"Underestimate who?" Jo asks, "who are you people?"

"That is of no concern of yours, Miss Yazzie. Why were you in Flagstaff asking questions about the airbase?" Peterson persists.

"How do you know what I was doing?" Jo asks, "You swooped on me minutes after I was in the diner. How could you know what I was doing or talking about?"

"We have eyes and ears everywhere, Miss Yazzie, we know more than you can imagine," Peterson replies. "Whatever you're involved in with Hunter, it could get you locked up for a very long time."

"If you have eyes and ears everywhere, then you already know why I was in Flagstaff and what I was asking," Jo replies. Peterson ignores Jo and continues reading her notes.

"I don't think you know the gravity of the situation, Miss Yazzie. This is a serious matter," Peterson tells her.

"No, Mam, I don't. I'm looking for cattle rustlers, stealing cattle off the reservation. So, unless you know a cattle rustler or have any jurisdiction over the Indian reservation, I suggest you release me and let me get on with my job," Jo says, raising her voice in anger.

"Take her to the holding cells," Peterson tells the two men. They walk to each side of Jo, one puts his hand under her arm to help her up, and they both hold her arms and walk her out of the room. Peterson remains seated. Jo looks back as the woman turns to the mirror and shakes her head. Now she is sure someone was watching her, but she did not understand who.

The men take her along a dark corridor, pale gray walls on either side. At the end, they turn left and on the left is a line of cells, with black metal bars as the front wall. They open the first cell door and push Jo inside. Neither men speak. One of them slams the door shut, the metal lock clangs into place. Jo stands for a few minutes, taking in the space. She looks through the bars, trying to see up and down the corridor. There are CCTV cameras up near the ceiling, watching the length of the corridor, both ways. Inside her cell is another camera, up in the front right corner, secured behind a metal grill and clear Perspex. There is a single bed with a gray blanket and a pillow. A metal chair, locked down to the floor in front of a small metal table, also secured to the floor. In the corner on the back wall is the toilet. No privacy, just a stainless-steel toilet, and stainless-steel sink and a roll of pink toilet paper. Jo thinks this is odd. In this gray grim prison of concrete and metal, someone put a roll of pink toilet paper in her cell. She wonders if they knew they would have a woman guest. Perhaps it was just all they had, or maybe it was an attempt to soften the situation, the government morons showing some compassion, win her over, so she would tell them everything she knew. Jo is thinking she is going mad. Now she is thinking about conspiracies, government tactics, spies and all manner of stuff. She sits on the end of the bed, thinking about what to do next. She listens to see if she can hear anyone else in the other cells, but there is just silence. Perhaps she is the only prisoner. Now she is thinking of herself as a prisoner. This is all strange. She lies down on the bed, staring up at the concrete ceiling, wondering what Hunter is up to, if he has been successful in his quest, if Hunter or Jaii are coming to her rescue. She drifts into a light sleep, trying to figure it all out in her head.

Chapter 9.

Hunter's cell phone rings. He answers.

"Hey Hunter buddy, it's Brennan. Are you still on the base? Wanted to catch up with you again."

"No, sorry Brennan, I had to shoot off," Hunter replies.

"Where are you, buddy, let's get together for a coffee or a beer later? Where can I find you?" Brennan asks. Hunter is not sure if he can trust his old pal.

"I'll call you in a bit, Brennan, a little busy just now," he tells him. Hunter hangs up. He turns to get into his truck, only to find Jaii standing next to the driver's side.

"You requested my help," Jaii states.

"Bloody hell, Jaii, can you stop doing that," Hunter tells him, startled by his appearance. "You took your bloody time," Hunter tells him. "Someone has taken Jo. She went up to Flagstaff to dig around, got taken by some agency or other. I need your help to find her."

"I suspect the government may know of our presence here on Earth," Jaii explains, "perhaps they have taken your friend as a bargaining tool, to get to you. Is this not how they operate?"

"Yes," replies Hunter, "or perhaps they weren't government agents, perhaps they were Nezulli soldiers?"

"This is also a possibility, Hunter. They can move among you, unnoticed. Like my species, they can create many looks. Whilst we, the Anunnaki, can change organically, the Nezulli create soldiers in your image. It is almost impossible to tell them apart from a human," Jaii explains.

"I just had a call from Brennan," Hunter tells Jaii, "asked me to meet him. I could ask him to investigate, ask around, see if he can find any info. Is there anything you can do with your superpowers and all that stuff?"

"I will instruct my fleet commander to locate your friend and keep watch over her, but I do not see her retrieval as a priority. It would not be safe for us to rescue her, it may jeopardize our mission here. One soul cannot take precedence over many souls. I hope you can understand?" Jaii replies.

"Yeah, I know, the bigger picture and all that," replies Hunter.

"I take it by your presence here and not in prison, that your mission was a successful one?" Jaii asks.

"Piece of cake," Hunter tells him. Jaii frowns, confused why Hunter would offer him food?

"I do not eat cake," replies Jaii.

"No, I mean, it's a phrase… never mind. Yes, the mission was a success." Hunter says, giving up trying to explain.

"Good, we have much work to do, Hunter. Time is not on our side. We can decrypt some files, but we will need your help with others. The Nezulli computer you retrieved will aid us. You must access it and find a certain code. When we developed the software for medical usage, the security was efficient. However, as is usually the case, the developers created a portal in which they could access the code and redevelop elements. We believe the Nezulli used this to create the AI and closed access to it. I believe there is still access. They must have made it accessible to continue developing it. You, Hunter, must find a way into it, find a weakness in their system that will allow us to destroy the Nezulli forever."

"Okay, find a backdoor. No pressure then," Hunter jests. Jaii looks at him blankly.

"I'm gonna need some tools. I need you to supply one of your supercomputers, something with some guts, that can deal with a lot of processing and one that can change IP address automatically every minute. We don't want to be traced back to a terminal by the government."

"This I can do," replies Jaii, "you can work from our base. Come, I will take you there." Jaii indicates his craft is over the hill. Hunter locks his truck and joins Jaii to fly back to the mountain base.

"I have so many questions," Hunter tells Jaii.

"Why didn't you just use your superpowers to retrieve the files from the base yourself. You could have got through undetected, I'm sure?"

"The Nezulli craft in one of the hangars emits a signal. This signal cancels our ability to time transport. If we are within a certain range of the signal, our powers are reduced. We cannot counteract this signal," Jaii explains.

"So, the UFO is still active?" Hunter asks.

"Yes, the craft is still active, regardless of damage. The material it is made from carries the signal, and many more. We believe it was crashed here on Earth purposely. This was the Nezulli's way of making contact, but also set up a signal for their fleet. They knew your government would hold on to the craft and any occupants. They would not destroy something that could advance their knowledge. It was the perfect plan. Where better to hide your surveillance equipment than in a secure government facility? Anyway, Hunter, as I have said, time is not on our side, we must hurry." They land back in the base. Jaii leads Hunter into the office. He touches a panel on the wall and a virtual computer terminal appears from thin air.

"You may use this computer to work on the code," Jaii tells him.

Hunter pulls up a chair from the office desk and sits at the virtual terminal. He studies it for some time, touching the screen and keyboard, getting familiar with it. He has never used a virtual computer, which looks like a projected image on the desk in front of him.

"How do I upload the files, there is no USB port?" Hunter asks. Jaii takes the flash drive from Hunter and sets it on the desk. A light appears under the flash drive and the files become visible on the virtual screen in front of Hunter.

"The screen is touch sensitive, Hunter, you can swipe, hold, move and open items on the screen."

"Cool, we have the same technology, maybe not as advanced, but getting there," Hunter explains. He concentrates on the files in front of him, searching through them to find anything that might help him understand the Nezulli's code structure. He places the computer part that he retrieved from the base onto the surface next to the flash drive. A light appears beneath it and strings of code roll up on another screen in front of Hunter. There are thousands, maybe millions of lines of code. Hunter's task is daunting, but this is his specialty. In the agency, he was valued by his peers for his coding skills, whether it was writing code or decrypting foreign enemy's communication codes. He was a genius in this department.

Hunter sets about finding a weakness in the Nezulli code. As he trawls through lines of digits, he realizes just how complex it is. He knew from working on the code from the crashed UFO that they had a sophisticated code structure, but the files he is examining are further advanced than he expected. He is fascinated by the information he uncovers. There are detailed schematics on an unknown power source, information on their fighter craft defense shield, a plan for the main control panel on fleet craft. Hunter kept digging into the files. How long had the government been sitting on this stuff, gathering dust on a shelf in a storeroom, deep underground? The stuff he worked on whilst with the government was only a tiny portion of what they had. He was thinking the government collusion with the Nezulli was deeper and more profound than he first assumed. He sets up an algorithm to search for the components of code he needs. The system runs through millions of lines of code, scrolling up the screen. Jaii leaves the room, then returns a few minutes later. He sets a tray down next to Hunter. Hunter looks down at it. His face lights up. He is looking at a Big Mac, large fries and an ice-cold cola.

"Thanks Jaii, I'm starving," he says with a mouth full of burger. "Do you guys have a McDonalds down here?"

"No, we get it delivered," Jaii says with a laugh.

"Tell me Jaii, why did you choose me for this task? There are many skilled operators out there who could do the job just as well, if not better. And why set up your base in the mountains on the reservation?" Jaii walks around the desk and sits in the seat behind it, sitting forward, resting his arms on the desk. Hunter swivels around to face him, still eating.

"We needed to trust someone who had inside knowledge of the government and who believed in the existence of extra-terrestrial life forms. You fitted the profile. You are open to alternative possibilities. You question motives, you analyze situations, as you did when you first met me. Also, as a person of Native American origin, you and your people have, for a long time, believed in and even conversed with our ancestors. Your people have a great understanding of the Earth and the stars. You know that you are only custodians of the Earth and you show respect to nature. This is the reason we based ourselves in your region. Only a few people would venture into the area and they would be indigenous, therefore they would accept anything they found as meant to be, as did your friend Johona. I orchestrated her finding us and bringing you together."

"You mentioned about when I first met you," Hunter replies, "I remember that. You asked to meet me, said you had information on UFO sighting in Nevada. I met you at a house in Greenvale. Was all this the reason you wanted to meet me?"

"Yes, I had to make contact. But you didn't believe me. When we met, you said my information was phony, I was a fraud," Jaii replies.

"Well, yes. The images of a UFO you showed me were too good to be true. No-one would believe they were real, they looked Photoshopped," Hunter tells him. "Also, some of the information you gave me seemed like something from a sci-fi movie."

"I now know it was all too much to take in. My judgment was not at its best. I could have handled it better, but time was running out, I had to take a chance," Jaii explains.

"And then I wake up in the bloody desert," Hunter tells him.

"I am sorry for that," Jaii continues. "When you got irate about me wasting your time, I felt I needed to give my story some credibility, so I touched your shoulder as you were leaving, putting you to sleep, transporting you to, well as you know, it was the desert."

"And the next time it happened, do you want to explain that?" Hunter asks.

"Yes, I found you in the bar in that diner out on the highway. You had a few of your alcoholic drinks. When I tried to explain my reasons for transporting you, you wanted to fight me. We went outside to the parking lot. I hoped you would be reasonable, but not so. You punched me in the face on that occasion." Jaii tells him.

"Good," Hunter replies, "I hope it hurt." Jaii smiles.

"No, it did not hurt, but it was a good punch. You needed to let your anger and frustration out, I can understand that. You were concerned for your daughter's wellbeing. So I dropped you in the desert once more."

"I could have died out there, heatstroke, bitten by a rattler, murdered by a hobo. Anything could have happened," Hunter replies.

"You were well protected, my friend. You were under our surveillance at all times. You were safe."

"I need to see my daughter, where is she?" Hunter asks.

"She is quite safe, off your planet, in the safety of our fleet. Your daughter will be returned when Earth is safe from the Nezulli. She will be a leader one day, Hunter. She will be given knowledge far beyond your imagination. We will give her the knowledge, skills and leadership qualities needed, so people will follow her, they will have confidence in her, they will take what she says and apply it to your future. This is our gift to humanity. We have done this many times, with outstanding success. We have chosen humans to carry your species forward. Albert Einstein, Nikola Tesla, Edison, DaVinci, Archimedes, Newton. The list is long. Even now, we have implanted knowledge in people to help save your planet. A lovely young lady, not much older than you daughter, is now spreading the word for climate change. Have you heard of Greta Thunberg? Greta is an exceptional young lady. She has been tasked with empowering the young people of your planet to reverse the climate catastrophe you have created for yourselves," Jaii explains.

"So, all of those prominent figures of history, you're telling me, that was you guys? They were aliens?"

"No," Jaii replies, "they were humans, we just helped them with knowledge, unknowingly to them. We implanted the ideas, the designs, the formulae in their brains when they were sleeping. We chose members of humanity who were already outstanding in terms of ability, then gave them the direction needed to move your species forward a few thousand years. In all honesty, Hunter, your human race is an embarrassment in the multiverse."

"What?" Hunter asks. "We are an embarrassment to aliens?"

"Sadly, yes. Other species on planets similar to yours have progressed far beyond your capabilities. They make fun of you. They say things like - Don't be so human - and - You're as dumb as an Earthling- Sorry, other species can be unkind."

"So, exactly how far behind other alien races are we," Hunter asks.

"Well, roughly, about ten thousand earth years, give or take a thousand," Jaii says.

"Bloody hell. Anyone of them could come here and wipe us out."

"This is true. However, not all species are war-faring. Most other planets live in peace and protect their planets from self-destructive behavior such as nuclear weapons, drilling for minerals and polluting their air. Only a few are dangerous, such as the Nezulli, and of course you humans." Jaii explains.

"What happened to your planet?" Hunter asks. "You said the Nezulli took it over?"

"Yes. We were a peace-loving race, creating technology to aid our existence, exploring other planets within the multiverse, gifting them with our knowledge as we have done with your planet. The Nezulli, on one of those planets, called Rema X, took our gift and turned it into the artificial intelligence that is coming here. They overran our planet, destroying it as they went, enslaving my race to carry out mining for minerals, killing the weak and infirm. They took everything from us."

"How did you escape?"

"Many of us were in transit. I, along with my team, were exploring another colony in a distant galaxy, when we heard of the Nezulli invasion. When we returned, although to us it was a brief time period, a matter of Earth days, using a wormhole as you call it, to travel back to our planet, the time equivalent on our planet was months. So much was gone. Our loved ones, our families, our homes, all destroyed. The Nezulli had left, raided the resources and gone onwards. I have been tracking them ever since, trying to warn other planets of what is coming. Unfortunately, this has not always been successful. Others have perished at the hands of the Nezulli."

"And your family?" Hunter enquires, uncomfortably.

"Gone, killed, no trace was left, it was as if they never existed." Jaii replies, "now, my mission is to track and destroy the Nezulli, for my family, for my planet. There are a few us left, the Anunnaki that is. Around two hundred thousand. But we have been joined by many others from planets taken by the Nezulli. Other races with no homes, no purpose in life, other than to find and extinguish the Nezulli."

"So how many fighters do you have, including those who have joined you?"

Jaii thinks for a minute.

"Perhaps half a million. But the Nezulli number over one million AI fighters. You see the problem, Hunter. We are outnumbered and their technology is more advanced than ours. To defeat them, we must use their own technology against them. We must outsmart them, we cannot outnumber them."

"I see. And their technology is advancing continually, they are reprogramming themselves all the time to adapt and overcome additional problems, environments, that sort of thing?" Hunter asks.

"That is correct, each time we think we are close to a solution, they upgrade and become stronger as an entity. This is a new battle. Your people have been fighting for centuries, using physical combat. This is of little use against the Nezulli. It aids them in reprogramming their strategy, learning from you, taking your knowledge and using it against you. Therefore we must fight them differently. We must get into their systems and fight from within. We need to cut off their supply of information. That is the key to overcoming the Nezulli," Jaii explains.

"And if we fail?" Hunter asks.

"If we fail, Hunter, there is nothing more. You will most likely be enslaved if you survive, put to work in a labor camp. Once you have been worked until you can work no more, you will be eliminated, killed, you will be of no further use to them."

"Great, thanks for clearing that up," Hunter says sarcastically. "Let's hope it doesn't come to that."

"Indeed," Jaii replies, "this might be our only chance to defeat this menace."

"If our planet is so backward, and our technology is inadequate, why have you not hooked up with a more advanced planet to defeat the Nezulli?"

"Good question, Hunter. This is something we have tried before. But the skills required to examine, interpret and redesign the coding have been lost by advanced civilizations. This part of the process is machine-learned, computers supply the code, but they cannot do what you can do. For this, we need a civilization still developing, still learning. We need you. We can develop off-the-shelf code, so to speak. You can provide the answers lost to us."

"So, we, the dumbest planet in the universe, no, actually the multiverse, an embarrassment to civilizations everywhere, dumb Earthlings, we are your only hope of defeating the Nezulli? Bloody hell, Jaii, we are in trouble."

"Perhaps I was a little harsh with my analogy. But this is your chance to show the multiverse that humans have the ability and desire to contribute to the stability of the multiverse, Hunter."

"Until only a few hours ago, I didn't even know there was a multiverse, Jaii. I, like many others, assumed there was only the universe. Our universe. So, all this is a little difficult to accept so quickly," Hunter replies. Behind Hunter, the computer screen continues scrolling through lines of code.

"I know, but we have very little time to explain everything. If we are successful, your world will change forever, for the better. If we are unsuccessful, well, you know what is in store if that happens." Jaii tells him. Hunter nods in acceptance, thinking about the worst-case scenario. The computer pings behind him. Hunter turns to face it.

"Good news, Jaii. The computer has found a flaw in their system. A kink in their armor, if you like."

"What is it?" Jaii asks. Jaii stands up and walks around the desk to stand next to Hunter. They both stare at the screen.

"Well, I'm not sure yet. It looks like this line here." Hunter points to a line of code. "It tells the system how to input information from other sources. Analyzing the content, then either allowing it based on a set of variables, or denying it based on the outcome of the variables," Hunter explains. "This might be useful if we can reassign the variables or the algorithm it uses. I need more to go on, but it's a step in the right direction." The office door opens and a young Anunnaki man, a member of Jaii's crew, enters. He looks almost like any other young man. Wavy fair hair, piercing blue eyes, physically fit. He could be a young air force recruit, Hunter thinks, except his eyes are a little too large, like Jaii's, and his ears and nose are just a little too small for his head, again, like Jaii's. They could easily pass as humans, but you might take a second look on first meeting them, he thinks. But other than the minor discrepancies, he seemed normal. He looks to Hunter with caution, then to Jaii for approval. Jaii nods and tells him he can speak freely in front of Hunter. The young alien man talks in a language unknown to Hunter. It is a series of noises and gestures he is not familiar with, but from the tone, Hunter can guess it is a serious matter. Jaii replies in the same language, their native language, Hunter assumes. After the brief discussion, the young alien man leaves the room and closes the door behind him.

"Hunter, there is a development. My observation crew has identified several Nezulli craft, mustering on the dark side of your moon. We are now sure of the imminent attack on Earth within the next day or two.'

"Jaii, even if we can break the code to stop the Nezulli AI recreating themselves or even updating, if they have Nezulli members within our government, isn't it possible that they will still be able to carry out the attack, regardless?" Hunter asks.

"Yes. There are some in your government who can be trusted. One such person is a state senator called Brent Carter," replies Jaii.

"Yes, I've heard of the senator. He visited the complex in Nevada when I was stationed there, but I never met him. Old school, former fighter pilot I'm told, very experienced in combat. He turned to politics when he left the military. How do you know we can trust him?" Hunter explains.

"I have spoken with him," Jaii continues. "We took him onboard one of our command craft. I believe you refer to it as alien abduction. He took some convincing, wanted to fight us with fists. We had to tie him down. But once we explained the situation and what might be to come, he understood the gravity of the situation. I have told him you will be in touch. He can help within the government."

"How much does he know?"

"He is aware of impending danger worldwide and that it could change the future of humanity if nothing is done to stop it. He knows it will be air, water and food supply contamination. He knows also that some members of your government are not what they seem."

"How did he take the news?" Hunter asks.

"It was all a lot to deal with during an abduction. But his military background helped. He seemed to grasp the severity. He knew we would not take him and deliver this information unless it was true."

"Why has he not contacted me? Surely he would have found me and explained all this?"

"Would you have believed him?" Jaii asks him. Hunter considers his own reaction when Jaii had attempted to explain it to him.

"No, I guess not. What can he do to help us?"

"He can influence the loyal members of your government, the honest members, those not under the power of the Nezulli. There needs to be support inside the government to help prevent this catastrophe. We, and you, can only do so much. We will require help from others. Senator Carter is one such person. I will bring you to him. But first, we must find the solution to stopping the Nezulli AI," Jaii says. Hunter looks at him. His face has a seriousness he has not seen before. An urgency.

"I must go speak with my crew." Jaii leaves the office. Hunter turns back to the computer screen, the digits flowing quickly up the screen. He ponders the code he found displayed on the second screen.

"What is the one thing they rely on?" he voices to the empty office. "What can they not do without? What is it that makes them tick? There must be something, a common denominator, one thing that they all need?" Hunter devises a list. Power, an obvious one, he thinks, but the Nezulli use a power supply which they make themselves, according to Jaii. This would not work. Each individual AI generates its own power. There would be no way to knock them all off-line, he concludes. Code? Okay, he tells himself, but the code is complex, could he rewrite that amount of code in forty-eight hours to break their system? He decides this is a possibility, adds it to a list on the screen, calling it 'maybe'. Weapons are his next thought. The Anunnaki have weapons that could take out the Nezulli. Jaii has shown Hunter his gun. However, their weapons are more advanced and they have many more personnel. Hunter discounts a traditional attack. He is sure the Nezulli would win. He leans back in his chair.

"Time is running out, this is impossible," he says out loud to himself. He sits for a moment, considering how his life might end within the next two days. Had he done all the things he wanted to do? Is there still time to do the ones he hadn't done? How would his daughter survive? He could ask Jaii to take her with him, assuming Jaii and the Anunnaki survive and get off the planet. That's what he would do. Jaii could keep her alive. Hunter didn't care much if he was taken prisoner, given hard labor. He could handle it, but others, like his daughter, couldn't. What about Jo? He had just met her. He liked her a lot. But he hadn't had the chance to tell her, or even really get to know her. Now he might not get that chance. Time was running out and so were his ideas to solve the problem. Perhaps Jaii had over-estimated his abilities, he thinks to himself? Perhaps he wasn't as clever as he thought? Just then, another thought entered his head. Time. He sat upright. Time. Time is running out. He didn't have time to do those things.

"God damn it," he expresses, "is time the one thing the Nezulli AI rely on?" His mind is racing, excited. He could be wrong, but just maybe, he was on to something. Hunter jumps up from his seat. He flings open the office door.

"Jaii," he yells across the vast cavern. He runs over to the crew members at the nearest craft.

"Where's Jaii, I need to speak to Jaii?" he asks them, agitated.

"Hunter," comes Jaii's voice from across the cavern, "what is it?"

"Time, Jaii. It's time," Hunter tells him excitedly, waiting for Jaii to probe.

"Okay, it's time for what," he enquires.

"Come, let me talk you through it," Hunter explains. He jostles Jaii back into the office, slamming the door behind them. Jaii stands behind the seat at the computer panel, Hunter sits in the seat. On the screen, Hunter types a long formula.

"I think this might be the key we are searching for," Hunter tells him.

"Okay, explain."

"Well, what if time is the key? Not time as we know it on earth, but as you know it. Time for us is relevant to our planet and our existence. What if the Nezulli requires the same time relevance? How else would they be able to sync their machines, re-apply code, regenerate their own existence? They need some type of clock to synchronize to."

"Yes, I see. Our systems rely on a time-base corrector system to allow them to synchronize and update as required. The time-base is relevant to our systems, not to where or when we are in the multiverse. So, if you can locate their systems time-base corrector, which keeps everything in sync, you can disable it. Is that the plan?" Jaii asks.

"Yes, pretty much. It is the one piece of software code that all their systems require. Without it, they could no longer update. If I can break the time-base link, would that give you enough time to upload the destroy code?"

"It depends on how long they take to get back online," Jaii tells him. "Is there a way you can break the link but delay the information feed to and from their master computer? Even an extra few minutes would give us enough time to ensure the virus upload completes. How long it takes to propagate their systems, I do not know," Jaii explains, "we don't even know if it will have any effect on them at this stage." Hunter taps away at the virtual keyboard on the desk, running lines of code up the screen, looking for anything related to the systems time-base corrector. After only a few minutes, the computer pings. On the screen is a code showing the time-base corrector.

"This is it." Hunter turns to Jaii. "I think this is what we need. Obviously, this is not linked to their systems as it is on a file, but I can manipulate this code, then we can upload it to their live system to cause the break we need."

"Excellent work, Hunter," Jaii praises his efforts.

"How do we get it into their system?" asks Hunter. Jaii pauses before replying.

"This is something I will do, Hunter. There is a small window of opportunity. I can get myself to their command craft under disguise and upload it to the master computer. If I fail, well, you know the outcome."

Chapter 10.

Jaii knew the risks involved in getting himself into the Nezulli craft. He didn't want Hunter to know. The task was dangerous. If he got caught, they would eliminate him. That will be the end of the mission. He needed a back-up plan, something to ensure if they killed him, there was still hope. He needed help. He could take one of his crew. They are a loyal group, dedicated to Jaii and he can trust them implicitly. But would they have the skills and knowledge to carry out the mission in Jaii's demise? There was only one solution. Jaii had to break it to Hunter. He had to come with him on the mission. He had gotten to know Hunter well over the past year. His attempts to get Hunter to listen to him, to hear the truth, had not always gone to plan. Jaii was aware he was a little less than sympathetic or even sensitive in dealing with humans. He knew his flaws, his experience with humans was limited. He didn't trust them much, and he sometimes felt they deserved what was coming to them. But his role in life, as with all Anunnaki, was to help nurture and better civilizations. To help them flourish, to contribute positively to the multiverse. Jaii had grown fond of Hunter. Although he was rough around the edges, Jaii felt he was a good man, with good intentions. He wanted to help people and his ancestry was one which made him a distant cousin to the Anunnaki. Jaii knows he can trust Hunter.

"I think the time has come to rescue your friend, we will need her help soon," Jaii tells him.

"Let me just copy this to the flash drive, then we can go," Hunter says. He drags the files to the flash drive, grabs the drive, zips it into the front pocket of his rucksack, stands up, slings the bag over his shoulder.

"Ready." He follows Jaii to his craft and they take off towards the facility holding Jo captive.

Hunter and Jaii arrive at the secure facility. They look across at the granite block building, with stone square turrets and armed guards high above the ground, with 360-degree views of the facility and surrounding areas. The gray granite stone walls stand in contrast against the red sandy desert landscape, imposing, intimidating, serving a purpose to withhold and frighten even those who just come close to it. Jaii and Hunter are about three hundred meters from the building, hidden in a rocky outcrop. The building, which covers at least 50sq acres, Hunter reckons, looks like many of the prison buildings built around the states of Arizona, Utah, Nevada and Texas, over the past fifty years. Unappealing, practical design and just fit for purpose. There is one road in and out, lined with tall twin head sodium street lights, facing both the road and the desert on each side of the tarmac road. It stretches from the main highway to the building for a half-mile straight, leaving no possibility for anyone to reach the facility by road undetected. Hunter and Jaii watch for some time. A variety of vehicles heading to the gates, checked by guards with sniffer dogs. Other guards use mirrors to check under the vehicles and open the truck hood and search inside. They watch the same process for any vehicle leaving. Both in and out use separate gates, leading to the one road. Security is tight. Guards patrol the perimeter of the building, lights scan the surrounding desert seeking any movement.

"This won't be easy to get into, unless you can get us in?" Hunter asks Jaii.

"Perhaps," Jaii replies, "I can get us to the maintenance area of the facility."

"Do you have a weapon with you?" asks Hunter.

"Yes," replies Jaii, as he pulls a strange weapon from his belt. It is not a model that Hunter has seen before.

"What the hell is that," Hunter asks.

"This is an 8th generation light spectrum weapon. It uses part of the light spectrum you can't see or probably even know about. As we are more advanced, our weapons technology is also far advanced."

"How does it work, what effect does it have?" Hunter asks Jaii.

"It generates a powerful light ray, so powerful and fast, it can vaporize a body. Unfortunately, this only works on organic matter, like you. Electronics and mechanical devices are not affected by the light ray, so it is not suitable for fighting the Nezulli AI," Jaii explains. "Do you also have a weapon, Hunter?" Hunter pulls out a gun from the belt at the back of his pants.

"What is that?" Jaii enquires, looking at a small dark metal gun Hunter has produced.

"This is a Gen 5 Glock, standard issue for government agencies."

"Should you still have it, now that you are no longer with the agency?" Jaii asks.

"No, but until someone comes and collects it, it's mine," Hunter states. He holds the gun up, admiring its sleek design and balances it on his hand, showing Jaii it is balanced for perfection. He slips the weapon back into the belt at the back of his pants. Jaii puts his weapon into a holster under his jacket.

"Right," Hunter begins, "we need a plan." He looks at Jaii.

"What," Jaii replies, "why are you looking at me?"

"Well, as you said, you are far more advanced than us, therefore, it stands to reason, you will be far more advanced in warfare, planning, ideas, everything, really."

"It's true, yes, we are much smarter than you. In fact, we had dumb creatures on our planet, not unlike your sloths, that were so stupid, they kept falling down because they would forget how to stand. They were smarter than you," Jaii replies, teasing Hunter.

"Okay, smart-ass. Let's hear your plan."

"We don't have ass's, Hunter, smart or otherwise. You humans are obsessed with asses. Talking about them, making them rounder, bigger, smaller, higher. Obsessed. So, our best option from my observations is to enter drain seventeen, over to our left, the fifth drainage tunnel along. This leads to the main holding area, which has corridors with cells along one side. The drainage maintenance entry point is in a small room off the main corridor. Presumably, this will be locked from the outside, but this should be easy to overcome. This facility is very well built and planned for holding people in, however, they have overlooked the fact that someone might want to break in. It is much easier to get in than it is out. The guards and their routines are standard, no real deviation. There will be guards internally on the holding wing. This is where we might be presented with some resistance, Hunter."

"That is something we will deal with if it comes to it," Hunter says.

"I would prefer it if we can carry out this mission without harming any of your fellow man, but I understand this is a time of necessity and what must be done will be done." Hunter shrugs. He is set on saving Jo, if anyone stands in his way, he will take them down. The pair wait for the sun to go down, to allow them the cover of darkness.

"Ready?" Jaii asks.

"Ready," replies Hunter. They stay low and crawl to the drainage tunnel. Inside, they have to crawl on hands and knees. They reach the end and Jaii uses a laser tool to cut through the wire mesh to gain entry. They climb a metal ladder up into a small room. They are inside a maintenance room, on the ground floor of the cellblock.

"Your friend is being held along the corridor at the other side of the door," Jaii whispers to Hunter, pointing to the entrance door to the room. "There are armed guards patrolling the area. Two, one is sitting at the far end of the corridor, the other is walking up and down the front of the cells. Your friend is the only occupant on this floor. She is in the first cell along from this end. The cell doors are activated by a switch panel at the far end where the guard is sitting."

"Okay," replies Hunter, "I will run out when the guard is close and overpower him. You get yourself to the other end of the corridor and take out the other guard. We won't have a lot of time before the alarm is triggered, so we need to get in and out fast."

"Okay, I'm ready," replies Jaii, as he unlocks the door with another tool. Hunter opens the door enough to peer out. He can see the guard ambling along the cells on his left. Partway down, he turns and walks back towards the door. Hunter gently closes the door and waits. He listens for the footsteps. They get closer and louder, slowly walking towards them. The soles are hard leather and the heels rubber. Prison guard shoes intimidated. Loud and hard to let prisoners know they were there and meant business, Hunter thought. A swift kick from one of those would bring on some serious pain for sure. The footsteps are nearing. Hunter waits until he hears the distinct change in direction, when the guard turns, his shoes making a sliding sound as one sole spins on the concrete floor. As soon as the turn is made, Hunter makes his move. He bursts out of the door, grabs the startled guard from behind, locking the guard's right arm around his neck and forcing the guard's left arm up behind his back. Jaii sprints to the other end of the corridor. Jo jumps up from her cell bed on hearing the commotion. She holds the bars, trying to see up the corridor, to find out what is going on. The guard and Hunter are entangled at the end of the cellblock. The guard puts up a struggle, wrestling to get to his gun, holstered in a hip lock on his waistband to the right. Hunter grabs the weapon with his left hand from behind, trying to unlock the strap. The guard tries to scrabble for the gun, they both have their hands on it. The guard gets the better hold and rips the weapon from its holster. He flicks the safety off with his thumb, raises it and points backward towards Hunter's head. Still holding the guard around the neck, Hunter ducks his head as the guard fires a shot in his direction. He misses. Hunter releases the guard, pushing him forward to unbalance him. Just enough time to allow Hunter to pulls his Glock out, unlock the safety as he brings it around his body. As the guard turns to face Hunter, they both raise their weapons. A shot rings around the cell block, a flash of fire, the smell of sulfur fills the air. At the other end, the guard is startled by the sudden appearance of someone behind him. He stands up and goes for his weapon, but Jaii just takes the guard by the shoulder. The guard falls down into his seat, unconscious.

The discharge of the weapon at the other end of the corridor stops Jaii in his tracks. He watches as the guard and Hunter stand, only a few feet apart, facing each other, pointing their weapons at each other, neither one moving. A few seconds later, the guard slowly falls to his knees, then collapses forward, face down onto the concrete floor. A pool of blood seeps out from under his body. He is dead. Hunter gathers his thoughts. He had shot his weapon before, in a few situations of danger, but he had killed no one before. He accepted it was part of his job, that there would be times when he had to draw his weapon, but the reality of killing a man, taking away his life, a father, brother, husband, son. Gone forever, only a memory. These were the thoughts flashing through his head in milliseconds of the body hitting the floor. Logic dictated that it was him or Hunter, it was a matter of preservation for the greater good. Hunter and Jaii's mission is to save millions of lives. The cost of one life was small in comparison. But Hunter still felt sick inside. He was not an evil man; the guard was only doing what he was paid to do. Was it worth his life? How much did he get paid to die? Hunter's mind raced around, searching for logic, searching for reasoning, searching for something to make this all right. He never felt so alone in his life as he did at that moment.

Jaii pushes a button on the panel and the cell doors slide open. Jo peers up the corridor. She sees Hunter, standing over the body of the guard, his gun still in his hand. He doesn't look up, just staring down at the dead guard. Jo can see he is in pain, he is trying to make sense of it. She walks over to him, takes his weapon, and slides her hand into his now empty hand, the hand that had just killed another man. She holds his hand tight, to reassure him, to snap him out of his grief. He raises his head and looks into her eyes. She had not seen his eyes look so tired before. She holds his gaze and nods a reassuring nod, letting him know it is okay to be emotional, okay to be afraid, uncertain. His eyes give a faint smile. He takes his weapon, flicks the safety switch on and places it back in his belt. He has had the time he needed to process his thoughts. Jaii joins them. He can hear footsteps running towards them, sprinting up the stairs at the far end of the corridor.

"We need to go, Hunter. There is nothing you can do for this poor soul."

Jaii opens the maintenance room door, Jo follows, taking Hunter by the hand, leading him into the room. Hunter takes one last look at the man he killed, trying to memorize it, not wanting to forget him, for the dead man's sake, but also wanting to forget it for his own sake. Once inside the room, they close the door. The running footsteps are now in the corridor. They hear the click of weapons being primed. Just as the weapons are discharged at the room door, Jaii, Hunter, and Jo climb down the metal ladder. Jaii closes the hatch behind him to stop the guards following. They follow the tunnel out to the open and race to Jaii's craft. Alarms are going off at the facility and searchlights are scanning the desert.

"That was too close for comfort," Jo tells the guys as they take their seats in the craft and take off towards the mountain base. "You okay, Hunter?"

"Eh, oh, yes, I'm fine. Just been a long day, too much excitement," he replies. "It's good to see you again, Jo. I thought we might not meet again, after hearing your abduction on the phone."

"Those clowns, government idiots, they do not understand what's really going on. I think they suspect you of spying or espionage or something," Jo tells Hunter.

They return to base. The three of them enter the office. Jaii takes his seat behind the desk, Hunter the seat by the computer panel and Jo, the seat in front of the desk.

"So," asks Jo, "what's been happening since I've been away?" Jaii speaks.

"Hunter has found a way to delay the Nezulli systems for a short period. Enough to allow us to get into their systems and release the virus code."

"Excellent," replies Jo, "when do we go, how do we do it, where do we do it?"

"Well, that's where there is a slight problem," Jaii explains.

"Go on?"

"The code Hunter has been working on and the virus, need to be uploaded to the Nezulli master computer."

"So, tap into their systems and destroy those crazy bastards," replies Jo.

"Not that simple, is it Jaii?" Hunter adds, looking to Jaii to elaborate.

"The only way to do this is to physically install it in the master computer system. We cannot gain access remotely. This is something we must do in person unless we have a Nezulli computer, which we don't," Jaii explains.

"In person?" Jo stands up and walks around the room, thinking. "Where exactly is this master computer?"

"It's on the command craft of the Nezulli fleet, we believe, mustered at the dark side of your moon."

"So, what do we do," asks Jo, "just walk up to the craft and knock on the bloody door? Hello, can we come in and use your computer, please?"

"Yeah, Jaii, how are you going to get into their craft?" asks Hunter.

"We, Hunter. We will get into their craft and we will upload the virus. You know the time-base corrector side of things. I need you with me, I can't do it alone. We must all go, there's no other way."

"Right, I see. But how are we going to get into the craft, parked 240,000 odd miles away?"

"I don't know yet, I'm working on that," replies Jaii. The three sit in silence for a moment, thinking about the almost impossible task ahead of them.

"First things first. I need to take you guys to see Senator Carter."

Chapter 11.

Nezulli Command Fleet
Shadow of the Moon
Vok stands in front of a huge control surface that arcs around the front of the command craft. The entire front wall is a window, with a view out to space and beyond. He watches other craft docking to long tunnels coming out of other stationary craft. These crafts are docked to more craft, creating a network of stationary craft all connected by tunnels. The network goes on for miles, as far as the eye can see, a city, floating in space, under the cover of the moon's shadow.

The control panel in front of Vok is a mass of lights and touchpads, blinking and flickering, some lit, some not. Screens in the panel show satellite images of Earth. USA, China, Europe, Australia, all the major continents. The Nezulli have tapped into the humans' satellite network. The room is semi-circled, only the wall at the back with sliding doors is flat. A huge space, mostly empty, with a few staff operating control panels along the room edges. No seats. The light is dim. Vok stands with his hands clasped behind his back, head raised, looking confident. His being is human-like, tall, slim, black hair slicked back, skin color similar to Caucasian, but a little iridescent. His troops look similar, with minor differences in height and stature. Although completely artificially built, these entities looked every bit the real thing.

"Progress report, Commander." A member of his team hands Vok a thin black tablet device, which he stands and reads for a minute. The team member stands behind him, waiting.

"We are behind schedule. Assemble another crew to increase output," Vok tells the crew member, without turning away from the window.

"Right away, Commander." The crew member takes the instructions and leaves the room, placing a hand on a panel to the right of the sliding doors, which open briskly and quietly, sliding closed behind him. Vok's second in command comes over to him.

"Several of the fleet have been held up because of a solar storm in the Caxtol Galaxy, Commander. The route is treacherous. They must wait for another wormhole to open. How should we proceed?"

"We will wait for another 24 earth hours. If they cannot join us within this time, destroy them remotely," Vok replies.

"Yes, it shall be done. Do you for-see any problems with this planet, Commander?"

"These humans are just basic organic matter. They have primitive weapons and their thought functions are very limited. But, I have learned over our many missions, to never underestimate even the lowest forms of life, when it comes to saving themselves."

The Nezulli command fleet sits in the moon's shadow, a hive of activity with craft moving into position to join the network, others leaving on recon missions. The craft are a mix of shapes and sizes. Transportation and engineering craft are huge silver cigar-shaped vehicles, with windows running the complete length of the craft. Fighter craft are black, triangular-shaped, thin from top to bottom with weapons protruding from the two outer-most corners on each side. The front angle is sharp with a cockpit flush with the body, only a small window for the operator. Other miscellaneous craft are saucer-shaped, or range from small modular blocks up to large long tubular craft. Below the Nezulli craft network, on the dark side of the moon, the Nezulli have set up a base, centered in a vast crater. This is a supply post, with communication to the command fleet. The post is undetectable from the earth. Manmade satellites are positioned between the moon and earth, so they cannot pick up signals from this position.

The Nezulli run their operation with the precision of a well-trained, disciplined army. With many thousands of years to evolve from organic matter to artificially intelligent machine-based entities, they were forever re-testing their needs and their systems, using quantum computing to forecast future events across the multiverse. This gives them the advantage of predicting which planets would be beneficial to them, looking at the state of the planet's environment, technology, political status and resources. With this kind of information, the Nezulli had the upper hand against any civilization less advanced than their own. And Earth was one of those planets, an easy pick, very little resistance, technology a thousand years behind the Nezulli's, political turmoil and excellent resources. The Nezulli's quantum computers had pinpointed Earth as their next target. Earth was a sitting duck. The Nezulli had also developed the ability to create programmable matter. This was something scientists on Earth could only dream of, but the Nezulli had been successful. With this, they could replicate any object and make it look like the original inanimate object, then when they need it, it could be programmed remotely to become anything they wanted, such as a weapon or a spying device. These objects could also come together to create a larger, more effect object. If they deployed this technology to Earth, there would be no way to detect them or to destroy them. They were fighting with technology far beyond the capability of humans.

The Nezulli did not have families or any kind of relationship. They are emotionless vessels, without empathy, and did not reproduce like humans. They are machines, built by machines, to act and behave like humans, but without the added baggage of caring. Their brains are highly advanced computers and they thrive by striping the resources they need to survive from other planets. Vok had become commander after many successful missions, leading his team into battle across the multiverse. He was a superior entity, programmed with strategy and battle skills.

#

Jaii and his crew had watched over humans for thousands of years, protecting them from various other species set on invading Earth. Unbeknown to humans, these battles had been carried out in space, unseen by humans, occasionally craft would burn up in the Earth's atmosphere. Humans at the time would believe it was the Gods sending them a message or a sign of something. The Anunnaki had invested their time and resources in protecting Earth, but now, they were up against their biggest challenge ever. They could defeat other species on a par with their own technology and abilities, using strategy and surprise, but the Nezulli were far too advanced for the Anunnaki to use their usual tactics. This battle may be their last, and Jaii knew it. He had not come up against Vok in person, but he knew of his history, the planets he had destroyed in command of the Nezulli fleet, including Jaii's own planet. He was aware of his ruthlessness and lack of empathy. He did not possess the traits of organic, carbon-based life forms such as Jaii and humans. This made him and his race even more dangerous. They could exist without food or water and had no need for personal interaction such as relationships or love. This meant they did not care for anyone other than their own entity and keeping it in operation. They had no feelings, no sympathy, no remorse. They were just killing machines, which killed to exist. Nothing more, nothing less, just exist.

Jaii had feelings and memories of his own family, killed by the Nezulli. He had empathy and sympathy and all the other feelings a human had. Hunter, too, had feelings. He loved his daughter, he was on this mission for her, to keep her safe, to give her a future. He was also falling for Jo. He had only known her for a short time, but he often thought about her, he knew he was bonding with her, to fall in love and he hoped she felt the same. These feelings both Jaii and Hunter had made them vulnerable. They did not possess the machine-like existence of the Nezulli. Emotions gave them a weakness, which could mean defeat. But they could also be beneficial. It might give them an advantage in certain situations. The Nezulli had no feelings, they would not stop to think about someone, they were programmed to react to a situation with computational precision. Jaii and Hunter had emotions. If they hesitated to think about someone, they could be killed. This weakness could be exploited by the Nezulli, if it came to face-to-face conflict. Jaii and Hunter had to be ready to fight, with no emotion or restrained feelings. Jaii was not convinced Hunter could do this. He had watched him when he killed the prison guard at the desert facility. He had taken a life and his emotions were running wild. It took a minute for Hunter to pull himself together. Jaii was concerned. This could get him killed, if he hesitated with the Nezulli.

Chapter 12.

Charlottesville, Virginia.
Jaii, Jo and Hunter arrive in the garden of Senator Carter's home in Charlottesville, Virginia. A huge white, wood-framed mansion, with carefully tended gardens, set back from the suburban street with a long winding driveway leading up to a turning circle with a mock Italian Renaissance style fountain in the center. Not tacky, but not suited to the environment, thought Hunter. The house looked like it had been in the Carter family for generations. Hunter could imagine the General Carter, sitting on a rocking chair on the porch, sipping iced lemon tea, served by his black slaves. Not a history the current generation of Carter would be proud of, presumably some events written out of their history or rewritten with a different slant. This was not uncommon, Hunter had known such things to happen, when up-and-coming families tried to hide their ancestor's murders of Native Americans, like Hunter's ancestors. He gazes at the house, the history flooding from it. He looks at Jo and Jaii.

"Shall we?" he indicates for them to step up onto the porch to the front door. Jaii lifts a heavy brass ornate knocker in the middle of a large oak door and gives it two forceful knocks. The sound resonates around an empty passageway. After a about half a minute, an elderly lady opens the door. She is short, plump, slightly bent forwards with years of drudgery. And she is African-American. This takes Hunter by surprise. Perhaps, he thinks, they have not hidden their racist, slave-owning past. Maybe they still embrace it. Maybe they are proud of it. The old lady speaks.

"Yes, my dears?"

"We are here to speak with Senator Carter, please tell him it is Jaii, with some friends."

"One moment," she replies, "please come in and wait."

The three step in past the old lady as she closes the door behind them. They stand in the passageway. Carrera marbled floor, ornate winding staircase to the right and left, meeting at a landing on the first floor, with doors and hallways leading off it. The old lady disappears down a hallway to the left. Hunter can hear a discussion in the distance. After a minute, she reappears.

"Please, this way." She summons the group and they follow her to a room with a brown oak door. She beckons them inside and she leaves. The room is a study or library. Brown oak panels around the walls, three walls full of books, the other a white wall with French doors leading out to another well-tended garden. In front of the window is a large antique desk with a red leather high-backed chair behind it. Sitting in the chair is a middle-aged man. A black man. A middle-aged African-American.

"Good to see you again, Senator," Jaii reaches across and shakes his hand as he gets up. Hunter now understands the help being black. The Carters weren't slave owners or landowners, or old money. In this county, they were most likely slaves. The old lady is Carters mother, still in servitude, but by choice, not because she has to be, but because she wants to look after her successful son and his family, and they look after her. He was the first in the family to go to college, to join the air force and serve his country, to get a career in law and to become a State Senator. Hunter feels a little ashamed for jumping to conclusions, but also relieved not to have to pretend to like someone with a terrible family history. He could feel empathy with Carter, he now understood his back story.

"Welcome, I'm sorry we meet under these extreme circumstances. Jaii has kept me up to date with the situation and the severity of it. I must admit, it took me some time to believe all this and come to terms with it." Carter shakes hands with Jo and Hunter. He looks down at Hunter's feet.

"Nice boots, Mr. Hunter."

"Thanks," Hunter replies, "Everything Jaii has told you is true, it is happening and we have little time to figure out how we can stop it, if we can."

"Quite," Carter replies, "but anything I can do to help, I will. I have set up a meeting with members of the government at the Pentagon via satellite link this evening. I'm not sure who we can trust, but some are old friends and colleagues, others I'm not sure about," Carter says.

"My team has examined the members who will be in the meeting. We do not believe any of them are Nezulli or working with the Nezulli. We believe you can trust them," Jaii explains, "but how you convince them that this threat is real, I do not know. They will be skeptical."

"Can you be present at the meeting, Jaii?" Hunter asks. "If you can do something that would convince them, that might get things moving quicker. Perhaps shape-shift into someone else or teleport yourself to one of their locations, that type of thing?"

"Yes, perhaps this is called for," Jaii replies.

"Wait," Hunter stops them. "You can teleport? Why didn't we do that before?"

"I can, but you can't. It could kill you. And it takes a lot out of me doing so, a lot of energy is needed."

"Fair enough."

"What will the government do, Senator? Jo asks, "how will they respond to this threat, are there procedures?"

"Well, there are in theory. On paper. But no-one ever thought the threat would come, not in our lifetime, so there is no tried and tested method. The closest we have are the emergency plans put in place during the cold war, during the Cuban missile crisis. There are nuclear bunkers scattered around the country, for people in government positions and with certain skills. They have maintained the bunkers, just in case. Chosen scientists and officials will be notified of imminent danger and will be taken to the bunkers. Standard protocol, but about fifty years out of date. No-one has updated the protocols since then. The list of important people gets updated every few years, but we are not even sure who is on the list, many might have died or changed address or moved overseas. But what we are looking at here is an extinction protocol, a whole new world is developing and we are ill prepared."

"If you don't know who is working with the Nezulli or who might be one, what happens if those people are among those chosen for safety in the government bunkers?" Jo asks Carter.

"I really don't know. If they are already inside our government or science institutions, then we have a major problem. They have access to many secrets." Carter replies. The room falls silent. The old lady appears at the door, carrying a tray with teacups and a teapot on it. Hunter rushes to help her under the strain of the weight. He takes it from her, thanks her, and sets the tray on Carter's desk.

"Well," the old lady says not looking at anyone, eyes fixed on the floor, like she was seeing something happening on the ground, "when we was small, to coax out a rattler from under the porch. We's had to get close as, and poke the damn thing with a stick. Sure did. Get it all worked up, make it come to you, make it leave the nest, sure as, it worked every time. Get it in the open, chop its damn head off, one cut clean through. Sure as, works every time." The old lady turns and leaves, closing the door behind her, still muttering to herself. The group stands silently for a few seconds, absorbing the old lady's wisdom.

"Seems logical, Carter says, "like my Mom said, root them out to us before we get to the lock-down stage. Make them show themselves, make them play their hand first. We need something to get the infiltrators to expose themselves. We need a hook."

"She's a wise old lady," Hunter tells Carter, "but what? What will bring them out of hiding? These guys are clever, super clever. We haven't found a weakness in them as entities. We have in their system, but that won't help filter out the rogue agents in the government or any Nezulli entities in the government who command them, if there are any?"

Hunter and the group consider their options. The Nezulli are here for resources. They can take the resources, with or without human interaction. For them, enslaving humans to do the work, makes the process faster, allowing them to move on to their next planetary victim. They have the resources and technology to wipe out humanity quickly. They know through Jaii, the Nezulli will use organic viruses to extinguish life, including countries the US government infiltrators want dealt with. They know the Nezulli will eventually turn on the government and extinguish all human life on Earth. They agree that the one thing important to the Nezulli are Earth's resources. Without these, their journey to the next galaxy may not be possible. This is the one thing the Nezulli will do anything to protect. This is their essential shopping item in the mission. This has to be what draws them out into the open.

"Do we know which resources they need, Jaii?" Jo asks.

"There are several resources your planet can offer. Plutonium, for example, is one element they can extract to use in their quantum computer chips. Beryllium and Boron will both be useful for their fuel systems. They can both react with dark matter to create immense power, which will carry them across billions of Earth miles before they need to refuel. On Earth, you use a propulsion system for flight, whereby you push the air behind, thrusting forward. This is an antiquated method of travel. We, like the Nezulli, do not use propulsion. We use a system that pulls dark matter towards us. You can't see it, but it is there, everywhere. With this technology, you could create a craft that uses this dark matter. It can bend time, create a portal to take you to another dimension almost instantly. It draws the dark matter in, opening up space and time ahead of you, therefore, literally moving it around you as you move forward, but not just in distance, also in time. This is yet beyond your technology, but not too distant in your future. Although your bodies would need to evolve to cope with the immense pressure. The Nezulli rely on resources to make their craft move this way. These are the elements that will be important to them. This is how we draw them out." Jaii takes a seat at the opposite side of the desk to Carter.

"What do you think, Senator?" Jaii asks.

"Whilst this whole thing sounds crazy, you make a very strong case, Jaii. It sounds plausible. But how can we make them expose their cover?"

"Your government keeps reserves of these elements. In the depository at Los Alamos, this will be a target for the Nezulli. If you let it be known the reserves are being moved to another secure depository, this will create a flurry of activity from those with a vested interest. You use your Homeland Security surveillance methods to track phone calls, emails, movements and look for patterns, look for unusual activity among government employees. I know you track every one of them."

"Well, I'm not sure that's entirely true," Carter replies, "and how do you know about Los Alamos?"

"Trust me, Senator, if I can find that information, the Nezulli will also have it."

"I will speak to some colleagues, see if we can get the rumor mill working, hopefully, it will draw the right attention," Carter replies. He picks up the telephone and makes a call.

Chapter 13.

Jaii takes Jo and Hunter back to the Anunnaki base, deep in the cavernous tunnel in the mountains on the Navajo reservation. They enter Jaii's office.

"We must plan," Jaii tells them, "we will monitor activity around the movement of the elements from the depository, but the next step must be timed right."

"What is the next step?" Jo asks.

"Presumably getting to the Nezulli supercomputer?" Hunter adds.

"I will inform my team of events, then we will discuss ideas," Jaii tells the pair. He leaves the office. Jo and Hunter stand in front of Jaii's desk.

"Hunter," Jo turns to face him, "this will get real dangerous, real fast."

"I know, but we have to try, we have to do something. We can't sit and do nothing. No-one else can do it. The government, well, who can you trust in the government? I hope Carter is genuine, seems to be," Hunter tells her.

"We have only just got to know each other," Jo looks into his eyes, "I kinda like you, Hunter. Not sure why, you're a bit of a grouch, but you are all right."

"I'll take that as a compliment. I've been thinking about you a lot too. I don't go in for all that romantic stuff, not great at expressing myself, you know. But you are, well, I guess, you're, sort of…" Before Hunter can finish his sentence, Jo moves in close to him, standing on tiptoes, she puts her hands on his shoulders, and reaching her neck up, presses her lips onto Hunters. Hunter is taken by surprise, but he holds still. He likes it. He tilts his head to the right, and Jo does the same, embracing each other. Hunter holds her by the waist, feeling her soft warmth in his hands. The kiss continues for a moment, before they separate their bodies, just as Jaii enters the office. They both look a little embarrassed, walking off in different directions. Jaii goes behind the desk and sits in his chair. Hunter and Jo glance at each other, then they sit in the two chairs in front of the desk.

"Ok, a progress report," Jaii explains. "We know how to delay the Nezulli systems, with the time-base code that will need to be installed in their computer system. Correct?"

"Correct," Hunter replies.

"We don't know how we will get the code into their system, but it may involve physical access to the computer. Correct?"

"Correct," Hunter replies.

"Senator Carter is setting the scene for the element transfer from Los Alamos, although no elements will be moved. He will monitor activity in the government if any."

"Yes," replies Hunter.

"We know the government is interested in your movements, Hunter, because they detained Jo. Correct?"

"Yes," replies Jo, "but I didn't tell them anything, and they don't know what we are up to, they or Homeland Security are just listening to chatter and reacting."

"Okay," replies Jaii, "but they know something is going on. We can't trust them, any of them could be with the Nezulli."

"Sure," Hunter adds. "Homeland has access to everyone in America. They keep track of anyone of interest. I'm of interest because of my work at the agency. Nothing else, just that. I don't think they have any idea. They can track my phone and see where I've been. They might see I visited an old buddy at the base, even spoke to him on the phone. That's it. They can't connect all the dots without more information. I wouldn't worry too much about those clowns."

"You killed a guard at the facility," Jo explains, "that might raise some questions. They will look for you for that."

"Well, they can't track you down here, so you are safe for now," Jaii tells them. We have prepared some sleeping quarters for you both and meals for this evening. I'm sure you are both exhausted. We will get a fresh start in a few hours. I will let you know if Carter hears anything. Please, let me show you your quarters for this evening. Jaii gets up and walks to the door, the pair follow. He walks them across the compound with the flight craft scattered around, crew members working on them. They reach another office type building. They enter through the only door, inside is a long corridor with blue doors on both sides. Hunter looks down the corridor, he reckons there must be fifty doors on each side. The corridor then comes to a T junction and shoots on left and right, presumably with the same layout on each off-shoot. Jaii stops a few doors down and opens one on the right.

"This is yours, Hunter," he explains, "number twelve. Jo, you are opposite, number eleven." Jaii opens a door for Jo on the left of the corridor. She walks inside. The layout is basic, not unlike one of the cells back in her Ranger station. A single bed on the right, against the prison gray wall. Pillow, bathrobe, nightwear. A bedside cabinet, gray painted aluminum, a washbasin, white, and a small cubicle in the corner at the foot of the bed with a toilet, shower and washbasin, white. On the left is a small writing desk, a chair and a wardrobe, gray. Dark gray carpet, plain. No windows, no need in an underground tunnel. Hunter's is the same layout, but reversed.

"Meals will be delivered to you for seven o'clock this evening," Jaii tells them, "get some rest, we have much to do." Jaii leaves.

"Hunter, can we talk later," Jo asks, "you know, about earlier. I will knock on your door in a bit," she tells him. They smile at each other, then both close their doors.

Hunter sits on the bed and struggles to pull off his boots. They are dusty, scratched and dirty, but still look great. He thinks so, anyway. He studies the image on the side of the boots. A silver flying saucer, with red lights around the rim, shooting upwards to the stars. He had it designed by a specialist, the only ones in the world. He loved his boots. He sets them side by side at the foot of the bed, ready. Hunter puts his head on the pillow, swings his feet up onto the bed and drifts into a sound, deep, sleep. He is startled by a banging noise. He sits up, still half asleep, trying to figure out what is happening. It's the door, someone is knocking. He gets up to answer it.

"Jo, it's you," Hunter says in a partial yawn, "what time is it?"

"It's gone after seven." Jo is standing in a red bathrobe, her hair still wet from the shower.

"They tried to waken you, the food guys, but you were sound asleep, we could hear you snoring. Here, this is for you. Can I come in?" Jo hands Hunter a brown paper bag with golden arches on it. She has one and a cardboard tray with two cold drinks.

"Sure, come in." Jo enters and takes a seat at the small writing desk. Hunter sits back on the bed and opens his food bag, containing a large fries and cheeseburger. The pair eat in silence, happy to be eating after a long day and happy to sit in each other's company. Jo finishes first, putting her rubbish back in the bag and starting on her cold drink.

"Tell me about yourself, Hunter," Jo asks, "where is your daughter's mom, are you not together anymore?" Hunter finishes the last of his fries and grabs the cold drink, stalling for time as he tries to talk about family.

"No, we got divorced a long time ago. Nothing to tell, really. She didn't like me working all hours, in secret places, not being able to discuss the job with her. The usual thing. She wanted more of my time, but so did the government. It just didn't work out."

"So, there's no special someone in the wings?" Jo asks.

"No, just haven't had the time. I look after my daughter, she lived with me, her mom moved out to California, so it's pretty much just me and Laura. That was until she was taken by Jaii and his crew."

"But you know she's safe now, she will be okay."

"Yes, but I didn't, that's why I've been chasing Jaii, to get my daughter back."

"I think it was an elaborate plan by Jaii, to get you here, otherwise you wouldn't have come, you wouldn't chase him if you didn't have to."

"Yeah, I see that now," Hunter explains, "but I didn't before. I guess desperate times call for desperate measures."

"What's she like, Laura? What is she into?"

"She's beautiful, long dark hair, tanned skin, big bright eyes, always smiling and laughing. She listens to music a lot, always got those little headphone things with no cables in her ears. Like most girls her age, always got her face down looking at her phone. Seriously, what can be so important? They're all into this 'Instantgram' thing or 'The Facebook' or whatever they're called." Jo lets out a laugh, almost choking on her soft drink.

"Instagram, Hunter, it's Instagram and no-one has called it THE Facebook since two thousand and four."

"Well, you know what I mean, those social media websites. They can't be good for them."

"Maybe, but that's the youth of today, it's what they were born into, they know nothing else."

"What are you going to do when this is all over, Hunter, assuming we survive, that is?" Jo asks.

"I don't know. I might retrain as a ranger, move back to the reservation, work my way up, become your boss," he replies with a grin.

"Sure, I don't think you would pass the physical. Look at you climbing up the mountain, you nearly had a heart attack," Jo jests. Jo sets her drink on the table and gets up from her chair and sits next to Hunter on the bed.

"It would be nice to have you around, on the reservation, if you decide to move back."

Hunter sets his drink on the floor, turns to Jo and with his left hand behind her neck, he pulls her gently towards him. They kiss.

"Wait. Just hold me, Hunter. Let's just hold each other for a bit." They lay down. Hunter puts his arm around Jo and she lays her head on his chest, comfortable, warm, safe. Laying on the bed in an embrace, they both fall asleep in this position.

Chapter 14.

Senator Carter sits in his oak panel-lined office at the back of his grand old mansion. It is past nine-thirty in the evening. He has called a video phone conference with colleagues to discuss the situation Jaii explained to him. On his computer screen, small boxes populate with video feeds from various offices and homes, with the heads and shoulders of important government officials, as they log in to the live feed conference. Some still wearing suits, others in evening wear, one woman in pajamas. Once all twelve boxes are filled with faces, Carter can begin.

"Thank you for joining me at such brief notice, ladies and gentlemen. I'm sorry to ruin your evening, but this is of national importance. Please remember, you are under the official secrets act and this is a secure closed feed." Carter continues. "Our nation and humanity are under great threat. Please bear with me. This might sound crazy, it did to me when I first heard it, but I have been convinced it is genuine. We are under threat from entities from another world, actually, another universe." There are some mutterings from the people in the live feed. One man asks Carter to clarify his statement. Just then, Jaii materializes standing next to Carter. There is alarm from the conference attendees.

"Please don't be alarmed," Carter insists, "this is Jaii, he is the one who told me of the impending fate. He is here to help us, to protect us."

"Is he an alien?" asks the lady in pajamas.

"Yes," replies Jaii, "I am from another world in a distant galaxy. As Senator Carter was explaining, your world is in grave danger, and humanity may not survive." A few of the attendees disconnect from the conference, believing it to be a hoax. Others laugh at Carter, applauding his theatrics. The rest sit in astonishment, not knowing how to react.

"Please folks, this is a serious matter," Carter persists, "we have little time. We need to get the President onside. I need your help to convince others of the gravity of the situation. We need a plan of action. We need to get the President and key officials into the government bunker and notify other world leaders."

"If this is true," one attendee speaks up, "one, how can you prove it, and two, what exactly are these aliens planning to do?" Just then, Jaii disappears from beside Carter and teleports next to the official who asked the question. She is startled by the appearance, but Jaii just smiles and talks.

"My friend, this is not a magic trick, this is real. Your futures are limited unless you act now. To answer your second point, the Nezulli, as they are known, will strip your planet of all resources, enslave the strong to do all the work, kill the weak and infirm, then when all is gone, kill those still alive, if anyone is." Jaii then reappears at Carter's side.

"So, what can we do to save ourselves?" asks the attendee.

"There are members of our government who are in collusion with theses aliens, they believe the Nezulli will give them ultimate world power, in return for resources. Jaii has explained the Nezulli cannot be trusted. We must weed out the officials working with the Nezulli, and help Jaii and his people to defeat the Nezulli," Carter explains.

"How do you know one or more of us in this conference are not working with the Nezulli?" asks one of the attendees.

"Jaii has assured me he has done a background check on each of you, no-one here is involved. His team will help, they can gain information for us and verify any contact with known Nezulli, but we each need to check and recheck our own teams. No-one can be overlooked. We must take a systematic approach to this, make sure we do the research, we don't want to accuse someone incorrectly. Anyone found to be working with the Nezulli, will be detained indefinitely at one of our secure facilities."

"What if the President is working with these aliens?" one man asks.

"In that case," Carter replies, "he, too, will be detained in a facility. I will send you each further details later tonight. Please be careful. Do not talk to anyone about this until they are confirmed cleared." Carter ends the conference.

"Well, Jaii, do you think anyone believed us?"

"Yes, it will take some of them a little longer than others, but they will get there. Thank you, Senator, you are a good man. I hope your influence will spur these people into action. I must return to my base, I will be back in touch soon. Please continue with your work to find the infiltrators." Jaii disappears.

Chapter 15.

Jo and Hunter are waiting, sitting in the chairs in front of Jaii's desk.

"You two look fresh, did you have a good rest," Jaii inquires. They look at each other with a smile.

"Yes, very good, thanks," Hunter replies. Jaii sits in his chair.

"Senator Carter is progressing with some resistance, but he is moving forward with the government," Jaii explains.

"So, what's next?" Jo asks. A crew member knocks on the door and enters, handing Jaii an iPad type device. Jaii reads the writing on the screen. His expression changes to a frown.

"Hunter, how well do you know your old colleague, Mr. Brennan?"

"Well enough, why?"

"My team ran a check on his movements and contacts, it seems he, or at least his cell phone, has had contact with a known Nezulli operative."

"Nonsense, there must be a mistake. Brennan and I go way back, right back to the training academy. That's, what, nearly thirty years? He was the best man at my wedding, for fuck's sake. You're wrong."

"Perhaps," Jaii replies cautiously, "maybe he loaned his cell phone to a colleague. It might not have been Brennan. I just thought you should know. He might not be as trustworthy as you believe."

"This is bullshit!" Hunter gets up and storms out of the office, slamming the door behind him. Jo looks at Jaii.

"I'll go speak to him," she says, "he'll be fine when he calms down a bit." Jo leaves the office to go find Hunter. She sees him marching along the huge cavern, still annoyed.

"Hunter, wait up." He stops and looks around as Jo approaches.

"You're such a hot-head, do you know that?" say asks.

"Yeah, I know. But Jaii really winds me up sometimes."

"What if it is true, though?" she asks, "what if Brennan has been won over by the Nezulli, promised a prominent position or offered money or something. Do you think he would take it?"

"I don't know, maybe. He's always been there for me, getting married, when Laura was born, going through a divorce. He has been there every time. I can't believe he would double-cross me."

"Well, we don't know for sure, yet. So, don't dwell on it, focus on what needs to be done to sort out the bloody Nezulli," Jo tells him. She takes his hand in hers and they walk along the cavern in silence, hand in hand.

Chapter 16.

Senator Carter leaves his mansion, heading for the Pentagon. It is over a two-hour drive on a good day, a trip he makes at least twice a week. It is night, close to 11 pm, he reckons closer to two-and-a-half hours in the dark. His automobile is a large BMW 4x4, smooth ride, Satnav, air-con, a comfortable vehicle for long trips. Carter heads out of town, towards the I-95. Traffic is light, no major roadworks reported on the Satnav. He puts the radio on, picking up the local news channel. After a few miles, he notices car headlights in his rear-view mirror. The car is keeping pace with Carter. He speeds up to put more distance between him and the vehicle behind, but it too speeds up. He continues on for a few miles, each time he speeds up, so does the vehicle behind. He slows to well under the speed limit, the vehicle behind slows. Carter is sure he is being followed. It could be Pentagon security, he thinks, he knows they sometimes monitor him and his colleagues in times of high alerts. Perhaps Homeland Security, wondering why he is traveling towards Washington at night. Carter thinks he is becoming paranoid. He settles for a steady speed and continues his journey, with one eye on the rear-view mirror.

After about forty minutes, he takes the off-ramp at Wilderness to head east. As he turns, the vehicle behind has approached at speed. It rams the back of Carter's vehicle, sending him into a spin. He struggles to control it, turning the steering wheel hard left, then hard right, to rectify the direction of travel. He gets the vehicle back on course, as he steers right, going around the off-ramp towards the highway traffic. He increases his speed, just enough to gain distance from the other vehicle, but it gains on him. He reaches the light traffic flow on the interstate, and puts his foot on the throttle, trying to lose the other vehicle. He slips into the traffic, weaving in and out across three lanes. The other vehicle does the same, gaining ground. Carter tries to use his cell phone to call the police, but fumbles with it and drops it on the floor. He reaches down to find it with his right hand, still trying to watch the traffic ahead. He finally gets hold of it and picks it up. As he sits up straight with the phone, he looks to his left. He sees the other vehicle beside him, the window down, then a flash of light, the sound of breaking glass, instant sudden pain in his head. Within a second, black. Carter's vehicle goes out of control as he slumps forward over the steering wheel, dead. The other vehicle slows down, keeping clear behind Carters. The Senator's vehicle drifts to the left, hits the safety barrier, bounces back, hits another vehicle and somersaults into an airborne spin, finally coming to rest over the barriers, down a slope in the darkness. The hitman's vehicle drives slowly past the wreckage, looking for any movement, then drives away at normal speed, whilst other vehicles stop to help.

Chapter 17.

"The attack fleet is ready," Vok announces,

"Preparations are complete," Vok commands his army from the command craft, passing orders to his Lieutenants, who pass orders to their crews. The craft fleet stretches for miles in space, hidden in the moon's shadow.

"By sunrise tomorrow, we will be stationed just beyond Earth's atmosphere, over every major city on the planet," Vok tells his crew, "send the forward crews to release the viruses into the planet's atmosphere. In a brief space of time, humanity will be sick, the weak will die, the strong will be enslaved. We must be swift. I have been informed of the Anunnaki's involvement with these humans. They will try to destroy our mission. We must not let this happen. We must hurry, but they are no match for us." His crew busies themselves with carrying out orders, the forward craft leaves the shadow of the moon on their mission to infect humanity. Hundreds of small forward craft shoot away from the base station in a long string of moving space ships.

#

The morning sun rises over the Anunnaki base, deep in a mountain range in Arizona. A member of Jaii's crew enters his office with a note. He hands it to Jaii with some urgency. Jaii reads the note. He leaves his office in search of Hunter and Jo. He finds them walking among the hundreds of craft stationed in the tunnel base.

"I have been informed that Senator Carter was killed last night. He was shot dead on his way to the Pentagon."

"Fuck," Hunter expresses.

"What the hell," Jo adds, "this is getting seriously crazy. Poor Carter. He was such a nice guy."

"Do we know if he alerted the President's team before he was killed? Where are we with the government? Someone in his conference must have double-crossed him, someone must have been working with the Nezulli?" Hunter tells them.

"Maybe," Jaii adds, "this seems to run deeper than we thought. His people will continue in his absence, but we must assume the Nezulli are now aware of our presence here. They will bring forward their plans if they know there is resistance."

"Who do you think it was, who killed Carter?" Jo asks Jaii.

"It must have been someone within one of your government agencies," Jaii explains. "Someone who could monitor the Senators movements, his contacts, perhaps they even had a feed of the secure line conference. Whoever it was, they needed to stop him before he went higher with his quest. Before he could convince the President. Let us know they mean business."

"They have broken cover," Hunter adds, "They have played their hand. A dangerous thing to do at this stage. They must be worried. What would happen if we alerted the world to what is happening? Would it help?"

"I believe it would create a major crisis, panic across nations. Some would consider it the end of the world, others would embrace it, most would panic, causing food shortages, water shortages, fuel shortages. It would help the Nezulli, as these are their principal areas of attack," Jaii explains, "if they infect the resources that people stock up on in times of crisis, it speeds up the results. Alerting the world at this stage would be counter productive."

"Okay," Jo adds, "but if we don't, millions of people could die. How do we prevent that from happening?"

"We don't," Jaii replies, "unfortunately, we cannot save everyone. But we can try to save the majority. That is the best-case scenario."

"Right," Hunter says, "the sooner we can get to their supercomputer the better, the more lives we can save."

"Indeed," Jaii replies, "but we must wait for the command fleet to come closer in Earth's orbit. Only then can we try to gain access. We need Vok, the Nezulli commander, to come out of hiding with his command craft. And I believe it will be soon, as things appear to be moving fast. Once he is in range, we will attack. I have a plan, well sort of."

"What do you mean, well sort of?" Jo asks.

"I mean, it hasn't been fully planned, but basically, we create a diversion, involving some of your air force fighter jets, to intercept Nezulli fleet craft. We can provide locators. Once they are engaged in a chase, we will head to the command craft, which will have less protection during the fight."

"Not much of a plan, is it?" Hunter replies.

"Like I said, it needs some work."

"When do we do this, what's the soonest we can get access?" asks Hunter.

"In the next few hours. That's my best guess. They will get into position for their mission. They will strike fast, first release the viruses and contaminants, then shortly after, make themselves known around your planet. By this time, the sickness will head towards a pandemic, panic will takeover, chaos will ensue. Governments will attempt to fight, send in their armies, but the armies will protect facilities, resources, keep the peace, maintain some stability. They won't have the resources to protect and send soldiers to fight against alien technology. It will become a case of self-preservation. Each government will close its doors to protect itself. The US government members working with the Nezulli will take charge, believing they will gain world dominance. But they too will soon discover the truth. There will be no world to dominate, no resources, little or no human life. Extinction is a rapid process. A few might survive and live hoping to rebuild a new society, but this is highly unlikely. If they do, it will be like no society you have experience of. But, with the changes to the environment, life might spring hope. No pollution, the toxins released by the Nezulli will dissipate, the water will run clear, the air will become fresh, the sea levels will reduce. Your ozone will redevelop. There may be some hope in the face of disaster. You must never give up hope."

"Were there any survivors from your planet who stayed behind to rebuild a civilization?" Jo asks Jaii."

"Our planet could not recover. The damage had been done. Maybe, if we had stayed, found a way to breathe life back into the planet, just maybe. But for us, we felt the safest approach was to keep moving, stay together, safety in numbers. The devastation was colossal. It was too much to bear. We chose, as a collective, to help others in danger from this scourge. This is our purpose in life, our future. We are increasing in numbers. Our society is procreating, we have newly born members each day. We will one day find our place in the multiverse, somewhere we can call our home."

"Perhaps you can stay here, on Earth?" Jo tells him, "if we defeat the Nezulli and Earth can rejuvenate itself, perhaps this could be your home. We could live side by side. Your knowledge would be of great help to us. I'm not sure what we can offer you that would benefit your race, though?"

"You have many things we could learn from you, or relearn I should say. We have lost many ways from our past, we could start over, you could teach us so much. But we must get the best outcome for any of this to matter. We must not lose."

"We need to know who betrayed Carter, who killed him. Otherwise the US government is in for a short sharp shock," Hunter says.

"Yes," Jaii replies, "they will close ranks, those with Nezulli connections will get into positions of safety, ready to take command. They will remove any threat, but not before they enter the secure bunker set aside for chief government officials and the President. Once enclosed, they have a smaller battle ahead, much easier than doing it in the White House."

"So, what can we do now, there must be something we can do, rather than waiting?" Jo asks. "There must be somewhere we could be to help?"

"Let's go pay Brennan a visit," Hunter suggests. If he is on our side, he will help. If, as you have said, Jaii, he might work with the Nezulli, then it's time to find out for sure."

Hunter, Jo and Jaii go to the Rangers station on the reservation in Jaii's craft. The station is a wooden built building, clean and well maintained, except for Jo's desk. Her desk is on the right of the open planned office, with only one other desk to the left. The walls are covered in maps of the reservation and there is a line of gray filing cabinets along the length of the back wall. A door on the right past Jo's desk leads off to a holding cell, out of sight. Her desk is a mass of papers, file binders, old coffee cups and bits of scrap paper. The other desk is tidy, everything well organized.

"Have you been burgled?" Hunter asks when he sees the desk.

"No, sorry, just haven't got time for filing reports, organizing my files, you know," Jo replies as she attempts to clear some mess up. "You will get a good cell phone signal here." Hunter flips open his cell phone and speed dials Brennan. After two rings, he answers.

"Hunter, buddy, how are you, what are you up to, we should catch up, go for a drink soon?"

"Hey Brennan, that's a good idea. Let's meet up again at the Rock Springs Diner again, say at around 11am?"

"Sure, the breakfasts are excellent there. See you later, buddy." Brennan hangs up. Hunter looks at the others.

"He sounds normal, didn't sound nervous or anything different, just the usual Brennan."

"Let's hope Jaii is wrong on this one," Jo replies, "Brennan could be one of the good guys." Hunter closes his cell phone and slips it into his jacket pocket.

"Jo, can we use a Ranger truck to head down to the diner?" Hunter asks.

"Sure, I'll drive," she quickly suggests. Jo grabs a set of keys hanging in a row of keys on the wall. She writes something in a journal on her desk.

"Just need to keep track of any vehicles used, my boss is a pain with the details," she explains. She grabs a cell phone from the department cell phone stock.

"I will keep you informed of any updates regarding the Nezulli," Jaii tells them as they prepare to leave, "please be careful, do not give any information to Brennan."

"I know," Hunter says, "we will only see if we can get info out of him. I can look him in the face, if he is lying, I will know."

Hunter and Jo leave the office. Jaii flies back to the tunnel base. She unlocks the truck. The truck is not as new as Jo's truck, but it is the same make and model, but dark blue, clean and full of gas. They buckle up and head away from the Ranger station, past the community center and the school house. They pass some residents of the reservation, going about their normal business, unpacking shopping from a trunk, brushing the yard.

"It's weird, isn't it," Jo turns to Hunter, "these people do not understand what might be in store for them," she explains, "they believe tomorrow will just be like today, business as normal. It's crazy. You want to shout out at them, grab your kids, get your stuff, run for the hills."

"It wouldn't make any difference," Hunter replies, "they would suffer regardless, short term or long term, they would be doomed. Let them have one more day to not worry about the end of civilization. One more day to hug their kids, make love to their partner, walk their dog."

"That was almost philosophical, Hunter. Are you mellowing," Jo teases him. Hunter smiles at her and turns to stare out the truck window.

"Knowing what we know about the future, Jo, makes you think. Think about the things you should have done, but never got around to."

"Like what?" she asks.

"Stupid stuff. Bucket list stuff, like write a book, travel around Europe, build something, make something, you know, leave a legacy for the future, if there is one."

"Yeah, I know what you mean."

"What do you regret not doing?" Hunter asks. Jo watches the dirt track road ahead, thinking about the question. After a few seconds, she replies.

"Kids. I wish I'd had kids. Or at least taken the opportunity. I have been so busy, absorbed in my work, I never really took the time. Never spent long enough with anyone to want to. Now, I meet someone who I would like to be with, maybe take that step to motherhood, and we will probably be dead within the week. Great timing, eh Hunter?" He looks over at her, he can see she is disappointed in herself. She has a sadness, a yearning that wasn't there before. But now, as time runs out, she may be too late. Hunter doesn't ask any further questions. They travel in a dust cloud towards the freeway in silence.

Chapter 18.

Rock Springs Bar & Diner
Arizona.
Jo turns off the freeway into the dusty parking lot of the Rock Springs Diner and Bar. There are a few vehicles scattered around the parking area. She pulls into a bay close to the diner, in the shade from the morning sun. Hunter scans the parking lot for Brennan's sedan.

"I don't think he's here yet," he tells Jo. "Let's get a booth facing the door. Get a good look around." The pair get out, Jo clicks the fob to lock the truck and they enter the diner."

"Hello, hun," the waitress with the dancer's legs greets them.

"Hi," Hunter replies, not looking at her, but looking around the diner for Brennan. No sign.

"Coffee?" the waitress asks them.

"Sure, we would love some," Jo replies, "we will sit over there." Jo points to an empty booth at the end of the diner, past where the counter turns left to the bar area. They walk to the booth and sit side by side, facing the rest of the diner. There is an old man at the counter, sipping coffee. A young couple with two kids in a booth by the windows on the long side of the diner, a girl about five and a boy, Hunter reckoned, to be about eight or nine years old. The kids are noisy, the parents trying to restrain and entertain them. Jo and Hunter have a window behind them. Hunter swings around, sitting partly facing Jo, with his left elbow up on the seatback, allowing him to see out of the window behind them. When Brennan approaches, he will have to drive past the row of windows on the diner's long side. If he parks around the corner, Hunter will have him in vision there. All angles covered, just in case. If he is followed by anyone, Hunter and Jo will have a good sightline for this too.

The waitress brings over a tray with two cups, a coffee pot, and two menus. She lays the menus on the booth table and pours them each a coffee.

"Help yourself to cream and sugar," she nods to condiments on the table, "let me know when you're ready to order or need a refill, my dears." She leaves them to go tend to the young couple with the noisy kids. Hunter and Jo take a sip of coffee in unison.

"Damn, that's good," Jo says as she takes another drink.

"How are you going to ask Brennan if he is involved with the Nezulli?" Jo asks.

"Damned if I know. How do you bring it into the conversation? Hey Brennan, did you see the game last night? Oh and are you working with aliens to take over the world?" Jo laughs.

"Yes, not an easy one. Especially as you don't want to give him any info," Jo replies, "Is he married, got kids?"

"No, still single, had a few girlfriends over the years, no kids that he knows of." Hunter sips his coffee, thinking back, looking for any clues that he should have seen, something to show Brennan was corrupt. He couldn't find anything. Everything had been normal between them. Brennan had given Hunter information on UFO activity at Flagstaff. He didn't have to do that, Hunter thought. He was helping him find his daughter. Brennan had been there when Hunter came to in the hospital after the accident when Jaii's craft hit his truck. Normal friend stuff. Brennan picked him up from the desert after Jaii had left him there. Hunter still didn't believe Brennan was a bad guy.

A cloud of dust precedes a vehicle leaving the freeway and entering the parking area of the diner. A black sedan. Brennan. The vehicle pulls into a parking bay two bays from Jo's pickup. Brennan steps out, looking around for Hunter's pickup truck.

"That's Brennan," Hunter nudges Jo, nodding towards the window. Brennan walks the length of the diner, past the windows on the long side, and enters by the door on the end. He sees Hunter at the far end and nods and smiles, giving a quick wave. He walks along the diner to the booth.

"Hey buddy, good to see you. Who's this?" Brennan asks, holding out a hand for a handshake with Jo. Hunter stands.

"Brennan, Jo, Jo, my pal Brennan." They shake hands.

"Lovely to meet you Jo." Brennan sits to the side of Jo, on the right side of the booth, with Jo in the middle.

"So, let me buy you guys breakfast," Brennan announces.

"No, you got the last time, my treat," Hunter insists. The waitress comes over to the booth with another cup and another clear pot of dark coffee. She pours Brennan a cup and tells them to call her over if they want anything.

"So, Hunter, I didn't have time to talk to you at the base the other day, you seemed in a bit of a hurry. What's going on, pal? Did you find anything of interest at Flagstaff?"

"No, Flagstaff was a washout, nothing of interest there," Hunter replies.

"What were you doing back on the base?" Brennan asks, "Was there something there of interest? Anything I can help with?" He sips his coffee. "Damn, that's good coffee." Jo flicks through the menu on the table.

"Maybe, Brennan. There has been something going on, but I'm not sure what it is, or even if it is related to the Flagstaff sightings."

"So," Brennan turns his attention to Jo, "what do you do? How did you get mixed up with this madman?"

"I'm a Ranger, up on the reservation. Hunter and I met by accident. I'm just tagging along, trying to keep myself occupied, you know," she replies, not wanting to give away too much information. Brennan nods and smiles, slightly disinterested.

"Hunter tells me you guys have been friends for years, worked together for the government," Jo says.

"That's right. We go way back. Back to the academy, happy days." Hunter looks across the table at Brennan, trying to pick up signals of deceit, or lies, changes in his tone or body language. He signals the waitress and orders them all pancakes and bacon with maple syrup.

"What do you do at the government?" Jo asks Brennan.

"I'm an analyst, boring stuff really. Just checking lots of numbers and making sense of it all." Brennan looks a little uncomfortable, like he wants to get to the point, cut out the chitchat and find out what he wants to know.

"But you work at the famous Area 51, right? There must be some weird, dark stuff that goes on there?" Jo asks.

"No, that's all hype, the movies and TV have made it all into something it's not. Maybe I'll take you there, show you around one day. Seriously, nothing to see," Brennan explains. Jo sips her coffee and thanks Brennan for the offer.

"Brennan," Hunter talks. "Have you ever heard of the Nezulli?" Hunter watches Brennan in great detail, watching for a flinch or eye movement. Jo looks at Hunter with a frown, trying to say he has given away information. But Hunter has no choice, he has to know if Brennan has gone rogue. And he gets his information. Brennan's left eyelid gives a minor tremor and his gaze drifts to the left for a fraction of a second. Almost unnoticeable, unless you were trained to look, and Hunter was. Brennan quickly makes eye contact, but the damage is done. Hunter has his answer. Brennan was also trained in body language and analyzing the human body under stress, so he knows Hunter might now know.

"What is that?" Brennan asks, "a new terrorist threat?"

"You have never heard that name before?" Hunter asks.

"No, can't say I have. Are you onto something big?" The waitress arrives at the table with their food, placing a plate in front of each of them. She leaves.

"Might be nothing, Brennan," Hunter adds, "just wondered if you knew anything, but clearly not. No worries, it's most likely a dead-end lead. Let's eat up, I'm starving." Brennan holds his gaze on Hunter for a few seconds longer, trying to see if he can find any evidence that Hunter doesn't believe him. He sees nothing. But he knows Hunter is onto the Nezulli. Brennan knows things will differ from this moment on. He knows if it comes to it, he will be forced to kill them both. He had killed a Senator less than twelve hours earlier. He was prepared to do it again. The three eat their breakfast, discussing the meal, the exemplary service of the diner, chitchat, uneasy, but necessary.

"So, what are your plans for today?" Brennan asks the pair, "going anywhere nice?"

"No, just cruising around for a bit, do some shopping," Hunter replies, "what about you?"

"Just back to the office, do some work, the usual," replies Brennan.

Hunter can see out of the window, over Brennan's shoulder. Another black sedan pulls in, in a cloud of dust. This one has blacked-out windows, like the one he saw the last time he visited the diner. Coincidence? Hunter suspected not. It parks up away from the diner, at the far side of the parking lot, facing the diner. No-one gets out. They finish their meals.

"Thanks for the breakfast, Hunter," Brennan announces, "I really need to get going. Let's catch up again soon. Lovely to meet you Jo." Brennan gets up and walks along the diner, turning at the door to wave back at the table. They wave back at him, smiling. He leaves. They watch him as he gets into his sedan and drives away, heading south. The other black sedan remains across the lot.

"Well?" Jo asks, "is he a liar?"

"Sadly, yes. He flinched when asked about the Nezulli. He knows who they are. Even if he had just heard the name in the office or read it in a report, why lie about it to me. He's in on it all right. We need to be careful."

"What will Brennan's next move be?" Jo asks, "what will he do now?" Hunter thinks for a minute, trying to think what he would do in the same situation.

"If he thinks we know he is involved, he will go to whoever he reports to with the Nezulli mission, tell them he has been compromised. He will probably get to the bunker at the base, safe and ready to double-cross his colleagues. If he is convinced we know nothing, or at least nothing that will cause a problem, then he will carry on as usual, until he gets his orders to go underground."

"Do you think he's doing it for money?"

"I don't know," Hunter replies, "it must be a lot of money if he is. Maybe they offered him something else, like a position of power, head of something or other." The waitress approaches.

"Can I get you anything else?" she asks.

"No thank you," Jo answers. The waitress smiles and leaves them to their conversation. Hunter sits and thinks about the situation, calculating what the next step should be.

"Let's head back up to the reservation," he tells Jo, "we need to speak to Jaii. I will contact him from up there." Hunter leaves money for the bill on the table, with a generous tip for the waitress and the pair head back up the freeway.

Chapter 19.

Jaii brings Jo and Hunter back to his mountain base on the reservation. They all enter his office and Jaii sits behind his desk, the pair take seats opposite.

"We have further intel regarding the planned invasion. It's not good news. The Nezulli have developed a whole new resistant coronavirus, designed to target the weak, old and very young among the human population. There is no known cure. Once released, there may be no stopping it globally, it will infect millions in days and could spread at a rate never before seen. This has serious implications for the human species. My team is working on finding the virus properties and I hope we can create a resistant antidote, but in a matter of days or hours, it is highly unlikely."

"Once released, do you mean the end of humanity?" Jo asks.

"Hard to say. Some humans might have a natural resistance, depending on their genetic make-up, which line of species they evolved from. But we believe they have designed it after studying the genetics of humans abducted by the Nezulli for that very purpose."

"Is there anything we can do, contact the World Health Organization or someone?" Jo asks.

"I don't think there is anything they could do. They have been working on antivirals for another strain of the virus, but this one is synthetic, the properties are different and much more effective against human's natural and man-made antibiotics," Jaii replies.

"Does this mean, even if we manage to get into the Nezulli computer systems and download the computer virus, it will be a pointless exercise?" Hunter asks.

"No," Jaii replies, "the situation has taken a fresh path, we knew they would distribute viruses across your planet, we were prepared for this with antidotes to build up human resistance, with many casualties, but with many lives saved. This new virus puts us back to square one, we have yet to develop an antidote for this one. But to go ahead with our mission to upload the computer virus is still vital. It is our best opportunity to wipe out the Nezulli permanently, to prevent this ever happening again, anywhere. We will continue to work on finding an antidote for the virus, but our mission has not changed."

"Okay," Hunter replies, "keep us updated. I'm going back to my quarters to come up with some plans for the mission. Jo, do you want to join me?" Jo nods her head and they both leave the office and walk back across the open hangar to the corridor to the accommodation rooms. Once inside Hunter's room, he closes the door quickly. Hunter paces the length of the small single room.

"I don't trust him," he announces, "all he is concerned about is getting rid of the Nezulli, revenge for his family. He doesn't care a fuck about us or humanity."

"You need to calm down, think about it. Yes, I'm sure there is some element of revenge, you would be the same," Jo explains. Hunter grunts.

"But I believe he is genuinely trying to help humanity. For him, it's a bonus if he can annihilate the Nezulli. We have to trust him, we have no choice. You have to trust someone, Hunter."

"I trust you. No-one else. Brennan has turned out to be a scheming, lying scumbag, Jaii might well be the same. You are the only one who has my back."

"You had mine back at the facility, I won't forget it. We need each other to get through this, to survive, succeed, flourish," Jo tells him, "but I think this mission to the Nezulli command center is suicide."

"I agree, we need a better solution. Any ideas?" Hunter asks. Jo sits on the end of his bed, thinking of another way to complete the task, one less dangerous, one where they won't each or both get killed trying. Hunter continues to pace the room.

"Brennan," Jo shrieks, surprised by her own idea.

"Brennan?" Hunter questions.

"Yes, why not? You know he is working with the Nezulli, you know he doesn't know that you know that. Right?" Hunter looks puzzled as he works out what she means.

"So, you give the encrypted file to Brennan, tell him to go to the government, it has info on a planned invasion or something he might believe, then ensure he must not, under any circumstances, let it fall into the hands of anyone else. I'm sure he will open it at the government base to decrypt it. When he fails, he will have remote access to the Nezulli supercomputer for decryption, right?"

"Sure, it might happen that way."

"Okay, let's assume it does. Once the supercomputer has it in the system, it can't be stopped. All you have to do is make sure the supercomputer doesn't recognize it as virus long enough for it to upload, hidden like any computer virus, masked or something." Jo is pleased with her idea.

"Bloody hell, Jo, you should work in the government's analytics department. That might work. I can write an auto-trigger into the code and a masking code to hide the actual contents of the container."

"Best of all, we don't have to get killed trying to break into the computer. We can stay here and wait for the virus to kill us all slowly," Jo says with a cheeky grin. Hunter smiles back, knowing it is humor, but in fact a real possibility.

Jo lays down on Hunter's bed. He joins her, nudging her over with his hip. He brings his arm up, and she lifts her head to allow for the cuddle. Jo snuggles her head onto his chest and throws her arm across his body, glad of the warmth of another human's touch. They lay on the bed in silence, thinking about the plan, the future and the lack thereof.

Chapter 20.

Jaii enters the lab, situated off the main craft hangar and close to the accommodation modules. He walks across the white under lit floor, to a bench with a range of glass vials, flasks, microscopes, and other lab instruments. The white-walled room has several workbenches, each with Anunnaki scientists, working with liquids, running experiments, testing and retesting. Jaii speaks to one of the scientists.

"What progress have you made on the coronavirus antidote?"

"Sorry, Commander, everything we have tried has failed. We need to wait for the spread to get enough samples to develop one that will resist."

"Once they release it, it may already be too late for humanity. I will work with you. I was a doctor back in our land. This is something I can help with. I have experience in developing resistant antibodies. Show me what you are working on now," Jaii insists. The pair set to work to find a solution for the impending virus release.

Jo lays in the embrace from Hunter, content in the moment.

"Tell me more about yourself, Hunter." He paused, thinking about his past, his upbringing, his career.

"Pretty unremarkable, I'd say, except for a few moments in life, like anyone, when things take on a new meaning. I think I told you before, I grew up on the north end of the reservation, about two hundred miles north of your settlement, so we probably never met in the past. My dad had been a traditional craftsman and hunter, before going off to fight in the second world war. He was one of the Navajo code writers. They called them the 'wind talkers'. He used to laugh when he heard that. But they were good at what they did."

"I've heard stories, on the reservation, about the men who went over there and used our ancient language to deliver messages."

"Well, my father was one of them. He never really talked about the war, though, seemed happier to forget it, move on with life. I know he was involved in communications during the taking of Iwo Jima. He went ashore with the Marine Corps and battled along with them. He relayed messages to ensure accurate fire cover from the fleet. Other than that, he didn't say much about it."

"What about your mother, tell me about her," Jo insists.

"Mana, that was her name. She was the glue of my family, the one who kept it all together. She made sure everyone was looked after, had enough food, could get an education, could progress in the world. There weren't many like my mother. Sadly, she grew old and passed away a few years back. Both parents gone, dad died about ten years before mum. I have a sister, though. Miri, she is a couple of years younger than me, works as a human rights lawyer in Los Angeles, very successful I hear."

"You don't keep in touch?" Jo asks.

"Not so much these days, she's busy, I'm busy, you know how it goes. We were very close as kids, loved to play out in the dust fields, climbing in the mountains up near our farm, cycling for miles along the old dirt tracks. It was a happy childhood. It always seemed to be sunny then, you forget the cold, dark, wet winters, just remember the sun-filled outdoor life, carefree, no concerns." Hunter goes quiet while he remembers his sister and him, playing down by the creek, enjoying the safety and freedom of life on the reservation back then.

"You said earlier, there were a few moments in life that change everything. What were yours?" Jo asks.

"Well, when I was about nine, maybe ten years old, I was heading back home, on my own, from fishing at the nearby creek. The sun was just setting, it turned dark quickly. But I had tracked along the route so many times, I knew it backwards. That's when I saw a light up ahead of me. I knew there were no houses up there and it wasn't a truck. It was a glimmering blue and white light, which just seemed to hover above the dirt track. It was masked by trees, so I walked a little closer to get a better look. Then I saw it in full. It was a disk, silvery, hovering about four or five feet off the ground. No sound, nothing. As a young boy, I was a little frightened but more curious about what it was, so I walked closer. It didn't move. I got right up beside it, reached out a placed my hand on the vessel. My mind suddenly became filled with numbers, binary code, a series of zeros and ones. Whatever it was, it was transferring the numbers to my brain. I remember little after that. It vanished, and I fell to the ground. My hand was hot. It was now dark and I could hear my mother and father calling my name. They were out looking for me. I ran up to them and asked why they were calling me, I had told them I'd be back in time for tea. That's when my father told me it had gone past ten o'clock. Somehow, in that encounter, I had lost about four hours. That was when my fascination with the unknown began, and when my interest with code, encryption, and decryption began. I couldn't explain it. I told my parents. They told me stories of visitors to our land for many years and not to be frightened. I wasn't anymore. I was intrigued. I wanted to know more, to find out where they were from and what they wanted from us. I guess I know now, sort of."

"Did you make any official report to the police or rangers?" Jo asks.

"No, my father told me· to just accept it for what it was. Telling the police would not change the facts. He was right, it wouldn't have made any difference and could have been on my record, maybe stop me working in the government in later years."

"Your father sounds like he was a smart man."

"He was. He had a way of looking at things I wish I had."

"Don't sell yourself short, Hunter. You have some wonderful qualities. You have good instincts. You can read people, that's a quality worth having. I mean, look, you chose me, what else can I say." Hunter laughs. Jo was one of the best choices he had made in a very long time. He felt lucky at that moment, but he knew it could end at any time.

"Okay, let's get to work," he announces as he sits up, throwing Jo to the side. He grabs his laptop and the flash drive from his backpack.

"This shouldn't take long, mask the container and make sure the encrypted files are uploaded to the time-base corrector before becoming visible. Then, by the time Brennan realizes what they are, if he does, it will be too late." Jo lies on the bed, resting her head on her arm, watching Hunter from behind, as he works on the laptop. She can see his excitement, even from behind. He is doing something useful, something he can do to help. He is in his element, his comfort zone, working his magic with codes and numbers and encryptions. She lays there, quietly observing. She felt she had known Hunter all her life, even though it had only been a couple of days. It was a connection that felt right. She only knew a little about him, but enough to know he was a good person, sometimes grumpy, sometimes annoying, but a good man. She felt safe around him.

#

Jaii worked alongside the other scientists, trying to figure out a solution to the coronavirus the Nezulli would dispense across the globe. Jaii called a meeting with the scientists. They all gather around Jaii in the lab.

"Perhaps the best approach is to recreate a synthetic coronavirus," Jaii explains to the team, "to use its properties to create the antidote."

"How do we know it will contain the same properties as the Nezulli virus?" one of the Anunnaki scientists asks.

"We don’t. But for the sake of argument, let's assume the Nezulli have used the known coronavirus strain common on Earth and known as the common cold. This virus is the most easily spread, it incubates at a fast pace and there is no known cure. So, it stands to reason, this is a likely choice for the Nezulli to use to build their synthetic version on. We take the virus, make it contagious and deadly to the human system, then from this, we develop the antidote," Jaii explains.

"It sounds too simple, Commander. Surely the Nezulli would have developed one far beyond the current coronavirus. Our technology is not on a par with theirs, I don't think we can do it, and not in the space of two Earth days," one scientist replies.

"I know, it's asking a lot. But we must try, we must persevere, for humanity. We, as a team, can come together, pool our skills and knowledge, and we can make this happen. We have the resources, we just need to believe, to have faith."

The scientists take onboard what Jaii has said and with renewed energy, they go about completing their work. They assign each one a task and a timeframe in which to complete and pass the work up the line to the next scientist to work on. They run several streams of work to find the best solution fast, each stream taking a fresh approach, but each with the same goal. Jaii hoped that they would soon find the ingredients for an antidote. It relied heavily on the skills of the scientists and luck, something they had had little of up to that point.

Chapter 21.

Nezulli Command Fleet.
The Nezulli attack force is ready, waiting for orders to begin their mission. Transport craft are fueled and ready. The satellite transmission team is set and ready to disable Earth's satellites when commanded. A ground team on earth provides up-to-date information regarding the political situation, ground weather reports, military movement and any breaking news that might show they are expecting an attack. If this was the case, then Vok had several plans which he could quickly change to gain the best outcome. He could compute for almost every known eventuality. He and his command crew are keen to get underway, but the timing is crucial.

"Contact our ally in Nevada," Vok tells one of his men. A minute later the screen in front of Vok, on the control panel, springs to life.

"Mr. Brennan, I hope you have some good news for me."

"Sure, Commander. Everything is good here. No major issues, nothing I can't deal with, anyway. There is some activity around the storage facility at Los Alamos. They might move the elements. Hit it sooner rather than later. I will monitor the data from the site."

"And you took care of our politic problem, the Senator?"

"Yes, he won't bother anyone again."

"Excellent work, Mr. Brennan. And what about your inquisitive friend, where is he now?"

"Hunter? Don't worry about him, he knows nothing. He's chasing his tail right now."

"His tail?" Vok enquires.

"No, it's just a saying, he is looking in the.... never mind, he is under control," Brennan explains.

"He better be," replies Vok with a forceful tone, "we do not want any surprises along the way. Your next mission, Mr. Brennan, is to take your place in the bunker in Nevada. You will be joined by some very important political figures, once the news of the virus is transmitted. Your mission is to persuade them to join us. If not, destroy them with immediate effect. It is a yes or no answer. Kill the first to refuse in front of the others. This might help them see reason." Vok cuts the transmission. He looks out across the mass fleet he commands, with the feeling of certain victory, an easy win.

Brennan's cell phone rings.

"Hey, Hunter pal, didn't expect to hear from you so soon after our meet up. What can I do for you?"

"I have some info on a flash drive. Brennan. I think this is related to the sightings over Flagstaff. I think something big is going down, and I think the government might know something about it. It could be an invasion or something."

"What's on the flash drive?"

"I don't know, it's encrypted, not one I've seen before. I tried to decrypt it, but I don't have the tools, buddy, my computer isn't nearly good enough to run this thing. Maybe you could run it for me, you'd be doing me a big favor," Hunter pleads.

"Hmm, sure, I'll give it a go. Can you get the drive to me?"

"Already on its way with a secure courier. I knew you would say yes. Thanks, buddy."

"Cheeky bastard," Brennan replies, "leave it with me." Hunter hangs up.

"Right, that's done, let's go tell Jaii about our change of plan," Hunter tells Jo.

They find Jaii in the lab, carefully working with the common cold virus. Hunter and Jo wait behind the thick glass in the observation space next to the lab. When they catch Jaii's attention they signal him to come join them. Jaii goes into a decontamination chamber, strips off his whites and joins the pair.

"We are making excellent progress on the coronavirus antidote," Jaii tells them, "we hope to have some good news soon, but there will need to be extensive testing, albeit in a reduced time frame."

"We have news too," Jo tells Jaii excitedly,

"Hunter has arranged for Brennan to introduce the computer virus into the Nezulli system, unwittingly."

"I don't understand," replies Jaii, "won't he know what it is when he decrypts the code?"

"No, it's been masked. Brennan's not the sharpest tool in the box, Jaii. He got to where he is on the strength of much of my work. He will try, but fail," Hunter explains.

"I hope for all our sakes your plan is watertight. Once the Nezulli systems detect a threat, they will shut out any intrusion."

"It was a suicide mission for us to go into the Nezulli command craft," Hunter tells him.

"Perhaps. But they could still release the coronavirus and other contagions before the computer program takes effect. The war is still very much on," Jaii replies. Hunter and Jo feel their news has not been met with the enthusiasm they expected. They leave Jaii as he suits up again to enter the lab. They return to Hunter's room.

"I thought he might be a little happier," Jo tells Hunter.

"I guess he's right, there is still a lot that can go wrong before the computer virus takes effect, assuming Brennan uses the Nezulli supercomputer."

"Maybe we should hold off on the celebrations," Jo replies. She lays back down on the bed and looks up at Hunter.

"We've got some time, maybe you can think of something to do?" she tells him, signaling for Hunter to join her.

Chapter 22.

Office of the Secretary of Defense
The Pentagon, Virginia.
Secretary Aimes is at his desk in his internal glass-fronted office. A young man enters. He hands Aimes a sheet of paper.

"Sir, we've noticed some unusual activity, satellite transmissions unaccounted for." Aimes studies the paper.

"What does this mean, Johnston? What am I looking at here?" Aimes says, holding up the paper.

"Well, as far as we can make out, there are satellite feeds being sent via our satellites and via some commercial ones we use, which are being bounced around. Some are down linking and up-linking several times, it looks like someone is trying to cover their tracks. Could be hackers, or enemies trying to control our feeds, sir. We're not sure at this stage, but we thought it best to read you in on the situation, sir."

"Feeds being up and down-linked several times is not that unusual, Johnston."

"No sir, but some of these feeds just end up shooting off out to space or towards the moon. I've checked with NASA, they have no activity out there to explain this, sir."

"Okay, good work, Johnston. Monitor it, see if your guys can track one feed to a destination, let me know if anything changes." Johnston leaves the room, closing the glass door behind him. Aimes looks down at the paper on his desk, waiting for Johnston to close the door. After he is gone, Aimes picks up the desk phone.

"Get me the Defense Chief of Staff." There is a pause while he is put through.

"General, how are you?" Aimes begins.

"I'm fine thanks, Bernard. What can I do for you?" General George Humphries replies.

"We might have a problem, sir."

In the Office of Defense satellite surveillance room, Paul Johnston sits at his desk, looking at the bank of flat-screen monitors in front of him. Each screen shows data and graphic charts from different satellites placed at strategic points above the earth. Each desk in the row either side of Paul's has similar data, with other government staff working, tracking movements, analyzing data. There is another row in front and at the front of the high walled dark room, is a video wall, also showing tracking and movement data, time zone clocks at the top, and a rolling CNN news feed across the bottom. Johnston reruns the data he presented Aimes with, rechecking if he made a mistake, looking for further anomalies, or something that might explain the data. Johnston has only been with the agency for a little over a year. He had been a dean's list student at Westpoint, served in the US Army in the Middle East, deployed with the 101st Airborne Division, the 'Screaming Eagles.' His military training had provided him with the skills of an analyst which he much preferred to battle. It was more intelligence work than sitting in a hole in the ground, getting shot at. He had done that and didn't much like going back to it. If he was wrong with his analysis, it might well be his future. No matter what method of analysis he used, the tracking data for the feeds always returned the same results. Somehow, there were feeds from US military surveillance cameras being beamed out to space via satellites. Johnston looks for mechanical and computer failures, which could send the feeds in the wrong direction. He had seen it before. It wasn't a major issue, as the feeds would need a decoder at the end of the line to be read, otherwise, they were just beams of digital radio waves which eventually would fall away to nothing as they became weaker. But this time it was different. The feeds going out to space appeared to be going to one location, even if bounced across several satellites. The endpoint is in one geographical location in space, somewhere near the dark side of the moon. Johnston is puzzled. The tracking telemetry and control systems were functioning normally. The transponders were not faulty, every maintenance protocol test had come back as satisfactory. He looks at the feeds being diverted, perhaps he can find a correlation between the information. The first feed he looks at is footage of what looks like a large factory. Using the image co-ordinates, he finds the images are of a water processing plant in Utah. The next feed shows co-ordinates for a cereal crop processing plant in Idaho. Next is a nuclear power plant in upstate New York. Johnston is realizing the significance of the images. The more he looks at it, the clearer it becomes. The images are of either highly secure nuclear facilities or utilities, including electricity, water, and food processing sites. If someone is hacking into their systems and gathering footage and images for an attack on US soil, these facilities would be key strategic targets. He is onto something, something big. Johnston rechecks his data several times. He doesn't want to go to Aimes with incorrect or half checked information.

Johnston asks one of his colleagues to check the information, get a fresh pair of eyes on it. His colleague comes up with the same data. It is correct. Someone is sending video feeds out into space. But who is it, and for what reason? These are questions Johnston can't answer. He thought about taking the data back to Aimes, but he wants further verification on the data. He has used the services of a government contractor before, an analyst he can trust, someone who has skills beyond his. He will contact him and see if he comes up with the same results. If so, then taking it back to Aimes is justifiable.

Chapter 23.

Hunter is asleep in an embrace with Jo, on his small bed, when his cell phone rings. He slips his arm from under her and leans over the edge of the bed, fumbling in his pants back pocket for the cell phone, now on the floor.

"Hi, this is Hunter."

"Hunter, hello, it's Paul Johnston, from the Defense Office in Virginia. Not sure if you remember me, you did some excellent work for us a couple of years back on the Iraqi project."

"Ah, yes, Paul, I remember, how are you?"

"Good thanks. Listen, I've got some data I need a new set of eyes on, would you be able to look? I might have it all wrong. The numbers look correct, but the results are all off. Something is amiss. We might have a hacker in our comms satellite system. If I send it over in an email, with the usual encryption, can you tell me what you think? I'd really appreciate your input. Just bill the department as before."

"Sure, send it over, I'll look," Hunter replies.

"Thanks, Hunter, speak to you soon." Johnston hangs up. Jo stirs on the bed, Hunter sits up on the edge of the bed and stretches and yawns loudly.

"What's happening, Hunter," Jo wakes.

"Nothing, just some work from the government, small job, probably nothing."

"You don't have time to take on jobs, now Hunter, this Nezulli situation is more important than anything else," Jo tells him.

"I know, I know. I just thought it might be related. Would be good to know what the government knows at this stage," Hunter replies. He slips his legs into his pants and stands up, pulling them up as he does. He pulls his shirt on over his head, then sits down to squeeze his feet into his beloved boots. Jo lies on the bed, resting her head on her hand, arm propped up.

"You never told me about those boots, what's the story?"

"It was a long time after the incident when I was a kid, seeing the UFO up on the reservation. After that, I saw them so many times, and not just on the reservation. It was like they were following me but never making contact. For a while, I thought I was going crazy. Anyway, when I worked for the government, part of my role was to investigate sightings, find out if there was any truth in the stories, or if they were imagined or if the UFOs were enemy counter surveillance planes drones or such like. The other guys used to tease me about it, they thought it all a bit of a laugh. So, I went to a bootmaker I had heard did great work, and drew him a picture of a silver disc-shaped UFO and asked him to make them for me. Then I wore them to work every day, made sure the guys could see them, sat back with my feet on the desk. I wanted them to know I was serious about the work, but could also take the jokes. They didn't bother after that. Seems it wasn't as funny if it didn't get a reaction. But I kept the boots, as a reminder of my experience as a child, that I knew there was something out there, beyond our existence."

"They are magnificent boots," Jo adds. "Not very practical, but magnificent." Hunter's laptop pings.

"That will be the email from Johnston," he tells Jo. He takes the laptop from his backpack and opens it. He reads the email, decrypting the message with his government-issued login.

"Seems Johnston has spotted some anomalies in the satellite feeds," he tells Jo.

"Anything to do with us?" she asks.

"Might be. I've got the data, I can see why he is confused. Feeds are going out to space from satellites, bouncing around a bit, then sent to beyond the moon. It must be the Nezulli."

"It would make sense for them to monitor activity on Earth, see if there are any large mobilization of military," Jo replies.

"Yeah, it looks like key targets, areas that might show additional activity if the government knew of an invasion," Hunter tells Jo.

"What about this Johnston guy, do you think he can be trusted?" Jo asks.

"I think so. He's a good kid, very smart, good military record, seems genuine to me."

"And the people he works for?" Jo asks, "do you know them. This could be a trap. It could be a set-up, to get you to meet him. Then they move in and arrest you for killing that guard."

"Could be, but I don't have to meet with him, just send my report by email."

"Could they trace you back to here with the IP address or something?" Jo asks.

"Jaii said the IP addresses they use here can't be traced, so I think it's safe." Jo gets up and dresses. Hunter sits at the small desk against the wall, staring at the laptop screen, full of data and graphs.

"I will see if Jaii and his guys have made any progress," Jo announces.

"Uh-huh," Hunter replies, engrossed in the data in front of him. Jo just smiles at the back of his head and leaves the room. She goes to the viewing area of the lab. Jaii sees Jo and enters the decontamination chamber, then goes to meet her.

"Well, Jaii, how are you guys doing. Any luck?"

"We have made some progress, I am hopeful we will find the solution we are looking for."

"Hunter is looking at some data from a government source. He thinks the data shows transmissions going to the Nezulli, at the back of the moon," Jo explains.

"Ah, once your government liaise with other government bodies and compare the data, they will soon notice a threat to your world. Things will move much faster at that point. Countries will lock down their borders, bunkers will be filled."

"How long do you think we have before they realize the threat?" Jo asks.

"Hours, rather than days, I would expect," Jaii tells her, "we are close with our antidote, but it may be too late if things escalate."

"I'll ask Hunter if he can stall his report back to the government. It might help a little," Jo replies.

"Good, I will continue with my work here. I will come find you when we make a breakthrough." Jaii re-enters the decontamination chamber. Jo returns to Hunter's room.

Chapter 24.

Office of the Defense Chief of Staff
General George Humphries, The Pentagon, Virginia.
Three people are seated around one end of a long mahogany conference table. An ornate mahogany desk sits at one end of the large office, flanked by two flags against the back wall, the stars and stripes and the Department of Defense flag, an eagle with the stars and stripes on its breast. At the conference table are General George Humphries, Chief of Staff, Secretary of Defense, Bernard Aimes and Head of CIA Counter Intelligence, Candice Peterson.

"Bernard, tell the rest of the team what you told me on the phone earlier," Humphries tells Aimes.

"One of my team has identified signal paths, transmissions, heading out to space, to the dark side of the moon. It's just a matter of time before it becomes known by others. They will find the signals and put two and two together. If the media gets hold of this, there will be widespread panic."

"You see, folks," the General adds, in his Southern drawl accent, "why I thought it necessary to call you into this meeting. We must contain this. We need more time. Vok is ready to go. Once the contamination begins, then things will move fast, but until then, we must keep a lid on this."

"I can put some of my team into action," Peterson adds, "silence this guy until the invasion begins, control measures. Do we know if he has shared this info with anyone else?"

"I'm not sure," Aimes replies, "we are looking at his outgoing calls and messages. If he has, then containment might be more difficult. There were several politicians who took part in a teleconference with Senator Carter the other night. He provided evidence of alien visitors and warned them that the government is involved. He died before he could meet with the President, but some of those in the conference call are asking questions, planning to expose the whole thing."

"We can discredit them, make them go dark for a while," Peterson adds. "No-one will believe them by the time my team has finished. They won't be able to get a job at McDonald's after this."

"You tried to control that ranger from the Indian reservation, Peterson. If I recall, she escaped and one of your team got killed. Perhaps you underestimate Hunter?" Humphries tells Peterson. "Whatever you need to do to keep this quiet, do it," Humphries insists, "We just need another half a day or so, to get the plans into action, all the pieces in the right places at the right time, so to speak. Feed the media with a distraction, if you have to. Point eyes in the opposite direction while we get ourselves into battle stations. I have mobilized some units, quietly to strategic points. The National Guard will be called in to deal with martial law, lockdown key areas and systems. The media will come under our control, so we can choose what the nation hears and sees, at least for a short while. We just need to coordinate our militaries when the time comes. We have invested a lot of time and budget in this plan. The Nezulli will provide us with the method. We can give them the resources they require once they have done their part. The population of earth will be restored to a manageable size, less pressure on resources, food, oil, gas. The period of change will be difficult for all of us, but worth it in the long run. Make sure you have your families, loved ones, pets, ready to join you in your chosen bunkers. You have been given passes for them, don't let the passes fall into the wrong hands. Right, let's get to work." The team stands up and leave the office. Humphries goes behind his desk and sits in the large black leather chair. He lifts the desk phone and makes a call.

"Hi, love. Listen, can you meet me here at the office later, say around eight o'clock, bring Mr. Jinks and a good supply of cat food. We need to go on a little trip. Pack a couple of bags for you and me. Okay. Thanks, see you later, love you." He hangs up. Humphries sits back in his chair and swivels around to look out of the window to the central garden area in the center of the Pentagon buildings. The grass is cut short, neat paths run through the garden making a cross in the middle. People, workers, are sitting around in the scattering of park benches, eating lunch, reading newspapers or chatting. The sun is shining, casting a shadow in one corner, where no-one is sitting, preferring the warmth of the summer sun. Humphries is deep in thought. Thoughts of what the world will look like in a few days, in a week or a month. He couldn't even imagine what it would look like in a year. The deaths of so many people is hard to comprehend. But he thought it a necessary sacrifice to make, to right the wrongs of his generation, of those who had created the world's climate problems and food shortages, through greed and progress of power. Even if he wasn't sacrificing himself or his family, he believed he and his colleagues were doing the right thing for the right reasons. He had searched his conscience many times, questioning the plan, looking for an alternative.

Humphries was chosen to assist the Nezulli with their needs, in return for helping him and certain members of his government to gain power over most of the world and thin out the population, control progressive third world countries and the supply chain for food, power, and medicines. Humphries was never certain if his meeting with the Nezulli was by chance or whether there had been a plan all along, to manipulate him, use him to gain trust with his government. But he believed strongly that this way was the only way to regain control of the climate issue and world hunger. Fewer people, less pollution, less food needed. Simple but effective. He knew the way they had fought for power in the past was over. They had new enemies, new ways of doing battle. Gaining power could be achieved with the help of visitors from another world. They were the new allies to the USA, a partnership that was mutually beneficial. Humphries had brokered the deal with the Nezulli and only brought in his most loyal and trusted colleagues, ones he knew would see the bigger picture, who could see how America could benefit from the cooperation. Humphries hadn't even told his wife. She was used to short notice packing, going with him on trips or packing him off on his own. She did not understand what lay ahead of them this time, that when they returned to the outside world, it would be dramatically changed. The couple didn't have any children, mainly because of Humphries's constant reassignments to all parts of the world. They had only each other to worry about, and their beloved cat, Mr. Jinks. Humphries was glad it was this way. It made life in the new world much simpler. The new world order would begin with the burial and cremations for millions of people. It was not something he would have wanted children to see. But it also meant the end of the lineage of his family genes. Many of the younger members chosen to join them in the bunkers had families or were young enough to start one in the new world. There would be restrictions on how many children someone could have, Humphries was certain that would be put in place straight away. The higher members of government he had met previously to discuss the plan had already drawn up policies to adhere to the new government. The policymakers had the same vision for the future as Humphries. He was guaranteed his place in the President's inner cabinet, with overall control of world military budgets and policies. But he wanted more, he wanted the Presidency. The General and his wife would be given the signal to get to the bunker before the coronavirus was released across the world. They would be safe, along with the others chosen to join them in the bunkers. These people were political figures, policymakers, scientists, doctors, nurses, surgeons, military, government agents, leaders in medicine, food production, natural resource exploration. Anyone considered to have important skills and knowledge to rebuild society after the virus had subsided and taken its toll. Most of these people knew they would be selected for their skills and jobs. They wouldn't be told the reason, other than a national security alert, and to get their belongings and loved ones together and make their way to a designated bunker. Humphries knew this could be a tricky part of the plan. People would turn up with the contents of their homes in trucks or with neighbors and friends in tow. His men would have the job of sorting them into the authorized and non-authorized personnel, strip them to just one suitcase each and send their friends and neighbors home. They would set up staging posts to carry this out with military precision. This is where chaos might ensue. People would get angry for being turned away, trouble could flair quickly. He would give the order to shoot if it came to it. People would die. There would be no civil order unless they controlled the situation with deadly force. Humphries was prepared for this.

Chapter 25.

Paul Johnston sits in front of his monitors in the satellite surveillance room. He waits for news from Hunter. He is ninety-nine percent sure he has found signals going to an unknown base or craft out in space. He doesn't know if it is an enemy collecting data from their comms satellites or something entirely new, an unknown entity somewhere out in space. He thought of all the possibilities, all the known pieces of machinery floating about in space. Perhaps an old satellite, thought to be dead or lost, had powered up again and was transmitting or receiving signals. He had searched for all the known space probes and dead technology circling the Earth. Other countries could have launched and lost contact with their own secret space race technology and didn't admit to it. There could be a dozen or more undisclosed satellites flying through space. Johnston did not understand how to find out where they were if they even existed. There was the possibility of extra-terrestrials. This was something which was often discussed in the office, but quietly. No-one wanted to be the one to shout about UFOs. Everyone had their own theories, some were believers, some non-believers, others were secret believers, afraid to hurt their chances of promotion by speaking up about UFOs. But the government knew there had been visitors from other worlds for years. It was kept well under wraps, with government officials issuing threats to those who spoke out. Johnston was a believer but kept his opinions to himself. Now he may have evidence of these beings, entities monitoring what was going on around the world. If they were out there, Johnston thought, why were they monitoring Earth? And why now? What happened that had taken their interest? Did they know something he didn't? He considered the government, if they knew anything. He had noticed no flurry of activity within military circles, no additional satellite feeds, other than the ones he spotted. No new orders had been issued to watch certain areas of the world. This was something that would happen with rising tensions with other countries, such as Syria or Iraq. Johnston would often be given specific coordinates for satellite or drone surveillance. The military liked to keep a close eye on their movements, know where the enemy was at all times. But Johnston and his colleagues had not been given any additional orders beyond the usual stuff.

The government sometimes used outside contractors with their own satellites for this work. They could use them for this, he thought, to keep their own satellites available for general issue. Several companies had grown around the communications business, winning large contracts with the government to research and build spy technology. They were currently developing Nano-satellites, small devices much more sophisticated than their current stock. Maybe one of these satellites had been launched and was being tested with signal feeds. It was a possibility. They would keep it a secret to minimize the data getting out and used by their enemies or competitors. It was big business.

#

Hunter is still at his computer when Jo returns to the room.

"Listen, Jaii asked if you can hold off on sending your report to Johnston, give them a little more time to work on the antidote," she tells him.

"Yeah, no problem. I'm sure it is the Nezulli. There aren't any other satellites or NASA bases out there, at that location. We know pretty much where everything is, even the space junk, mostly anyway. It makes sense for the Nezulli to muster at the dark side of the moon, out of sight from Earth. I wonder if Johnston has figured this out or is still speculating. How long does Jaii need for the antidote?"

"He didn't say, it seems like they are close, within hours I suspect. He seems more optimistic than before," Jo tells him. She sits on the end of the bed, watching Hunter scan the data, making notes in his notebook. She could imagine him working in some dark office, deep in the bowels of a government facility, tapping away at his laptop, solving codes and writing new ones, programming and encrypting, all the things he seems to thrive on. She wondered if she would have ever met him under different circumstances. If it hadn't been for Jaii bringing them together, she thought it unlikely they would have ever run into each other. She thought about the past few days together, how fast it had all gone, how much had changed in such a brief space of time and how it might all change again soon, for the worse. But she was happy to have spent time with Hunter, to get to know him, to help find a solution to save themselves and humanity. She wondered what would happen to them.

A member of Jaii's team knocks on the room door. Jo opens it.

"The Commander asked me to give you both these," the crew member tells Jo. He hands her two respirator masks, which look like gas masks.

"Do you think these will be necessary? We were hoping to avoid coming into contact with the viruses," she replies.

"It's just a precaution. The Commander is concerned for your safety. He needs you both to complete this mission. If one or both of you fall ill, we may not be able to defeat the enemy. We will tell you if you need to wear the masks. Please keep them with you at all times." The crew member leaves and Jo closes the door.

"Just throw them on the bed, we won't need them down this tunnel, I'm sure," Hunter tells Jo without looking around. He is transfixed with the data on his laptop. Hunter's cell phone rings.

"Hi, Hunter here."

"Hunter, it's Paul Johnston, any luck with that data set I sent you earlier. Just wondered if you had any news?" Hunter covers the mouthpiece with his hand and turns to Jo and mouths

'Johnston' to her. She indicates not to tell him anything yet. Hunter turns back to the laptop and uncovers the mouthpiece.

"Hi, Johnston. Sorry, it's too soon to give you a definitive answer. I'm still trawling through the data. Out of interest, what did you think this meant?"

"I don't want to stick my neck out, Hunter. Not here at the Pentagon, so just between you and me, it looks like someone or something is directing the signals to a point at the back of the moon, to monitor our feeds. I don't know who or what, but it looks strange."

"If you were to take a guess who would you say it was?" Hunter asks.

"If I was to take a wild guess, don't judge me on this, its pure speculation, even outrageous, but to me, it seems like it could be aliens. I know, crazy as it sounds, but that's my best guess. Off the record," Johnston tells him.

"Okay, well, not sure if I agree with you on that Johnston, but everyone's entitled to their own opinion."

"Really, because I heard you used to work on the UFO projects a few years back. Did you never come into contact with anything strange, anything that might have made you question what we know?" Johnston asks.

"Yeah, sure, there were lots of odd things, most of which could be explained, natural phenomenon, man-made attempts to deceive, cranks, hoaxes, that sort of thing. But, yes, there were one or two which remained unexplained."

"Did you ever come across signals being gathered from outer space, Hunter?"

"No, can't say I have. But this could just be a glitch in the system, gremlins at work. I'll call you in a bit when I've had more time to study the data. Have you discussed this with anyone else?"

"No, well, just my boss Aimes. He didn't understand it, asked me to carry on, look into it further."

"Is that normal procedure, you take it to your boss, he tells you to keep working on it, report further?" Hunter asks.

"No, not usually. I would go to him with a concern. It usually gets escalated to one of the special op's guys. They would take the data, look at what I found, take it to the next level, they have the security clearance above my paygrade."

"But this time, he told you to look into it, not the special ops guys?"

"Yes, that's correct. I didn't mind, it gave me a chance to double-check my data, and get your opinion."

"Okay, leave it with me, I will be in touch soon." Hunter hangs up.

"Hmm," he says, thinking hard.

"What?" Jo asks.

"Why would his superior change his way of checking data, not pass it up the line to special ops people with higher clearance? Something doesn't seem right. Why with this data? What does he know that Johnston doesn't know? I think Aimes is part of this. I think others in the Pentagon are involved."

"Well, we know there must be government collusion, insider help. Brennan is involved, who knows how many others," Jo tells him. "We know this from Senator Carter's murder. Someone in high office authorized his killing. This could go all the way to the White House." Jo sits on the end of Hunter's bed, thinking about it. It was only her and Hunter and Jaii's crew against the rest of the world, or at least it seemed that way. She didn't see how they could defeat a race of advanced artificial intelligence, the highest powers in government and a deadly virus. She was quickly losing her optimism. Hunter turns to her.

"Don't worry, we can still win. Sometimes it's about being smarter than the other guy. He might be bigger and stronger and faster, but intellect can be deadlier," he tells Jo.

"Do you believe any of that nonsense, Hunter? Give me an example of intellect beating a big guy in a fight?"

"Sure. David and Goliath."

"Seriously, that's the best you can do. A story from the bible, over two thousand years old."

"Yes, the little guy used his smarts and a slingshot to take down the big ugly guy. See. Intellect over size." Hunter smiles, which makes Jo smile. He was right, it could happen, unlikely as it might be, fighting a race of AI robots, but the seeds had been planted. The intellect had begun by giving Brennan the flash drive. Perhaps, she thought, Hunter was smarter than he appeared, which was not very smart on the surface.

"Let's talk about how all this might play out," Jo asks. "What are the stages if it goes to plan?"

"If it goes as planned, Jaii and his guys will have an antidote ready soon. Brennan will use the supercomputer to decrypt the flash drive, releasing the computer virus into the Nezulli system. How long that will take to propagate, I don't know. If it works fast, they could be destroyed before releasing the coronavirus on Earth. If it is slow or gets detected, they could stop it and go ahead with their plan. In scenario one, the Nezulli get destroyed, no virus is released, the world goes back to normal, and those involved will probably get away with it as no-one else will have known about their involvement. In scenario two, the computer virus is stopped, minimal damage caused, they release the virus, then our only method of fighting is to join Jaii's fleet and try to fight them in the air. This is not the one we want. It could end badly for us and millions of lives."

"There is a third option," Jo explains. "Jaii is sending some of his team away, to ensure there are survivors to carry on if they are defeated by the Nezulli. Some young men, their families, kids. They will continue the fight at a later date on another planet. We could go with them, start again, a fresh start, with your daughter."

"I couldn't live with the guilt of not having at least tried to save people. If we are being defeated and Jaii thinks it best we leave, then we can consider it. But we must try. This is our planet, our home. We can't let some bloody alien machines take it away from us.".

"I agree. But good to know the option is there."

Chapter 26.

Government Bunker
Nevada Desert.
Brennan makes his way down into the bunker, with his laptop bag over his shoulder, showing his pass to guards as he goes. He reaches the inner bunker and uses the retina and fingerprint scanners to gain entry. Inside, he makes his way to his quarters. The bunker is huge, with many corridors and rooms. Maps on the walls help guide people to the correct room. The bunker, like many across the US, was built during the Cold War years, to accommodate many government officials. The technology inside the bunkers had been updated in recent years, with introducing updated security protocols, computer systems, air-con, lighting, and all facilities to make the stay more comfortable, if ever needed. They had even installed vegetable gardens with UV lighting, to grow their own vegetables. 5G connectivity and satellite phones and government satellite intranet had been added, along with old-school landline telephones.

There are very few people in the bunker, as the call has not yet gone out to get to the space. Only Brennan, the guards, and several cleaning and maintenance staff are in the area. Brennan enters his living quarters. The walls are painted white, with a defused light built into one wall, to look like a window. The color temperature of the window and the room lighting can be adjusted to emulate daylight. There is a single size bed against the wall on the left, a small wet-room and toilet, a TV in the corner, a small sofa, a table and chair, and a wardrobe. Brennan didn't expect to have to stay in the bunker for any more than a few weeks, a month at the most, so it was fine for a brief stay.

He sits at the table and takes out a sophisticated looking laptop. It was one he was given by the Nezulli to communicate with them securely. The laptop is far superior to any human device, he can use it to decrypt the files on the flash drive. If he uses the government computers, they could look at the logs and see what he has been up to, so he figures it is safer to use the Nezulli device. The laptop doesn't have a keyboard; it is just a glowing panel which when activated by voice command, a keyboard appears on it. It also can allow the user to use two fingers to grab a screen item or the whole screen, swipe it off the laptop and enlarge it in thin air, in front of the user. The laptop projects the image and renders it in 3D, so it can be moved around, and observed from all angles. A clever bit of computer, Brennan thinks.

"Keyboard," he says to activate the keyboard. He types in a string of numbers and letters to access the Nezulli system. He places the flash drive on the laptop next to the keyboard. The surrounding area glows, as the data is read. Brennan navigates to the decryption program to decipher the data. The program springs to life, with strings of binary code shooting up the screen, sometimes just a single vertical line, then the whole screen would be filled. The ones and zeros flow up the screen, white digits on a black background. Watching it makes Brennan's eyes go funny, so he lets it run its course whilst he retires to the bed for a lie-down. He doesn't know how long it will take for the data to transfer and be analyzed and the results made available. He monitors it in his peripheral vision, whilst stirring at the ceiling.

#

"Commander, we have activity on our network from somewhere on Earth," one of Vok's crew informs him.

"What activity? Can you identify the source?"

"It looks like someone is using our system to analyze data, scanning it with our software. The source is one of our computers, but the location is unidentifiable."

"It is most likely one of our soldiers on the ground. I do not think we should worry at this stage, but just in case it is an enemy at work, set the command craft and base to restricted mode, internal communications only for the time being. Tell the technicians to keep a close watch on our systems."

"Yes, Commander, right away." The crew member leaves the command room, the door slides closed behind him. Vok walks around the room, arms held together behind his back, fingers interlocked, as he inspects the various screens and data over the shoulders of his team. He approaches his second in command, Taur, who is standing at a control console, with screens showing satellite video feeds from across the USA.

"Taur, is everything as we expected?" Vok asks.

"Yes, Commander. There is the expected movement of the military, as discussed with General Humphries of the US Army. His men will be in place before the attack, with suitable protective suits. Our human contacts on Earth are making their way to the safe zones for entry to the bunkers and our crew is monitoring the ally government agents we have recruited. We do not foresee any major problems."

"Good, our teams are mustering, they will leave within the next four earth hours. Expected delivery of the payload in eight hours."

"Commander, when will we take control of the US government? I'm concerned they could turn on us, as we plan to do to them. If we leave it too late, they could shut down contact and we will be left with no alternative but to engage in warfare," Taur asks.

"Our military capabilities are far beyond the human's technology. If they tried such a move, they would not live very long, Taur. They will not live very long regardless, but the end would be swifter than planned. It would leave us to mine the resources ourselves if humans are finished, so the better result is that they comply and we enslave the healthiest to do the work."

"I estimate we can get the resources required from this planet within six months, with enough human slaves. We will have more than enough resources to take us to our next mission.

Some of their resources are depleted, we will need to source these from another planet, but there is plenty of uranium, plutonium, gold, silver, and dysprosium. We can strip the reserves at Los Alamos. They have nuclear reserves we can remove easily and once we control the food chains, we will have complete control." Vok looks at the video feeds on the screens in front of Taur.

"We will hit the US, China, and India first. Their populations are the greatest. The spread will be rapid in the most densely populated areas. Then we will cover the other major areas such as Europe, Australia, the Soviet Union. Smaller islands will be last. Only the healthiest and fittest can survive the coronavirus, it is a natural select tool. We only need the healthy and fit. Everyone else is of no value to us."

"Quite, Commander. The delivery craft are primed, the payload ready. We await your command."

#

Brennan looks across the small room from the bed. The data streams have stopped. He gets up and sits at the table. His network link with the Nezulli supercomputer is still connected but shows a warning.

Network Limited. Command Module Disconnected.

He hadn't seen this message before when he connected securely to Vok in the command vessel. He clicks 'ok' and the streams continued. He sits and watches it, waiting for further warning messages. The results pop up on the screen.

Illogical number sequence. No known binary sequence. Would you like to run the program again?

Brennan didn't understand. If there was information regarding the Nezulli, the system should have decrypted it, the information would be readable. He thought about the earlier message and considered there might be a glitch in the system. He clicks 'run program' and starts the process again. After a few minutes, the first message reappears. Brennan clicks 'ok' and it continues, ending with the same result. He takes his cell phone from his pocket and calls Hunter.

"Hunter, hi, it's Brennan. Listen, I ran that encrypted flash drive you sent me, but there is nothing there but random numbers."

"Are you sure? I'm sure the files contained info on the UFO sightings."

"Unless the government or someone is using a new encryption method, it looks like random numbers, no usable data. I think someone is giving you the runaround, buddy," Brennan tells him.

"Did you use the government terminal with the latest software?"

"Eh, yeah sure, it came back with no known binary data."

"Okay, well, that's disappointing. I thought I was on to something. Another dead end. Listen, thanks anyway for giving it a go."

"No problem. Speak to you soon." Hunter hangs up.

"Job done," he tells Jo, "Brennan has uploaded the flash drive contents."

"Do you think he has used the Nezulli computer," Jo asks.

"I think so."

"If he tried the government computer, would the virus affect their systems too?"

"No, I've designed the algorithm to effect the supercomputer only, different technology, qubits. I hope it will take effect before they launch the coronavirus," Hunter tells her.

"What if they are already heading this way?"

"I'm not sure, but I think it should affect their craft and the Nezulli AI themselves, assuming they work on the same system. If it works, they should either fall out of the sky or never reach our atmosphere, drifting off into space."

"If they fall to Earth, the virus could still be spread, areas contaminated," Jo tells him.

"Yes, maybe, but the damage would be much less, more containable in small areas."

"How soon before we know it has had an effect?" Jo asks.

"I wish I knew. Could be an hour, could be a day. I'll get the news website up, we can see if any news breaks." Hunter brings up the CNN news website, looking through stories for anything that might show an attack.

Chapter 27.

Nezulli Command Fleet

Vok stands behind the line of crew standing at their control positions, busy sending and receiving information from the fleet. He reads a report handed to him by a member of his crew. He looks out across his fleet, stationed in the shadow of Earth's moon.

"We are ready. Initialize launch protocols. Attack fleet 1 released for advance under cover of darkness. Attack fleet 2, make your way to rendezvous point 2 and wait for the cover of darkness on the other side of the planet. You each have a grid to cover, once completed, move to the next grid on your charts." Vok's attack fleet heads out of the icy darkness towards Earth, in long trails of craft, coming into the light and glimmering in the sun, disappearing into the distance. Within a few hours, they would be in position and would release their deadly cargo.

#

Jaii found Jo and Hunter in Hunter's quarters.

"They've launched the attack," he tells them with urgency in his voice.

"How long before they reach our atmosphere?" asks Jo.

"Not long, a couple of Earth hours. Our antidote is almost complete, but untested. Without initial testing, we can't release it. It could cause more harm than good," Jaii tells them.

"We have introduced the computer virus into the Nezulli system, so, if all goes to plan, and it takes effect, their craft and personnel should fail soon. If not, then we have a big problem," Hunter reports.

"Good," Jaii adds, "it might buy us more time to finish our work in the lab and get the antidote completed." Jaii was trying to be optimistic, but he felt hopeless. He wanted to remain positive and keep up the pretense in front of them, if only to keep them hopeful. But deep down, he knew what the Nezulli could, and he didn't know if they could defeat them. Jaii left Jo and Hunter alone in the room and returned to the lab. Hunter took out his cell phone.

"I need to warn my sister Miri, try to get her and her kids to a safe place," Hunter tells Jo.

"Where? There aren't many safe places just now."

"There is a deep mountain facility I used to use near LA, not used much now, although it might be soon. It's just a storage facility really, but it has power and heating. I can give her the access code to get in. Hopefully she can get there before the attack. What about you, anyone you want to warn, Jo? Any family you need to warn?"

"No. My parents are both passed away. There's only my Grandma, really. She's ninety, still lives in the shack she grew up in on the reservation. No point trying to warn her. She couldn't get to here; the terrain would kill her."

"I'm sure Jaii could transport her, if you asked," Hunter suggests.

"Wouldn't make any difference, she wouldn't leave her home. She would stay and face what was coming, regardless. She's a stubborn old girl."

"Ah, that's where you get it from then, your Grandma." Jo smiles. Hunter calls his sister and tells her the situation and where to go for safety. It is all he can do. She is a few years younger than Hunter, but an accomplished person, stubborn, like Jo, determined and very practical. Hunter felt she should be okay if she can get to the facility. He has to turn his attention to the bigger picture, the world-wide attack on humanity.

"There's one more call I need to make," Hunter announces. He taps a number into his cell phone.

"Johnston, it's Hunter. I have some news. Are you sitting?'

"Should I be?" Paul Johnston replies.

"You were correct. The signals are being sent to the dark side of the moon, and I know why."

"Go on."

"You need to prepare for an attack. But you must be careful, not everyone in your department or government is on your side. The attack has been launched. In the next few hours, an unknown species, from a distant multiverse, will launch viruses across our planet, to wipe out the weak and take control of resources," Hunter explains. Johnston is quiet on the line.

"Johnston, are you still there? Did you hear me?"

"Yes, just trying to assess the information. So, aliens will attack Earth? With viruses and take over the world? From another multiverse, as in, there's more than one universe?"

"Correct."

"I knew it," Johnston replied, happy that he had been correct all along. "If this is the case, what can we do, I don't think we have any procedures in place for this. It has been discussed as a far off, probably never happen scenario, but nothing was ever put in place. You said to be careful. Do you think some government officials are working with aliens? That's far-fetched."

"This whole thing is far-fetched, Paul, but it's true, it is happening and happening right now. One of my old colleagues and former friend is in on it. His name is Jake Brennan, works at the facility in Nevada. He has contacts in your department, so assume there are those around you who can't be trusted, like Aimes."

"I have had my suspicions about Aimes, the way he handled my report on this," Johnston replies, "I'll do some digging around, see if I can find out more, flush the bad eggs out."

"Be very careful. We went to Senator Carter for help. I'm sure you heard what happened to him shortly after. He would take it to the top, the White House, but they took him out before he could. So, they will stop at nothing to achieve their goals. This is serious. We can try to fight the invaders in the open, but you are dealing with a hidden enemy within. Trust no-one and get to safety before the viruses are released. We need your help on the inside of government." Hunter tells him.

"Sure, Hunter, I'm on it. Be safe, keep in touch if you can, let me know what's happening at your end." Hunter hangs up.

"Let's hope they don't kill him before he can be of some help," Hunter tells Jo.

Most of the population of Earth did not understand what was about to descend on them. The world would be a very different place within a few days. Martial law will be called in many countries to control the people, panic will take over, riots, stock piling and looting for food will be rampant. Many people will self-quarantine, hoping to avoid the virus or minimize contact with others to keep safe. To begin with, they will not know where the virus came from or how they could be affected, but escape will be futile. Governments will collapse, militaries will struggle to keep control, life will change forever. It was human nature to panic in the face of a major catastrophe, mass hysteria could take place, causing even further deaths. Psychosis and mass suicides were a real possibility. Humans are not well equipped for such events as alien invasion or pandemics.

#

The attack fleet vessels are under the control of Vok's military commanders, with Vok in overall command. They, like Vok, are artificial intelligent beings, programmed to follow warfare procedures. They feel no pain or suffering, nor empathy or sympathy. They will destroy themselves and their craft, rather than be captured, and fall into the hands of the enemy. They have to prevent other civilizations from reverse engineering their technology. This was the one thing they must never let happen.

The first wave of craft enters Earth's atmosphere just after darkness had fallen across the Western half of the world. They waited until they were all within range, before fanning out across the USA and Canada, Mexico and South America, then they dropped to a level suitable to release the contaminants.

Once at a lower altitude, they would be picked up on Radar systems, and military jets would be scrambled to observe and intercept any unidentified craft in their air space. The first Nezulli craft flew low over the major cities. New York, Chicago, Washington, D.C., Philadelphia, Kansas, Dallas, Las Vegas. Others worked up the coast, covering Los Angeles, San Francisco, Seattle and onwards into Canada, over Vancouver and onwards north to Alaska. The craft flying up the East coast head up to Toronto and Montreal. Craft are assigned to rural areas of Nebraska and Utah and Ohio, areas with huge crop fields full of produce. Water supplies are targeted up and down the continent, every reservoir contaminated, feeding water supplies to homes and industry. Thousands of Nezulli craft cover the country, then turn West to cross the Pacific towards Japan and China. As they travel West, the sun will go down, so darkness will fall before they arrive, allowing some cover. USAF jets had already been scrambled and are in pursuit of the craft, but the Nezulli have far advanced craft, capable of speeds human craft could not match. They leave the jets behind as they head across the ocean, but they know there will be more to meet them. They are prepared for battle.

#

The joint Chiefs of Staff assemble in the war room of the bunker deep beneath the Pentagon. Key personnel have been called in to deal with the threat. Defense Chief of Staff General Humphries is among them.

"I'm sure you are all by now aware of the severity of this threat. We have set the state of alert to DEFCON One, folks. This is not a drill. This is an inbound threat to our nation," Humphries announces from his position at a large circular table in the center of the room. A digital screen covers the entire back wall with live updates of USAF fighters in pursuit of unidentified craft all across the US. Lights, lit lines with various colors, crisscross the map. Live video feeds from drones are shown down each side of the video wall, and key staff take their positions at computer terminals all around the large room. At the table are heads of departments, responsible for defending the country and keeping its citizens safe. There is a lot of discussion and chatter around the table.

"General, what's the status report right now? Do we know what the threat is, who it is, where they are from?" one senior staff member at the table asks Humphries.

"At this moment," he replies, "all we know is they have craft and weaponry far superior and faster than ours. They are all across our skies, from north to south, east to west. Thus far, they have dropped no bombs, but our USAF fighters have engaged with those they encountered and the craft have downed, as far as I know, seven of our F35's, killing, I believe, six of our brave men and women."

"Are they Soviets or Chinese? Who's attacking us?" a second official asks Humphries.

"Ladies and gentlemen, this is not an attack from our opponents. This attack is from another species, from another planet. This is not a terrestrial enemy we are dealing with. We are on a whole new level here, one we are ill-prepared for, one we never expected to become a reality. But here we are, faced with an unknown enemy, with unknown technology, attacking our country… no… our planet, for an unknown reason. How we deal with it is now up to us. Our futures are about to change. Our terrestrial enemies must now become our allies." Humphries turns to a woman standing behind him.

"Get all the world leaders you can and set up a video conference. The President is on his way here, I want it ready for when he arrives. He wants to address the world leaders and afterward the nation. Set up a press conference in the media suite, send a satellite link to the major broadcasters to downlink," he tells the young woman. She scurries off to set the conference up.

"People, we are in a state of emergency. Use whatever resources your department has available to combat this threat. But we must stay coordinated. The challenge is great, we must be greater," Humphries ends. The senior personnel get up a go to find their teams and track and analyze the threat, looking for weaknesses, patterns, anything that would help them fight this unknown enemy. Humphries knows more than his staff realizes. Along with Aimes, he has a hand in orchestrating the attack. Now they just have to keep up the pretense. Aimes finds Paul Johnston at his computer terminal.

"Seems you were onto something Johnston, good work."

"Thank you, Sir," Johnston replies, without looking away from his screen. He didn't want Aimes to know he suspected him of deception. Aimes might be able to tell by his expressions, so not making eye contact seemed like a good ploy.

"I'm tracking signals to and from the other side of the moon, lots of information flowing now, sir. They are on our comms satellites, using some of our radio waves to transmit unused higher frequencies. Nothing we can manipulate. They are clever little bugger's sir, excuse my language," Johnston tells Aimes.

"Keep trying, Johnston, find a way to break their comms, anything that will make life more difficult for them." Aimes walks off along the line of operators, speaking to each of them. Johnston looks up just in time to see Aimes glance back at him, trying to weigh him up. Johnston carries on working, hoping Aimes isn't on to him. He felt Aimes was too casual about the whole situation.

Johnston looks around the room, everyone else is running around frantically working, trying to figure out how to stop the attack. Aimes, on the other hand, is walking slowly around his team, hands held behind his back like it is a normal day in the office. Johnston scans the room. The only other person, sitting and watching, looking controlled and relaxed, is General Humphries. He is a calm and calculated person, Johnston reminded himself. He didn't get to his position without those traits, so it wasn't unusual for Humphries to look controlled under pressure. Johnston hoped the General was not involved, all he could do was carry on and observe the surrounding people. Hunter told him to trust no-one. That was his plan.

Chapter 28.

Jaii and his team of scientists have spent hours formulating the antidote. But they have a problem. They need a test subject, a human who they can expose to the virus and treat. This is the only way to test it. It is a synthetic product they have created, using the Anunnaki's own resistant antibodies and enzymes, and created a retrovirus solution to combat the coronavirus. Jaii considers sending a team out to abduct an infected human, but time is running out, he has to look closer to home. He goes to Hunter's room to discuss his predicament.

"So, the only way to test its effectiveness in humans is to infect someone," Hunter repeated, to check if he had heard Jaii correctly.

"Yes, that is the quickest and most accurate method," Jaii replies, "we have little choice." Hunter thought for a few seconds.

"Okay, give me the virus," he told Jaii, "I'll be the test subject."

"No, wait," Jo interrupted, "this is crazy. What if it doesn't work? What if you don't recover? You can't go through with this," she pleads with Hunter.

"Listen Jo, it's the best way. It could save millions of lives. We don't have time to find someone else."

"You don't have to. I will do it. I will take the injection. Think about it, Hunter, you know the code and all that computer stuff, you will be needed if anything goes wrong. And you have a daughter to think about. What will happen to her of you die from this test? It's too big a risk. I only have my Grandma, and she might already be dead for all I know."

"You have me, Jo," Hunter reminds her. She looks hard into his eyes. His sincerity is apparent. She has him. She is thankful for that. But she doesn't want his daughter to lose her father, her world.

"I do, don't I?" Jo replies. "But let me do this. Let me take the risk. If it works, then we will have a lifetime together, if it doesn't, at least your daughter has a chance of having a father. Besides, I'm in much better physical condition than you, better chance of surviving this," she smiled at Hunter. He nods, he couldn't argue with her reasoning. She was right, she usually was.

Jaii injects the virus into Jo's left arm. It stings, but no worse than a bee sting.

"I cannot inject the antidote until you are fully infected, to discover the best results and what concentration of the solution works best. Only then, can I give you the cure, and hope it works. If you believe in your gods or deities, now is the time to ask for their help," Jaii tells them both. Jo lies on Hunter's bed, while he takes a seat at the little writing-table by the wall. He doesn't take his eyes off her. He wants to witness every stage of the virus taking effect. It could be important. He wants to be sure Jaii can administer the antidote before it is too late. Jo looks peaceful on the bed, her long brown hair flowing across the pillow, her eye closed, a slight smile on her lips, like she is happy to be taking the risk over Hunter.

He watches her for an hour before the beads of sweat appeared on her forehead. He gets a flannel from the wet-room, rinsed it under cold water, and places it on her forehead. She opens her eyes and looks up at him standing over her and smiles. The smile quickly disappeared as she grimaces in pain.

"What is it?" Jaii asks, "we need to know every symptom."

"Sharp pain, right side of torso, ouch," she replies, struggling to tell him over the pain. She is writhing around on the bed, sweating heavily.

"Struggling to breathe, chest feels tight, lungs not working fully." Jaii gets a bowl from the wet-room and places it by the bed. Jo leans over the edge of the bed and vomits into the bowl. There is blood in the sick.

"You need to give her the antidote now," Hunter demands.

"Not yet, Hunter. This is just the start. When she is fully infected, I will proceed." Jaii takes a small torch from his pocket and checks if Jo's eyes were dilated. She is convulsing and foam at the mouth. Hunter finds it hard to watch, but he refuses to stop.

"Do it now," he demands again, "she's in terrible pain."

"No," Jo says through the pain, "wait, not yet." Hunter knows she is strong and stubborn. She won't give in. He tries to look confident, but inside it is tearing him up. He has fallen for this beautiful woman he met only a few days earlier and now, he could lose her. Jo stops writhing and breathes erratically. She is drifting into a coma. Hunter kneels by the bed and takes her hand in his and squeezes. He wants her to know he is still there.

"I think I love you, Jo," he whispers in her ear. It has been a long time since he said that to anyone other than his daughter. But he means it. The words flow easily, even for a man who didn't discuss his feelings or act romantically. He feels he has to let her know, to give her a sense of purpose, to make sure she fights the virus and comes back to him.

#

The public panics. Firefights between military aircraft and strange-looking craft are taking place over highly populated areas. People are becoming aware this is no ordinary threat. This is not a known enemy. The craft fire lasers at the military aircraft, destroying them in seconds. People try to flee their homes, taking what they can carry in their vehicles. Roads are becoming congested as the news spreads. The military has taken control of the media, but the internet and social media are unstoppable beasts. By the time the government had taken control of the internet, it was too late. Information travels across the globe in milliseconds, with hundreds of servers in various countries, storing and passing on little bits of information, allowing for speed. This means the first time someone tweeted news of the attack, it was stored in lots of places and distributed before the government could act. The world is waking up to a global catastrophe. Within an hour or two of spreading the virus, people are getting sick with fever. The sickness is not localized, as many medical staff had hoped, it is widespread and growing. Medical centers and hospitals can't cope after the first few hours. They have to send the sick away, they don't have beds for them or even suitable medication. They don't know at that point what the illness is, only that it is epidemic, or worse, pandemic.

In the towns and cities around the US, military vehicles appear on roads and streets, setting up roadblocks. Large desert sand-colored Humvees carry regular troops and National Guard troops to locations to take control. It will be dawn in Eastern parts of the country within the hour, and rush-hour traffic will be chaos. No-one is going anywhere fast. On the West coast, it is still dark and many people are still asleep, only the night dwellers are aware of the military movements taking place outside. Part-time National Guard volunteers are getting called in the middle of the night to go to emergency assembly points. Firefighters and police, all called back to duty and doctors and nurses, finishing a long shift, are expected to stay on to deal with the chaos. The same pattern is happening across the world as countries become aware they are under attack.

In the Vatican City, the Pope, along with his senior Bishops and key staff, is ushered into the tunnels beneath the Vatican, where a bunker has been constructed, deep below St Peter's Square. In London, the Prime Minister and his family take the tunnel from below No.10 Downing Street, leading down to the revamped war room in the bunkers below Whitehall, just around the corner. Churchill himself had taken the same route when faced with an invasion from a very different opponent. The French government and other members of the EU have been in contact with one another and are preparing a plan of action for Europe. In Britain, the RAF are scrambled to intercept the unknown aircraft, but most are shot down, unable to compare with the alien craft. The RAF have limited airpower. They couldn't allow all their aircraft to be destroyed, leaving them vulnerable to other predator nations. The Prime Minister quickly decides not to engage in air combat with the unknown assailants. They need to formulate a tactical plan with other nations to have a fighting chance. The President of the USA has called a video conference with world leaders.

Chapter 29.

Government Bunker
The Pentagon
The President and his family arrive safely at the bunker command center. His family retreat to the comfort of their exclusive suite. The suites are held for the very highest office officials. Everyone else has to bunk down in single rooms or communal dormitories. The President is ushered to the command room conference. He takes his seat at the end of a long table, populated by his senior staff members, Senators, Generals and everyone below. On the video wall were boxes, filled with the faces of heads of countries from around the world. China, UK, Soviet Union, and many smaller countries, hoping for guidance or support from the major players. The US President speaks. A team of interpreters quietly translated into headset microphones in the background, following his words to the letter.

"Fellow leaders, colleagues, friends and, I hope from today, former enemies, thank you for agreeing to discuss the current situation at short notice. I will cut straight to the point. We, all of us, our great nations, are under attack from an unknown enemy. This enemy is like no other we have faced before. Our usual warfare tactics and technology appear to be of little use in this battle. We are facing the ultimate force. Our only hope is to work together and try to minimize loss. But we must decide what our course of action should be. One option is to pool our military resources and attempt a full-on offensive and pray that we can defeat this enemy with numbers. However, my Generals inform me we may be outnumbered regardless of a union. Another option is to contact the enemy leaders and ask what they want. What are they after on our planet? To me, this seems like the best option. Would anyone like to discuss any other options?" The Chinese leader speaks, and the translation is carried over the room speakers.

"President Murray, I agree that we should communicate with these enemy beings, but we must also assume that they will not agree with a peaceful solution. If that was so, would they not have communicated with us first, and only threatened to attack? It appears they have an agenda and peace is not part of that agenda."

"Thank you, Mr. Jing-Tn. Everything you have said is true. We don't know if they would agree on a peaceful deal in return for whatever they have come for. But I believe we should try. If they choose not to communicate or not to agree on our terms, what is there left to do that will not destroy our nations and humanity. Our only real chance of fighting them is our nuclear weapons. It is a lose, lose situation for all of us," the President replies.

"I agree with Mr. Jing-Tn," the Soviet leader announces, "we should strike them hard and fast. Use every means available to each of our countries, nuclear bombs, ballistic missiles, whatever we have, fire it at them."

"Unfortunately, their craft is so fast, it might not be possible for our missiles to be effective. They can track the craft, but they don't have the speed capabilities to make contact. We need to find where their command base is and strike that. We are searching for a command center in our orbit. Our telescopes are scanning the skies right now. I would urge each of you with similar technology to reassign you telescopes to search for their base, they must be somewhere close to Earth." The Soviet leader spoke.

"We have already repositioned or telescopes and deep space monitoring station. We should, if you agree, use the International Space Station to monitor the atmosphere for anomalies. There is one other thing we can do if we can locate their command base." The Soviet leader is interrupted by an aide next to him, whispering in his ear.

The leader waves him away with his hand, a little agitated by the interruption.

"My colleagues are concerned that I am giving away our secrets," the Soviet leader laughs, as does the President.

"I suspect I am, but, my friends across the world, I believe now is the time to reconcile. We must each give up our secrets to help our survival, for humanity's survival."

"I agree," the President added. The Soviet leader continues.

"We have, and I apologize in advance that this is against the space warfare convention. But we have satellites in orbit with long-range nuclear missiles on board." The people in the boxes on the video wall shout and throw paper in the air to show their disgust at the Soviets.

"Wait, please people. Let us hear our friend. He has offered help at a great cost to his country's security. I think we owe him the kindness of listening," the President requests. The leaders settle down and the Soviet leader continues.

"Yes, I know we broke the rules of the convention. But this is not the time to discuss it. What I am offering is that we can reposition the satellites to take down their command base, if we can locate it."

"Thank you for your honesty and your offer," the President says, "I too have a confession to make." The President's people protest, knowing what he is about to announce. The President raises his hand to stop them.

"We also have armed satellites in orbit, just in case someone else did also," he adds with a smile. The Soviet leader laughs. "We will do the same and make them available to take down these enemy beings." The Chinese leader speaks next.

"I have a question for the US President. Do you think you are in charge of this offensive? It occurs to me that you called this meeting like you are taking charge. We must approach this with equal responsibility."

"No, my friend, I do not believe I or any of us are in charge, we must work as a collaborative entity to have any chance of survival. I called this meeting because my nation was the first to be attacked. We have a few hours advance in terms of sickness and death. I hoped we could help you and other nations who are being or about to be attacked. I suspect everyone is now in the same situation and suffered an attack. Please, do not think I am here to take charge. We must work together for the good of humanity."

"Ok, thank you Mr. President. In that case, may I also add, we too have nuclear-capable satellites in orbit. My apologies, but fear for my nation led my predecessor to launch these satellites. They are all at our collective disposal, should the need arise."

"Thank you. We have people trying to locate the command base for these attacks. I hope to have some news soon, but for now, if we can all stay close to comms and let each other know of progress, maybe we can find a solution before it is too late. Thank you all and God bless." The President ends his conference. He stands and addresses the people in the command room.

"Thank you each of you, please keep up the good work, America is depending on you." The room breaks out in applause.

"What's next," he asks his aide.

"Media presser next door, Mr. President," comes the reply. The President walks across the floor reading a script handed to him by his communications advisor.

Chapter 30.

Nezulli Command Craft
Vok watches data feeds from his fleet.

"Commander," a Nezulli crew member speaks, "several craft have lost contact. We have no visuals on them and they are not responding to communications."

"Nothing to worry about. The atmosphere on this planet could affect our signals. Carry on and let me know if you get any information," Vok replies, covering up his concerns. His craft and fighter crew are much more advanced than the primitive technology of humans, but he doesn't expect many loses, and not in the first few hours. He considers the terrain and the climate could play a part in the loss of craft, with a small possibility of getting shot down, a lucky strike by the humans. He has a second wave of fighters standing by, waiting for his orders. He will send some of them on search missions, to locate downed Nezulli craft and destroy them and their pilots to ensure their technology cannot be replicated. Humans had their technology since the Roswell incident and still hadn't cracked it, so Vok wasn't too concerned. It is possible the pilots had already destroyed themselves and their craft to avoid capture, as they were instructed to do, but he had to be sure. Vok gave the command for several craft to search for locator signals and assess the situation. He sends the second wave of craft to cover the smaller outer islands and most northern and southern areas of Earth. His plan was on schedule and his mission looked like it would be successful.

#

Jaii takes Jo's vitals. Her heartbeat is irregular and her pulse is above normal. He scans her head with a device Hunter is not familiar with. He assumes it was one of the Anunnaki's advanced tech medical devices.

"She's ready. I will give her the antidote now," Jaii tells Hunter. Jaii takes a syringe from a small medical tray on the table. He gently presses it into Jo's arm and releases the contents into her bloodstream.

"How long do you think before we notice any changes," Hunter asks.

"Unfortunately, I do not know. As with any new medicine, we do not have knowledge of the effect on patients until they have been tested. Everyone's metabolism is different, so each patient will take more or less time, depending on their body. My best estimate would be within the hour."

"Thank you, Jaii. I know you have done this for us and for humanity, with nothing in it for you and your guys."

"To rid the multiverse of the Nezulli would be payment enough for me. To end their tyranny and bring peace to worlds is all we want. It would fulfill us." Jaii put a cap on the syringe and dropped it in a dish on the table.

"Now we wait," he adds.

Hunter drags the chair from the table to beside his bed, where Jo lay in a state of semi-consciousness. A coma-like state, not moving, but breathing unassisted. Hunter watches for any sign of change. Her hair is matted with sweat and from writhing around in pain. Jaii stands by the table, entering data about Jo's condition into a tablet. He didn't know if the antidote would have the desired effect. They had tested it synthetically, ran samples through their computer simulation systems to map results and analysis. But this was the first test in the human blood system. The future of humanity could rest on the results.

A member of Jaii's crew knocks and enters Hunter's room. He indicates to Jaii he needs to talk. Jaii leaves the room with the crew member. He returns within minutes.

"My team are monitoring the attack on Earth. The Nezulli have covered around 80 percent of the planet. I have sent several craft to intercept their fighters, perhaps we can lessen the damage. They have reported a few Nezulli craft have self-destructed in flight. It is possible this is the computer virus taking effect. It could be they were hit by human-made missiles. They report that the command vessel and base station are functioning as normal, so perhaps there was a problem with your virus, or it didn't upload as you thought."

"They have supercomputers, quantum computing, which works on a different system to anything we have, theirs uses subatomic particles," Hunter explains, "so it may take longer to infiltrate or their system might have detected the problem. All we can do is wait and hope it kicks in soon. If not, then if this antidote works, at least we can save millions of lives."

"Live to be enslaved and worked to death by the Nezulli," Jaii reminds Hunter. It looked bad no matter how he looked at it. All Hunter wants at that moment in time was for Jo to recover. He wants her to meet his daughter. He thought she would get on great with her. He wants to spend more time with Jo, not just the few days they have had together, but proper time, a time when they are not trying to save theirs and everyone else's lives. Time when they could do normal things, like watch a movie or go for a meal. He watches Jo closely, willing her to open her eyes and smile at him.

#

The Anunnaki fighters enter the skies above Europe. They track the Nezulli craft as they fly over Germany, releasing their deadly cargo. The Anunnaki engage in a firefight, shooting with laser weapons mounted inside each wing of their craft. The Nezulli craft can outrun and outmaneuver the Anunnaki, but the skill of Jaii's team makes them strong opponents. The Nezulli weapons are similar to the Anunnaki, but upgraded to more powerful lasers and sonic blasters, which can render the computerized controls of its target useless, causing it to fail and drop out of the sky or leave it vulnerable for the Nezulli fighters to pick it off at will and destroy it. The Anunnaki are brave soldiers, knowing they are up against a much more advance adversary, yet they are loyal to Jaii and go into battle without question. Several Anunnaki craft follow Nezulli fighters across the English Channel, into British airspace. Within a few minutes, they are facing another challenge. The Royal Air Force has intercepted them and the Nezulli. They opened fire on both, not knowing if they are both enemies. They are not taking any chances, and anyone in UK airspace is a target now. The RAF fighter jets struggled to keep pace with the craft, but they give chase across the skies of southern England, heading north. Several Anunnaki craft fall in behind the RAF jets but do not open fire, they just follow from a distance, keeping an eye out for further interference from human military. One of the Anunnaki fighters gets in touch with the command center and tells them they are under attack from human military. They need someone to communicate with them to avoid having to take deadly action against the jets. This information is communicated back to Jaii.

"Hunter, you need to talk to your people in the government and convey our support for their cause, ask them not to engage in warfare with our fighter craft. We will send them the tracking code for Nezulli craft. These are the only craft to be targeted, any others they encounter will be ours." Hunter agrees to call Paul Johnston and pass on the message. He knows he can trust Johnston and the message will be escalated and passed to the UK military tactical team and all others across the world. He makes the call from the bedside, not wanting to leave Jo even for a minute. Hunter explains to Johnston the situation.

"Listen, Hunter, the entire world has gone crazy, martial law, rioting for food and water, people are locking down their property and arming themselves to the teeth."

"I know, but we might have a chance with the Anunnaki on our side. These guys have medical expertise way ahead of ours. They are working on something, if it works, millions of lives will be saved," Hunter tells him, "any news on finding out who is involved."

"Hang on, something's happening, an incoming feed. I will call you back later from a secure line." Johnston hangs up. The video wall feeds are interrupted, turning to digital snow briefly before a live image comes online. Vok appears on the video wall of the US government bunker, the UK, Europe, the Soviet Union, China and every leading country in communication with the others.

"As you will now be aware, we do not come in peace. We have come to your planet for the resources we require to continue our journey through your universe and onwards. It is futile for you to attempt to battle us, our technology is beyond anything you can even imagine. Here is what you need to do. Your weak, infirm and elderly will die soon, we have ensured this, they are of no use to us. Those of you who are fit, healthy and strong, will work for us to extract the resources we require from your planet. Anyone who does not do as we say, will be eliminated. Our terms are simple. Your leaders will orchestrate the resource mining and workers on our behalf, under orders from my commanders. Failure for the leaders to comply will result in their elimination and new ones appointed. When we have the resources we need, we will leave you to carry on with your primitive lives. I will contact you again when we are ready to position our fleet on your lands." The broadcast ends and the video wall goes back to normal. Everyone in the US command room stands or sits in silence, in disbelief. General Humphries speaks.

"Folks, let us continue to find a solution to this problem. I don't think talking will help. Everyone back to work." Humphries knew full well how this would all end. He had already set the plans in motion. He and a few others were preparing to put themselves into the top positions of power. Humphries was planning on taking the Presidency for himself and appoint Aimes as Chief of Staff, Candice Peterson would take Director of the CIA. Once the Nezulli had their resources, they promised Humphries they would eliminate the top officials, leaving Humphries and his people to step in and take over. His goal was in sight, or so he thought.

General Humphries is informed of the support for humans from the Anunnaki. Johnston watches him as he is given the information. As he reads the report, he is visibly disturbed. To Johnston, he looks like he has received bad news. He sits at the table, thinking for a few minutes, before speaking to the military personnel nearby.

"I don't think we can trust this information, folks. These Anunnaki could be working with the invaders. To me, this looks like a clever military ploy to allow them to get into strategic positions without reprisal. As far as I'm concerned, if your men or women encounter an alien craft of any type, they should consider it a bogey, an enemy craft. Shoot without hesitation. We are in this to win, folks."

Johnston asks his supervisor to be excused to use the restroom. He leaves the command center and goes to his quarters. Once inside, he takes out of his pocket a secure cell phone with encryption. He calls Hunter.

"General Humphries has given the order to shoot down Anunnaki craft if encountered. He says it could be a trap."

"God damn it," he says and looks at Jaii, "you need to pull your men back, Jaii. The military will shoot them down." Jaii leaves the room to give the order to pull back.

"Another thing, Hunter. Possibly, General Humphries might be involved in all this. It would make sense. He has the high-ranking authority to orchestrate this, with a little help from some lower ranks, like Aimes."

"Sure," Hunter replies, "he is an ambitious, cunning, calculated son of a bitch. I only met him a couple of times at bases, but can't say I liked him much. If he is up to his neck in this, then you will have to go higher, Johnston, find anyone who was in the conference with Senator Carter, who can verify Jaii was there and who can go above the General's head. I'm relying on you. I can't be there, we are fighting this from another angle, so you are pretty much on your own out there."

"I know, Hunter. I will do what I can. God willing, we can defeat these creatures."

"That's something I was going to mention. The attackers, the Nezulli. They are artificial intelligent beings. They destroyed their creators, then developed their own civilization. So, be warned, they cannot be killed conventionally. They can be destroyed, like any machine, but they are extremely advanced technology."

"Great, thanks for the heads up, good to know I might get killed by a super-advanced coffee machine," Johnston jokes. Hunter laughs, glad of the light relief. Johnston hangs up the call. Hunter sits on the floor of his quarters, holding Jo's hand, waiting for signs of improvement. There are none.

Jaii returns to the room to check Jo's vital signs.

"Her temperature is dropping. This is a good sign, Hunter," Jaii tells him. Jo was still unconscious, but her face was showing signs of color returning to it.

"We will soon know if our efforts have been worth it," Jaii continues. "If this has the desired effect, we will somehow deliver it to your population. However, if they do not trust us and deem us your enemy, this could prove difficult."

"Paul Johnston is working to get people at the top of government to weed out the Nezulli allies. If he can do this, then it will smooth the way to allowing your team to go public and distribute the antidotes."

"We will pass on our scientific research to your scientists. They can quickly reproduce the antidote on a much larger scale, across many countries. This would be the best method to save lives," Jaii explains. Jo starts to wake up. She is groggy, her eyes have dark rings around them and her forehead still has beads of sweat on it.

"Water," she manages to get the word out through a dry mouth and throat. Hunter takes a bottle from the table and gently holds her head up off the pillow and tilts the water into her mouth, a little at a time. She nods to indicate she has had enough, and he places her head back on the pillow. She drifts back into a restless sleep.

"This is good, right?" Hunter asks Jaii.

"Yes, Hunter, this is very good. Her recovery is beginning much faster than expected. I am pleased with this. The antidote could be better than we thought." Hunter is pleased and relieved. Though Jo still had a fight on her hands, he felt this news meant the odds were in her favor.

After about thirty minutes, Jo begins to come around. She is still quite ill, but beginning to speak.

"How long was I out," she asks Hunter.

"A good few hours. I thought you were a goner for a while. You look a lot better now, but you will need to have a shower when you get back on your feet, you stink something terrible." Jo tries to laugh, but the pain stops her short. Her body feels like it has been dragged through the back roads by a pack of horses. Her whole body hurts. Her mouth is still dry, and she is quite dehydrated, even though she is on a drip. The virus has taken its toll and her energy is near zero percent.

"Where are we with things," she asks Hunter.

"Don't worry about that now, just rest, get better and help us fight these bloody Nezulli." She smiles up at Hunter and closes her eyes. She feels safe with him by her side. But this is only the beginning for them both.

Chapter 31.

Government Bunker
The Pentagon
Paul Johnston sits down at the computer terminal in a private data viewing room. He accesses the video conference files for Senator Carter's conference a few days earlier. The files are classed as confidential, but Johnston's clearance level gives him access to much higher classification files than these. He plays the recording to identify those involved. He is looking for someone who believes Carter and who looks like they might be approachable. Someone in high office who he could ask for help.

He watches the footage from start to finish, in a private viewing room they sometimes use for sensitive material. He uses headphones to ensure anyone passing the room door can't hear what he is listening to. He saw Jaii by the Carter's side, then appear next to one of the attendees in another city. This was the first time he had seen an alien, and he was quite surprised at how much he looked like a human. Tall, thin, similar type of skin, hair slicked back, wearing a gray jumpsuit. If he didn't know he was an Anunnaki, Johnston would have assumed he was human. One of the attendees who appeared to support Carter's quest and who seemed keen to find out more about the situation was the Attorney General Gloria Usbana. She held an executive position within the cabinet and she would be very persuasive. Johnston watches her closely, gauging her interest and concern. He believes she is honest, and she is quite genuinely surprised by Jaii's appearance next to her at the conference. Her startle soon faded as she began to accept the situation and she wanted to know what she could do to help. He liked her resolve, her willingness to accept the facts. Perhaps these were qualities that got her to the position she was in. This is the woman, the person he would approach to convince the government of inside collusion with the Nezulli. His decision was based mostly on the information he found on her career. Working her way up from a lower working-class background, studying at night school whilst holding down two day jobs, until she gained her Law degree, after which she worked for a number of law firms and offered her services pro bono in poorer neighborhoods. But he also likes the look of her. She is an African American, aged fifty-six, has a grown-up family. She smiles with her eyes and looks happy and honest in her profile picture. He likes that. She would be his next call.

#

Gloria Usbana is sitting at her desk in a bunker about one hundred miles north of the Pentagon. She had been at a meeting and couldn't make it back to Virginia, so she was redirected to an outlaying bunker, used for mainly military personnel. She hadn't minded going to this one. Although smaller and not as up to date as the Pentagon bunker and no command center, she is pleased to have some quiet to catch up on paperwork and keep an eye on the news, following events. The bunker has live video feeds from news channels, fed through the government's network for censorship, but she also has access to the uncensored clips. Her security clearance allows her to override the censored feeds. She has both feeds on two computer screens, so she can see what the government was not telling the public. The news gives her a good understanding of the situation and she reflects on the video conference with the late Senator Carter. He had tried to warn them that this was coming and that they should prepare. She wanted to do something, but it had been too late. When she got the news of the Senator's death, she was stunned and shocked. But she was also a cautious woman. She knew how certain departments of government worked, departments that were deep and dark. Some didn't even have names, just numbers. Dept 36, she had seen this on documents, but even after trying to find out who or what it was, she hit a dead end. There were other departments just as mysterious. In her fifteen years in government, she had learned when to stop digging, when to walk away.

As Attorney General, her job is to investigate, to ensure everyone is doing their jobs in the pursuit of justice, to ensure they give their all and standards are maintained. But she is aware there were times when the government used unconventional methods for the safety of the nation, and that these departments were responsible for these dark methods. She and her staff didn't venture too far into their work, for fear of their own lives and the lives of their families. But Usbana felt she was letting down the memory of Carter, who may have died for opening the door onto one of those departments, for peering into the looking glass. Everything Carter told them was true. He knew what was coming. Now, stuck in a bunker, writing up pointless reports, Usbana felt helpless.

#

Johnston did a little more digging into the files in the data viewing room. He has targeted Gloria Usbana as a possible source of help. But he wants to find out more. If she has any connections with General Humphries or with Aimes, both of whom he suspects as being somehow involved with the invasion. He found files relating to Aimes, usually referring to his attempts at promotion. He wanted to climb the government ladder but often found himself side-lined. There is little available information on Humphries, other than his impressive military career, having fought in most of the major conflicts since Vietnam. Johnston, as a former soldier, admires his war record, but he can't accept that he would betray his country. Neither men appear to have any contact with Usbana, at least no paper trail is evident. Accessing personnel files can be traced back to the user log in. Johnston knows he is taking a huge risk, one that could end his career. But he weighed that up against the planet being overrun by an alien species. He believes it is a risk worth taking. Once he is satisfied Usbana isn't corrupt, he logs off and takes his notes back to his desk.

#

A member of Jaii's team knocks on the door and enters. He hands Jaii a tablet message and leaves. Jaii stands for a moment, reading the tablet.

"Good news, I hope," Hunter says.

"I'm sorry to say, no. It is not. My team has reported that they believe the Nezulli command craft may be working on a standalone system. Their surveillance shows some support craft are beginning to fail. This is good, but it looks like the command craft must have protected themselves before the computer virus could reach their system. They have a back-up, remote system."

"Does that mean we can't touch the command craft and Vok?"

"It will be extremely difficult, yes. But it might draw him out of the shadows. He will need to be closer to communicate with his teams, using your satellite systems to do so. This could benefit us. If he comes within range, we or your military could potentially launch an attack on the command craft. It will be surrounded by its own security craft, so it won't be unprotected."

"Do you think they knew about the computer virus?" asks Hunter.

"We should assume their system alerted them before it spread throughout. If it affects their fighters, then we still have a chance," Jaii replies. Hunter looks at Jo, still asleep on his bed.

"As soon as Jo is well enough, we need to get out there and start fighting."

"I agree," Jaii replies, "I will arrange with my team to instruct you in the use of our craft and weapons. We will need all the help we can get." Jaii leaves the room. Hunter turns to look at Jo. She is sitting up in the bed, looking rough.

"What was all that about?" she asks. Hunter hands her a bottle of water, which she takes short sips from.

"I don't think the computer virus has been as effective as we hoped. We might need a new approach."

"At least the antidote works, that's a relief," Jo replies.

"Yeah, you're looking much better." Hunter sits on the bed next to Jo.

"I must admit, you had me worried for a while there," Hunter tells her, "your temperature was through the roof."

"It felt like it. My mind was all over the place, weird dreams. I wasn't sure when I was conscious or unconscious."

"Well, you're on the mend now and thanks to you, millions of lives can be saved. I'm proud of you."

"Shut up, Hunter. You getting all soppy on me now?" Hunter laughs and stands up.

"I'll go tell Jaii you're awake, he'll want to know and to administer me with the antidote." Hunter leaves the room, leaving the door open, just in case.

#

Gloria Usbana's cell phone rings. She takes it from her handbag.

"Hello, this is Gloria."

"Hi, Mrs. Usbana. My name is Paul Johnston, I work in the Pentagon. I want to talk to you about the video conference with Senator Carter. Can you talk?"

"Yes, do I know you?" she asks.

"No Mam, but I know you took part in the conference, I have reviewed the footage and I really need your help. I know you saw the alien chap appear next to you. I know you believed the Senator and that you would have supported him if he hadn't been killed."

"Go on," Gloria tells him, curious to find out what he wants.

"Well, Mam, I have seen the alien as well. His name is Jaii, and he is on our side. He and his people, if I can call them that, have come here to help protect us. They want to help. The invaders are a species that will decimate the world and move on, like locusts stripping a field of corn, Mam."

"What is it you want me to do, Mr. Johnston?"

"You have the ear of the President. You can talk to him and his cabinet and convince them these other alien guys are okay. They are on our side. We need to protect them so they can help us. There is one very important thing. There are members of government, in high positions of power, who are working with the invaders. They are out to gain overall power, presumably. I mean world dominance, overall control, with the help of these invaders."

"Okay, let's assume I believe you. Let's assume there are good aliens and bad aliens. And let's assume there are people trying to take over control of the new world. How do you know I'm not one of them, Mr. Johnston?"

"Well, Mam, it's a gut feeling. I don't think you want to take over the world for one. You did a lot of pro bono work in poorer communities. Communities like the one you grew up in. I don't think someone who does that would kill their colleagues and collude with aliens to gain power."

"You've done your homework, Mr. Johnston. Yet, I know nothing about you. How do I know you are not working with the colluders and this is a ploy to capture and enslave me?" she asks.

"You don't, Mam. You will have to decide for yourself if you trust me or not." Gloria thought for a few seconds.

"Okay, I'm going to take a chance. You sound like a truthful young man. Brent Carter was a good friend to me. What can I do to help?"

"If you can get in touch with the President, explain to him what I have told you and that some of his people are corrupt, then he might be able to do something about it. I have my suspicions about a couple of staff members. There might be more."

"What if the President is in on it? This could go south real fast for us?"

"I'm sure he is oblivious to it, Mam. I saw his reaction when he spoke to the command center. He is as much in shock as the rest of the world."

"Could you not have approached him then?"

"No Mam, I don't hold a high enough office to get near him, certainly not for a private conference. This is why I'm reaching out to you. I need your help. He will listen to you." Johnston continues to explain about the Anunnaki and Nezulli, passing on the information Hunter has given him.

"Okay, Mr. Johnston. You present a good case. I will call his aides and arrange to speak to him on a secure line. I will contact you on the number you called from, if or when I have some information."

"Thank you, Mam." Gloria hangs up the call. She is happy to be able to do something positive, to carry on Senator Carter's quest. She sits at her computer and draws up a plan of action, a method to discuss the situation with the President, in a way that he would believe. She prepares the telephone conversation like a defense case, covering every possible question the President might throw at her. She needed to be prepared. If she got this wrong, her career could be over in one short call.

Chapter 32.

Anunnaki Mountain Base, Arizona.
Jaii and his scientists complete their work on the antidote. They create a computer file with the exact formula, to be distributed to science labs across the world. They carry batches of the substance on every fighter craft for delivery to the most in urgent need. Their primary concern is getting shot down by military or Nezulli fighters before they can distribute the medication. They must wait for clearance that they are safe to proceed. In the meantime, they get ready and wait. Jo is up out of bed and sauntering around the room, with help from Hunter.

"I need a shower," she announces.

"Please, for all our sakes, have one," Hunter replies with a laugh. Jo tries to laugh, but it ends in a cough. He helps her into the wet room and leaves her to shower. He talks loudly to her through the door.

"Jaii will need our help to distribute the meds. Do you think you will be up to it?" he asks her.

"Hell yes. I'm not staying here while you go all gung-ho in a fighter craft. I'm going with you."

"I thought you might. Good. We will leave after we have some training and they give us the all-clear to go." Hunter is happy Jo wants to go with him. It is a dangerous mission, but with her by his side, he feels they could take on the world, which is pretty much what they had to do.

"Do we know how many people have been affected by the coronavirus?" Jo shouts through the door.

"Not an exact count, but somewhere near four billion. Of those, it's estimated twenty percent have died and another ten percent likely to die. It's a huge cull."

"It's hard to imagine that many people dead. All those families, losing loved ones," Jo calls through, "having to go through that grief, with the knowledge you or other family members might be next." She rinses her hair with her face under the warm water, cleansing the sweat and germs from her body. She thought about her grandma, wondering if she survived, if anyone had gone by to check on her. The elders often visited her, almost daily, so she hoped if she had passed, someone would tend to her, respect her remains. She wondered what the world would be like if they survived and defeated the Nezulli. With mostly the old, infirm, people with underlying ailments gone, would the world be a better place. Would it be more sustainable, cleaner? Would those who survived take a new approach to how we treat our world and our people? Could something good come from this? But what would the world have lost. Generations with knowledge and stories of the past, gone. Ancient skills, gone. Links to the past, gone. She remembered a saying she heard somewhere once. 'From chaos comes great refinement.' She didn't remember where she heard it, but it seemed poignant now. Would global warming slow down? Would we stop cutting down the rain forests? Would we only use sustainable energy? She hoped there would be changes for the better. She dries herself off and wraps the towel around her body. She opens the door and enters the room. Hunter is sitting at the table, watching news feeds from US media channels. He turns to look at her.

"You look like new," he smiles.

"I feel so much better. Anything to eat?"

"Jaii will bring something shortly. He left clean clothes on your bed across the hall. Jo smiles at Hunter and leaves to go get dressed.

Jo returns just as Jaii is delivering a tray of food. Burger and fries, with ice-cold cola. Jo downs the cola straight away. The sickness has made her so thirsty, she takes Hunter's cola and starts on that too.

"Thank you, Jaii, for developing a medication that worked. I'm so grateful."

"We should thank you, Jo," Jaii replies, "you took the ultimate risk. You could have died if we got it wrong. That was a huge sacrifice you made."

"I knew you guys would pull it off. Glad to be of service." Hunter and Jo sit on the bed eating their burger and fries, while Jaii goes to ready the craft for their initial training.

#

Gloria Usbana calls the President's personal aide to arrange a telephone call back. Then she waits. She has her notes in front of her, ready to make her case. After about fifteen minutes, her cell phone rings.

"The President will speak with you now, just putting you through."

"Hello, Gloria, how are you, hope you're well?"

"Yes, thank you, Mr. President. I'm glad to hear you are safe."

"What can I do for you, Gloria?"

"It's to do with this invasion, Mr. President. There are things you need to know. Things that could change how you deal with it and who you turn to for help. This is connected to the death of Senator Carter, Mr. President." Gloria continued with her case, providing information when requested, giving the facts as she knew them, answering questions.

"These are very unusual times, Gloria. If what you say is true, and I have no reason to doubt you, then we need to close ranks and go fishing for those who do not have our nation's best interests at heart. I will inform our military to aid these Anunnaki and ask other world leaders to do the same. I fear it might be too little too late, Gloria."

"All we can do is try, Mr. President. Thank you for your understanding. I hope we can meet again soon. Give my love to your wife and daughter." President Murray hangs up. Gloria is relieved to have had the chance to do something for Brent Carter. Now it was up to the President to find out who he can trust. Gloria calls Paul Johnston and tells him the news.

"That's great, thank you Mam."

"You're welcome, Mr. Johnston. But just one thing. Please stop calling me Mam."

"Yes, Mam, sorry, Mrs. Usbana."

"Gloria will do, Paul. Now go pass on your news to whoever you need to." Johnston calls Hunter straight away. This is the news he was waiting for. He and Jo go to find Jaii.

"Okay, now you get a quick lesson in using our craft and our weapons, Jaii explains. He takes them on board a fighter craft. Like all the others, it is a dull gray aircraft, pretty much triangle-shaped, with rounded edges and a cockpit for up to four personnel, with a glass dome protruding out of the top of the craft at the front. They enter up steps from below the craft. It was the same as the one that took them back to the reservation cabin a few days earlier. They sit in seats next to each other, which then change to fit snuggly around them.

"One of you will fly the craft, one will operate the weapons. I will be with you and navigate. Also, I don't want to lose this craft, so I will be here for safety. Yours and mine," Jaii explains. He takes them through the controls, how to move in all directions, the speed controls, weapons and how to land safely. Hunter takes the craft up in the mountain cavern, hitting the walls and roof as he did so.

"Bit tricky, isn't it," he confesses.

"Let me have a go," Jo tells him. She lifts off smoothly, then turns on the spot three-hundred and sixty degrees. She takes off at speed along the tunnel, stopping abruptly, turning and returning with a smooth faultless landing.

"I guess we know who is flying and who is on weapons then," Jaii tells them. Hunter looks a little disgruntled but is soon over it as he learns how the weapons work.

"You may not have any need to fire these, but best to be prepared," explains Jaii. Hunter grabs the joystick type control arms and presses a button. A loud bang is heard outside and they can see bits of rock flying through the air. Jaii's crew members are running for cover.

"Oops," Hunter speaks, "sorry about that. Tell your guys I'm sorry, slip of the finger." Jaii shakes his head.

"Let's save the weapons for the Nezulli, shall we? Right, we will follow the others out of the tunnel and head for the nearest large town whilst they disburse across the US. I believe Flagstaff is closest," Jaii tells them. Jo takes the craft along the tunnel without incident, reaching the entrance and out into the bright sunlight. She then pulls the control arm back, and the craft shoots up into the sky. She levels off once she has the hang of it.

"This is great, Jaii. You should rent these out for kids parties," she tells him. Before long she is comfortable at the controls. She increases the speed, passing Mach 5 and overshooting the town of Flagstaff by fifty miles. The speed has no noticeable effect on their bodies, like a drive on the freeway. She slows and returns to the town, landing in an empty parking lot behind the diner she had visited a few days earlier. They leave the craft and walk around the buildings to the main street. The street is deserted and stores are closed or boarded up. Jo looks in the window of the diner. There are people inside. She tries the door handle. It's unlocked. They enter the diner.

"Hello folks," the waitress, wearing a face mask, greets them, "you all want some coffee? We don't have much in the way of food, I'm afraid, but we can offer you a cup of strong coffee."

"Where is everyone?" Jo asks her.

"Seems they don't want to come out due to the sickness. Some have died, sadly. Mostly the elderly or those who were already sick, I guess."

"Can you point us to the hospital, we have medication," Jo asks her.

"Sure, sweetheart. Just go left out of here, top of the main street, on your right."

"Thank you." They begin to file out of the diner. Jo pauses, then turns back to face the waitress.

"I spoke to an elderly gentleman here a few days back, his name was Charlie, Charlie Gates. Lovely guy, very friendly. Do you know what happened to him?"

"I'm sorry, sweetheart. Old Charlie didn't make it, died early this morning, got the sickness he did." Jo felt a tear well in her eye. She had only met him once, briefly, but he had left an impression on her. He seemed like someone who was of great character. She would have liked to have met him again, spoken at length about his life and family. She left and caught up with the others.

#

Government Bunker
The Pentagon
President Murray talks privately with his close aides.

"So, we need to find who is involved in this. We don't know who we can trust. I'm putting my trust in you. Please be careful. They could be in this bunker or in several government bunkers. We just don't know how deep this goes. We have enough on our hands dealing with this invasion, but to have our own people betray us is unthinkable. I need you to look at telephone and computer logs, see if there is anything unusual going on, start with the highest cabinet members, then work your way down. See if you can find a common link. Check out the analysts, make sure they are clean, then use them to research, but tell them to keep it quiet, not to report to anyone else but you." The President's team leave his bunker office to set about finding the government officials working with the invaders.

The aides look at the telephone logs of all their Generals. They didn't really know what they were looking for. They needed the analysts, the people who do it all day every day. They decide to clear the analysts first, so they can do most of the work. They all had high enough clearance to look at logs. They bring up the logs for Paul Johnston. It soon becomes apparent he has been making some unusual calls, mostly to a cell phone owned by an ex-government employee called

Hunter, and to the Attorney General. They ask Johnston to join them in an interview room. He goes without question. In the room, he sits at the table in the middle, with three aides across from him, one seated, the other two standing.

"Why have you been calling the Attorney General?" one of the aides asks him.

"To explain the situation. That there is a group of people in the government waiting to take it down and gain control." The aides all look at each other.

"Isn't that what you guys are after. Did the President not send you to find out who it is?"

"Well, yes, but how do you know so much?" the aides asked Johnston.

"I'm the one who got the information to the President. I think there are two people here involved. General Humphries and Bernard Aimes, my boss."

"Okay, we will look into it. Keep this quiet for now, whilst we do some digging around," the aides tell him. Johnston goes back to his desk. Aimes spots him coming out of the room, followed by the aides. He is sure something is going on. He goes to his office and calls Humphries. He tells him what he saw.

"Calm down, Bernard. We are almost there, just a little more time. I have started to organize people to control the work gangs for the Nezulli. Our army will be deployed when requested. For now, settle down and relax. And don't call me again, come find me and we can speak face to face. Don't want a log trail coming back to me." Humphries hangs up.

Aimes feels like they are closing in on him. He doesn't have the General's reserve or courage. He goes back to the command center room and watches Johnston, trying to judge what is going on. He watches the President's men, some on computers in private cubicles, others walking around, talking to people. He thought this unusual. They would take an analyst to the interview room, then they would return after a few minutes. Something was definitely going on.

#

In Flagstaff, Hunter, Jo and Jaii enter the local Community Hospital. The whole place was in lockdown, with people on stretchers in the hallways and nurses, doctors and cleaners all in hazmat suits. A nurse approaches them.

"You can't come in here, we have no beds. There is nothing we can do for you. I'm sorry." Jo speaks first.

"We are here to help you. We have medication that will fight this virus. I have recovered, please believe us," Jo pleads.

"Wait here." The nurse leaves, then reappears a few minutes later, with someone else in a hazmat suit. He approaches them. The nurse goes about her business.

"I'm Doctor Admed Hazan, Head of Medicine here, " he announces, holding his suit visor down to talk into the mic.

"My colleague tells me you have a cure for this virus. We are not buying anything, I'm afraid, there is nothing that will cure it."

"There is, we have it here," Jo tells him, becoming a little annoyed. "We don't want money for it, we just want you to administer it to the worst cases."

"I'm sorry, we can't just give patients untested, unregulated medication off the street. It's just not how we work." The situation looks hopeless. They hadn't considered the hospital's position and the risk of huge lawsuits if people suffered adverse effects or death from the antidote. It would be too big a risk for any hospital to take.

"This is ridiculous, we are offering medication, that we have tested and we know works. Under what circumstances would the hospital administer a medication they didn't have any history off, no known results from tests or actual case studies?" Hunter asks the doctor.

"Well, in a state of emergency, such as a pandemic, as we have now, then one provided by the government for the safety of the nation. In that circumstance, our legal obligations are waived, and the government takes full responsibility," the doctor replies. "But what you have is not issued by the government, we can't take the risk."

"Doctor," Jaii speaks softly, "people are dying needlessly. We can help stop it. We have developed this antidote to fight the virus. It works, we have proven evidence standing right here," he indicates to Jo. "What if you ask the patients or their next of kin. Ask if they wish to have the medication, that they waive their rights to sue the hospital. Use this as a case study group. Protect the hospital from lawsuits and group test the medication, to allow others to benefit from it, based on your results. Please, doctor, give these people a chance. I'm sure you do drug testing studies, it's the same thing. But without a lengthy medical check-up before-hand. These people don't have that sort of time. If it doesn't work, at least you gave these people hope in their final hours. That at least should bring them some comfort." The doctor is clearly moved by Jaii's speech. He thought for a moment, weighing up his options. He knows Jaii is right, there is little hope otherwise and to give them hope, even if they didn't recover, was better than the despair and anguish they faced.

"Okay. This could be the end of my days as a doctor, but hell, what else can we do. I need to get the paperwork sorted. I need their next of kin or guardians to sign the waiver. Once done, we will give them the meds. Tell me more about this medication." Jaii goes with the doctor to explain the antidote and how long it took Jo to recover.

Hunter and Jo walk through the corridors of the hospital, looking at the people on beds in the hall, writhing in pain, sweating, retching. The scene is upsetting. They see rooms filled with people dying, hallways cluttered with beds and sick pans. The stench of sick and faeces is overwhelming. Nurses do what they can in a hopeless situation. Jaii returns.

"I've given the doctor the medication. He will give it to those who agree to his terms. It is all he can do. He is a good man, taking a leap of faith. At least they will have some hope here. Let us return to the craft. We have much work to do. We must enlist the help of the government or military to issue the medication, otherwise, we face the same problem elsewhere."

Overhead, USAF fighter jets rattle the town as they fly over. Flagstaff was well used to low flying jets. The airbase was just on the edge of town, and many of the residents worked there. Hunter is worried they would spot their craft, neatly parked, although taking about four parking spaces. The jets were obviously on a mission to chase Nezulli fighters. He hopes they had all been given the notice not to engage Anunnaki craft. The US military had a long history of friendly fire. There was no guarantee they wouldn't mistake their craft for a Nezulli fighter, even with the trackers sent to them by the Anunnaki. They reach the craft and enter.

"Where to now?" Jo asks Jaii as she takes the controls.

"We're going to land on the lawn at The Pentagon," he replies. Hunter and Jo look at him with a look of shock.

"Do you think that's a good idea," Jo asks.

"You got a better one?"

"Okay, The Pentagon it is," she replies as she takes off from the parking lot in Flagstaff.

#

Government Bunker
Nevada Desert.
Jake Brennan watches the news feeds, as military personnel take control of towns and cities. Roadblocks are set up at intersections, people stand in long queues for food and water supplies. Gas stations are shut due to running out of fuel. Everything they expected to happen was happening. But Brennan has concerns. He hasn't had any contact with the command craft since before he tried to decrypt Hunter's files. It had gone quiet. He didn't know if there was a problem. He thought about who he could contact. One of the others, the General, Aimes or perhaps Peterson. One of them might know what was happening.

Brennan had been promised great wealth for his part in the invasion and subsequent overthrow of power. That was all he cared about. After giving years of his working life to the government, all they would offer is a standard retirement package, barely enough to live on. He wanted to enjoy his retirement when it came and enjoy it early with the money promised. Now he was beginning to feel he was being left out of the plan like he had been discarded. He needed to know the plan was still on track. He calls Humphries.

"What's happening, General?"

"Brennan, you shouldn't be calling me, it's not secure."

"With all due respect, sir, I don't care. I need to know what's going on. I haven't had contact from our friends up there," he says cryptically.

"There have been some problems, but everything is okay."

"What problems."

"I think the President's team knows someone in government is involved. They seem to be hunting for someone. Also, there is another visitor offering to help governments fight the invasion. I don't know much, but I have heard they have fighters in the air, working with our guys. This is not something we planned for or expected. It might get bumpy now, son, but nothing to worry about."

"Okay, thank you, General. I think I might get out of here and head to the mountains, probably safer there."

"Best to stay where you are, son. It's safer and we can contact you when the time comes. Just stay put." General Humphries hangs up. Brennan didn't like the idea of the government closing in on him. Did he cover his tracks well enough? He had used government phones and computers to contact people like Hunter. These would show up in logs. But he had used the Nezulli computer to contact Vok, this was untraceable. He could explain all or any contact with Hunter and Aimes or Peterson. He would often contact people at their levels in their departments when investigating sources or analyzing data. This was not unusual. He had used a non-government vehicle to deal with Carter. He didn't think he could be tracked to that. He took the vehicle to a scrap yard and paid cash to have it crushed. He watched them crush it. It was unlikely they could trace it now. But sitting in the bunker, waiting for the door to burst open with a SWAT team throwing him to the floor and arresting him, didn't feel like something he wanted to wait around for. He had to decide for his own sake.

#

General Humphries calls Peterson to his bunker office. He sits behind his large mahogany desk. Peterson enters and sits opposite him.

"Yes, General, what is it?"

"Brennan. He's becoming a liability, getting a little jumpy, becoming sloppy."

"How do you want it handled, Sir?"

"The President's team is looking for someone working with our friends. Let's give them someone. But make it a Dept 36 job, no loose ends."

"Yes, General. Where is Brennan now?"

"The Nevada bunker. Take a small team, make it look like suicide, easier to explain with a confessional note." Peterson leaves the General's office and prepares her team. They put on N95 respirator masks, and head to the airport to take one of the CIA's private jets to the Nevada base.

Chapter 33.

Nezulli Command Craft

"Commander, we have further reports of losses of our fighter craft. It appears there is a problem with the computer system. Instruments are failing, craft are exploding or crashing. Our crew cannot control them. We are also receiving messages regarding personnel failures. We believe the system error is causing fighter crews to stop functioning," the Nezulli Communications Chief tells Vok.

"This can't be happening. Our systems do not fail. This must be caused by a rogue element. Someone has entered a virus into the mainframe system. There is no other possibility. We do not make mistakes, we are programmed to succeed. You must find this viral code and take care of it immediately." Vok spoke forcefully. He did not have the ability to become angry, but his program provided him with several simulated emotions, such as raising his voice. This was as close as he could get to anger. Vok walked around the command room of his craft whilst his team dealt with the equipment in the consoles around the space.

"How many vessels have we lost? I need that information. Quickly." A crew member turns and speaks.

"Commander, we estimate around one thousand."

"Send more, send them to the areas not covered by the loss of these crafts. We must work fast."

"Commander, we are out of communications range on our old standalone system to give the order."

"Then we take the command craft to them. Prepare to move closer. We must be able to communicate on our own systems. And find that virus in our systems, we must get back online with our quantum computer." Vok's crew prepare their craft and outlying security craft to move to a closer position to the action. Vok knows this leaves them exposed, but communication is the key to the success of this mission.

"We have identified the base for the Anunnaki. In a mountain range in the US state of Arizona. Surveillance shows no sign of movement, Commander."

"Tell your team to keep watch over it. If they leave or return, notify me immediately." Vok knew the capabilities of the Anunnaki. They were not as technologically advanced as his species. They were organic living beings, who suffered from emotions and feelings. This was seen as a weakness by the Nezulli. Vok had commanded the destruction of the Anunnaki's planet. Those who were not present during the invasion were the only survivors. Jaii and his crews had been on a mission to another planet and had returned to the devastation. Vok knew that they were after him, but it never worried him. He would kill them when the time was right. If they were on this planet, helping the humans, he saw it as an opportunity to end their existence once and for all. He particularly wanted to come face to face with Jaii and destroy him personally.

#

Candice Peterson lands at the airbase in the Nevada desert, with two of her operatives. They jump into a black SUV waiting for them on the runway and head towards the government bunker a few miles East.

Peterson is an ambitious woman. She had fought her way up through the agency, in a man's world, but she had gained the respect of her colleagues for her ruthless interrogation methods and her willingness to take whatever action was needed to beat the enemy. She was cold and calculating. The perfect CIA operative.

The SUV is cleared at the security gates and drives into the bunker, parking in the bays provided for government staff. They are sent through a decontamination chamber. After this, they enter a room with benches around the walls. They are clear to remove their respirator masks. The three walk along a long corridor, with security guards opening a series of blast doors for them. Once through the final set of blast doors, they take the lift at the end of the last corridor. There is only one direction, down. The first floor down is the reception. They stop at the floor to ask where they can find Brennan. With the information, they proceeded to the tenth level down, where his accommodation is situated. They march along the hallway, turning left and right in the maze of rooms.

The rooms are numbered and they are closing in on Brennan's. They slow their pace as they arrive at his room door. One operative takes out his weapon and holds it close to his face as he quietly goes to the door and listens for any sound from inside. He signals to the others it is silent. He gently turns the doorknob. To his surprise, it is unlocked. Peterson and the other operative both draw their firearms from their holsters and hold them with stretched out arms. Peterson is at one side of the door and the other two operatives are on the other side. She gives the nod to enter at speed. The first operative pushes the door open fully and Peterson and the second operative barge in, one high, one low, sweeping the room with drawn weapons. There is no-one there. The toilet door is closed. They all point their weapons at it and one operative kicks the door open. They move forward, only to find the toilet and shower cubicle empty.

"Damn it," Peterson expresses, "look around, see if he is still around or left any clues to where he might be."

"The drawers are empty, Mam, looks like he has left for good. Nothing here of his. The room is clean." Peterson leaves the room and stands in the hallway. She holsters her gun and takes out her cell phone.

"General, the marque is gone. He's in the wind."

"Find him, Peterson. Check his comms, see who he spoke to or emailed. Think like him. Where would he go, why would he go? We need this wrapped up, no loose ends."

"Yes, General. We are on it. I will let you know if we get anything." She hangs up. She is visibly annoyed at not catching Brennan.

"Right," she tells the operatives, "let's find this son of a bitch. Download his cell phone records. He is likely to have more than one cell phone, so look across all data. Get his email trail and see if he made plans with anyone, somewhere to stay for a few days. I want to know who he talked to, who called him, who he met. Get the kit from the SUV, we will set it up in his room." The operatives leave to collect their gear. Peterson sits on the edge of the bed, trying to think where Brennan would have gone.

#

Jo gently lands the craft on the lawns, in the center of the Pentagon buildings. As she touches down, the craft is surrounded by armed US Marines in hazmat suits, all pointing their weapons at the craft.

"What now?" Hunter asks.

"Perhaps we should go out and say we come in peace," Jo says with a giggle.

"Hunter, call Johnston and tell him to clear us with the military. Let them know we are not the enemy." Hunter calls Johnston and explains their situation. After about five minutes, someone gives the command for the marines to stand down. Jaii opens the door below the craft and the steps set down onto the lawn. They exit the craft, watched closely by the marines, as they make their way to the nearest entrance.

"Can you tell us how to find the bunker?" Hunter shouts to one of the dumbfounded marines. He points to a door to their right. They enter and make their way to the lifts. Inside, there are buttons for the lower floors. They head to the deepest one. From here, they are directed through a decontamination chamber, then out through a changing room, into the corridor, leading to another set of lifts, going even deeper. Then travel another twenty floors down to reach the bunker. Hunter had been in some government bunkers before, but when he sees the command room, he is amazed at how hi-tech it has been fitted out. They had obviously spent a lot of time and money on it.

Perhaps they knew this day was close. Hunter asks a young lady at a desk where he can find Paul Johnston. She directs him to the data analyst's cubicles across the large command room floor. They find Johnston and ask to speak to him privately. He guides them to a data viewing room. Inside, Hunter and Jo sit opposite Johnston at the table. Jaii stands, pacing the room.

"This is amazing," Johnston speaks. "I'm actually in the presence of an alien being, how cool is this? I guess a selfie would be out of the question?"

"Maybe later, Paul. Listen, who can we trust here?" Hunter asks.

"Well, me, the President and his closest aides, a few other analysts for sure."

"Okay. Here's our problem. We have the medication that can fight this virus, but hospitals are afraid to administer it, for fear of reprisal, like lawsuits. We really need this to come from the government, for them to issue it under the guise of an antidote they have developed. This way, it can be distributed quickly by the military and government agencies, and the World Health Organization. We have some with us and other Anunnaki craft can drop it off wherever they need it. We will also give the governments across the world the formula to make large batches of it. We need to act fast before more lives are lost."

"What can I do?" Johnston asks.

"Speak to whoever you spoke to, to get the President to believe the Anunnaki are on our side," Jo adds. "We need to ensure this goes through the correct hands and isn't stopped by someone collaborating with the Nezulli."

"No problem. Gloria, she is very persuasive. I will give her a call, see if we can get the ball rolling on this. Listen, there are reports of the invader aircraft falling out of the sky or exploding, lots of them. Not sure if it's your virus code or not, Hunter, but it sure sounds like it's starting to work." Johnston leaves the room to call the Attorney General.

"We will leave the antidote and formula files with Mr. Johnston," Jaii tells them, "but we must go and assist my crew with their mission. The Nezulli will send back-up fighters soon. Our work must continue."

#

Brennan had weighed up his options. Leaving the bunker was a huge risk. He could catch the virus but probably survive. He was fit and healthy, so he knew his chances were better than those with underlying medical issues. If he stayed in the bunker, the government could easily arrest and detain him, he would have no chance. This was his best option, get out, get away and hope the rest of the plan is carried out accordingly. He turns off his cell phone and drives his sedan up the freeway, heading to a mountain range he knows well, stopping only for supplies. He often visited a cabin in the area, on hiking trips or on government business. With the state of chaos in the US, he figures it would be a good place to hide out. It was only used by colleagues at the agency, usually as a place to have a few days rest and was owned by the government. He didn't know which department, but his team had use of it. It had been used as a safe house, only known to those who had access.

Brennan drives through several military roadblocks at intersections. They are controlling the movement of people, trying to keep the public in order. Brennan slips through with his agency ID, given the priority lane to go around the general public. He is making good time. He leaves the freeway and takes the small road leading to Pine Valley. After another half hour of driving on dust tracks and winding mountain roads, he arrives at the little cabin. Hidden by trees and well away from the road, it is the perfect hideout. There are no other cabins for miles and few people ventured up into the mountains this far, unless they knew the area. Brennan is off-grid but still had the Nezulli computer if he needed to get in touch with them. He has the satellite phone with him, but using it could alert the government to his whereabouts, so that was a last resort.

The little cabin is basically one room, with an outside composting toilet. No luxuries, somewhere to sit, somewhere to cook, somewhere to sleep. It has an open fire and a generator out the back for power. Brennan settles in for what could be a long few days until he can contact someone to find out if the plan was still in operation.

Chapter 34.

Jo has gotten the hang of flying the Anunnaki craft and is beginning to enjoy being in control. She still feels a little rough from her illness, but having something to do keeps her mind off the pain and focused on the mission. Under Jaii's instructions, she has mastered the controls, which are much simpler than flying a traditional plane. She has over twenty flying hours in a Cessna, so she was quite competent in the air.

Her job on the reservation involved covering a huge area, so they arranged flying lessons for her and her colleagues. They leased a small plane which they used for search and rescue mostly, as well as carrying medical supplies and personnel to outlying areas. Now, she is in control of a vehicle that could go faster than any known human-built aircraft. Hunter, on the other hand, is idle. Jaii had given him control of the weapons, but until they engaged in a firefight, he had very little to do. He sits next to Jo, swiveling around to face the right-hand side of the craft, which had a bank of screens showing the view around the whole craft from cameras built into the body of the craft. Jo has a dome window to look out and a bank of screens just below it. If needed, the seat could go down and the glass dome shield would come up and she could fly using the screens for view. Jaii has a seat behind her facing the left-hand side, also with a bank of screens and an array of instruments for communication and navigation.

Jaii instructs Jo to head north, where some of his crew have encountered Nezulli craft. Both she and Hunter are excited by the thought of getting stuck in, but Jo is nervous. She could fly okay, but she has never been in a dog-fight with another craft, she doesn't know if her judgment and reactions are up to it.

"What happens if we take a hit?" she asks Jaii.

"We are pretty well protected and we have a magnetic shield that I can activate. It will give us a little more protection but uses a lot of energy, so it will only be used in an emergency. I have programmed the craft to react to incoming objects, so you may feel the system take control briefly, to turn or flip the craft. Don't be alarmed. This will only be for a few seconds, then you will regain full control. Hunter, when we engage the Nezulli, fire at will. There are two different weapons. On your right is the laser firing control, and the left controller is the pulse weapon. This fires a series of pulsating light waves, which, if it reaches its target, can disable electronics and weapons. Again, this takes a lot of our energy, which we must conserve to get the craft back to base, so don't overdo it."

Within a few further minutes, they reach the area of the reported engagement. Jo can see Anunnaki and Nezulli craft in the distance. One of the screens in front of here shows the Anunnaki craft with green outlines and the Nezulli with red outlines, to easily identify them. Hunter and Jaii both have the same images on their screens. Hunter watches the screens from all sides of the craft. He sees a small red mark, coming at them from behind, growing larger by the second.

"Incoming at our six o'clock," he tells Jo. She reacts by turning the craft sharply ninety degrees to the right, then straight up to thirty thousand feet and levels off.

"Bogey still on our tail," Hunter tells her, "engaging." He moves the laser weapon control arm, lining it up with the incoming craft. He presses the button, and the weapon fires a series of laser beams at the craft. The Nezulli craft weaves left and right as it avoids the lasers, still gaining ground. Jo takes evasive action, turning and flipping the craft as the Nezulli fighter opens fire with a laser. Hunter can hear the beams whizzing past them, some hitting the protective field and dispersing with a fizzling sound. Hunter opens up again, with continuous fire, striking the Nezulli fighter several times. Smoke billows out of its engine, but it keeps coming at them. As it comes closer and flies over them, Hunter fires into the belly of the craft, causing a fire to break out. The Nezulli craft begins to spin and lose altitude. Before it reaches cloud level, the craft explodes into thousands of pieces, leaving only a cloud of smoke where it was and a rainfall of metal particles.

"Great work, Hunter," Jo shouts over her shoulder, "that was some scary shit."

"There will be many more," Jaii adds, "we must be cautious."

"The underside of their craft seems to be its weakness. If we engage again, try to get under their craft, I will aim for its undercarriage," Hunter explains. They are joined by several more Anunnaki craft, just as a fleet of four Nezulli craft come into view for attack. Jaii speaks in his communications headset.

"Get ready, incoming enemy, aim for the underside of their craft. Break formation." The crafts break away and head in different directions. The Nezulli craft gives chase and the dogfight begins. Jo controls the craft like a professional, taking it down to the ridges and valleys of the desert, weaving through openings and over peaks, then braking hard to allow the Nezulli craft to go above her, so Hunter can take his shot. Another one hurtles to the ground, exploding into a fireball. The battle continues for another hour, with the Anunnaki sustaining three casualties. Jaii reckons the Nezulli downed craft was eleven, Hunter thinks more like twenty. No more Nezulli come at them, so they make their way back to base to refuel and rest.

#

Paul Johnston is asked to meet the presidential aides in one of the interview rooms in the bunker beneath the Pentagon.

"How is your investigation going?" Paul asks.

"We are sure we know who is involved, maybe not everyone, but certainly some key players," one of the aides tells him.

"Who is it?"

"General Humphries for certain and your boss, Bernard Aimes. There is someone else in the CIA, but we are not sure who. Humphries has been looking closely at the Los Alamos reserves, checking movements in and out. He has sent a unit there, which appears an odd thing to do, given the push on military resources right now."

"What's the plan, will you have them arrested?" Johnston asks.

"Soon, yes. We want to be sure, and we want to see their reactions when questioned. We would like you to view these meetings from behind the glass, tell us if you think they are truthful or not." The aide indicated to the two-way mirror, where Johnston could observe from.

"Sure, happy to help. These guys are doing a great injustice to their country, I won't allow that to happen." The aides and Johnston leave the room. Johnston goes in the next door, leading to the space behind the two-way mirror. A couple of minutes later, Aimes is lead into the interview room, flanked by two US marines and followed by two of the aides. Aimes is directed to sit facing the mirror and the aides sit opposite him.

"Tell me about your relationship with General Humphries?" one aide asks.

"Relationship? Well, it's a colleague relationship. He is my senior, he gives the orders and I carry them out. That's it. Why?"

"How long have you known General Humphries?"

"I guess about ten years or so. What's this all about? You have taken me from my work when all hands are needed on deck. I demand to know what this is in relation to?"

"I'm sorry, we can't divulge that information at this time," the other aide tells him, "but it is on the orders of the President, so if you would like to make a formal complaint, I will let the President know your concerns."

"No," Aimes relents, "it's fine, just a bit stressed at the minute, what with all this alien virus stuff going on."

"Have you had any contact with the alien invaders?"

"What! Hell, no, what are you asking? This is ridiculous."

"Has General Humphries had any contact with the alien invaders?"

"No, of course not," Aimes tells them, "why would he have contact with the enemy?" Aimes is visibly disturbed by the question and getting beads of sweat on his forehead.

"You tell me," one of the aides asks. "You look a little warm, are you okay?"

"I'm fine, it's just warm in here. Listen, I don't know why you're asking me questions about the General, go ask him. I need to get back to work."

"Okay, you're free to go," one aide tells him. Aimes gets up and is escorted out by the two marines. Johnston joins the aides in the interview room.

"Lies," he tells the aides. "He knows the General has contact with the invaders. Aimes might not have spoken to them himself, but he knows the General has. They're both in on it." The aides are happy with the results.

"Next step is to get a warrant and have the police make arrests," one aide tells Johnston. "We need to do it all by the book, make sure they don't get off on a technicality." They go off to round up the personnel and paperwork they need to carry out arrests. Johnston returns to his work station, watching Aimes as he nervously walks around the command room, trying to catch the eye of the General, to notify him of a possible problem. The General is in his office, head down reading reports, oblivious to Aimes's predicament.

#

Jo lands the craft on the end of a line of returning fighters in the Anunnaki base in the mountain. Jo, Hunter and Jaii exit the craft and head to Jaii's office. He is handed a report, which he reads as he walks to the office.

"Good news, my friends," he explains, holding up the report. "Nezulli craft are self-destructing and we now know that the command craft is heading closer to Earth, presumably to be able to communicate and command the invasion, ready to land when they have finished the first phase. This is good for us. It leaves their command vessel exposed."

"Can we point a missile at it and blast it off out into space?" Hunter asks.

"Not quite. It will have strong defenses, but it could still be breached. It is the link between the fighter craft and the supply base on the moon. If it can be taken down, the others will follow. They will not be captured. For us, this is a good position," Jaii explains.

"What's our next move?" Jo asks. Jaii looks more serious than usual.

"We go after Vok."

Chapter 35.

Government Bunker
Nevada Desert.
Candice Peterson and her operatives trawl through data on government networks and telephone records. They are looking for anything to indicate where Brennan has gone. He has covered his tracks well.

"Mam," an operative speaks, "we have some data on a safe house used by the agency. It looks like Brennan checked the records for it earlier today, presumably to see if it was occupied. It's up in the mountains, some eighty or so clicks from here."

"Let me know when you have all the data, we need to get out of here and start covering some mileage." The operatives study their screens, making notes and entering information into their tablets.

#

Jaii looks at a large computer screen on the wall in his office. He touches it, swiping data and maps left and right onto a smaller screen on either side. On the main screen, he zooms out to show the Earth from a satellite camera feed.

"We know the Nezulli command craft will be within range anytime now. We need to locate it before they bring the rest of their fleet and land. They will be able to disable all your missiles and nuclear armaments once they are within range. Earth will not be able to launch a counter-attack," Jaii explains.

"Then we need to tell the government to get ready to strike now," Jo adds.

"We will monitor the movement of the Nezulli and locate the command craft," Jaii replies. "When we have that information, then we will know what the right thing to do is." In the bottom left-hand corner of one of the screens on the wall is a news feed from CNN. It catches Hunter's attention.

"Jaii, can you enlarge that feed and turn the sound on," he asks. Jaii brings the feed up full screen and enables the audio.

Newsreader: We are getting reports that many of the alien attack aircraft are beginning to explode in mid-air or simply fall to the ground and explode on impact. Sources say they have not been shot down by military aircraft or surface-to-air missiles, they are simply failing…

"It's working," Hunter announces, delighted with himself. "The computer virus is working its way through their system. It might all be over soon."

"Vok will step up his assault now. He will have no choice but to send in the whole fleet and hope they don't start to explode before he carries out his plan," Jaii replies.

#

Johnston watches from his work station as two presidential aides and two US Marines enter General Humphries office. He can't see the General through the glass in the door, but he hears the distinctive Southern drawl of the General raising his voice in anger. What sounds like a scuffle taking place is followed by the dull thud of a body hitting the floor. Thirty seconds later, the General is marched out of his office by the two marines, with his hands cuffed behind his back. The General looks straight ahead as he follows one of the aides across the floor and out of the command room. Everyone in the room watches. The room falls silent. As soon as he is gone, the room breaks out into chatter, as the staff discusses what could be going on, speculating. Johnston looks around for Aimes. He catches a glimpse of him, slipping out another exit. Johnston gets up and follows him, staying well back, observing. Aimes takes a corridor to the accommodation area, continuing past long rows of yellow doors. He walks hurriedly, looking around as he enters one of the doors. Johnston slows and waits at the corner of the corridor. It must be Aimes's living quarters, he thinks. Johnston considers what he should do. Go back and tell the aides, but Aimes could leave before they get here. Stay and watch if he leaves, and follow him, maybe. He stands on the corner for a minute, then moves closer to the door. He decides to confront Aimes and take him back to the aides and marines, by force if he has to. Johnston cautiously approaches the door, putting his ear to it to listen for the sounds of packing. He hears none. Still, with his ear to the door, he hears a distinctive double click. A sound he is familiar with. The sound of the trigger of a revolver being brought back and locked into firing position.

#

Peterson and her team, wearing their government-issue N95 respirator masks, roar up the freeway, slowing only to show their ID's to military roadblock personnel. This is their best lead, and even better for them, it is secluded. They could carry out their task without anyone knowing they had been there. The day is hot and dry and the roads are clear. People are either staying at home to avoid contamination or being turned back at the roadblocks. Presumably many were dying or dead already. The only traffic the CIA team encounter is military trucks, carrying personnel or supplies. They drive through small roadside towns, deserted. Gas stations closed due to a lack of fuel. America is in lock-down.

Peterson sits in the back of the government SUV, with her two operatives in the front. She takes a few minutes to close her eyes and rest. She finds it hard to turn off work, to stop thinking and planning. She is a workaholic. She rarely dated and preferred to stay late at the office than attend parties or functions. The agency is her whole life. She is desperate to get to the directorship of the CIA, at any cost. She thought about how her life would change after she had been given the position. She is a firm believer in the scheme with the General.

She trusted him and his plans. But she had some nagging doubts about the future. The world would be so different. People would be different, it could never return to the same condition. People are now aware that we are not alone in the universe. That there are other species that could come at any time and destroy us. How would this affect humanity? Would her new role be more challenging, would she face a new type of threat, of terrorism from beyond as well as from within? She reflects on her decision to not have kids, to focus solely on her career. Had she made the right decision? She would be the end of the line. She didn't feel the world was right for bringing kids into, but she wondered if it would be after all this. Had she left it too late? There are lots of cases of women in their fifties, having IVF or conceiving naturally. Why was she even thinking about this? Maybe, she thought, what she really wanted wasn't what she thought. The SUV jolted as it left the freeway and took the secondary road towards Pine Valley. It wakes Peterson out of her half-sleep. She looks out the window, through the dust thrown up by the vehicle. This part of the country is beautiful, she thought. It is a mix of vast flat desert, with high mountains to the north, green with forests and vegetation. The very highest peaks have small patches of snow on them, so different from the dry arid flatlands.

"ETA about thirty minutes, Mam," the operative in the passenger seat tells Peterson. She nods. She takes her firearm from her shoulder holster and checks the safety is on. She pops the magazine out, checking that she has a full clip. She clicks it back in hard, checked the safety switch again, then clips it back into the holster under her jacket.

#

Hunter anxiously paces the floor of Jaii's office.

"Let's get back out there and kick some Nezulli ass," he tells them. Jo sits in the seat opposite Jaii, at his desk. She is tired but also wants to get back to the fight. She feels like they are achieving something by fighting. It had tangible results, something she could see and hear, something that made her feel useful.

"How long do you think we have until the Nezulli go full-on invasion?" Jo asks Jaii.

"Within the next couple of hours, I would imagine. They will come in fast with full force. Every craft they can enable will be sent, their personnel carriers will drop off their military to take control across your planet. They will kill anyone who does not cooperate or who is of no use to their mission. Let's hope Hunter's computer virus takes full effect before they get to that stage."

"Then the sooner we get out there the better," Hunter replies. The computer virus is working, although slower than we thought. The medication is in the hands of the government, they should be able to distribute it soon. You sent each nation's leaders the formula to recreate the meds. So now, all that's left to do is defend ourselves, before they get a foothold on Earth." A member of Jaii's team knocks on the door and enters. He hands Jaii a note.

"They have located the Nezulli command craft. It is closing in."

#

Johnston listens at Aimes door. He is sure Aimes is armed.

"Aimes, it's Johnston," he calls through the door, "do you have a minute? Can I talk to you, please?" Silence.

"Aimes?" he tries again. Silence.

"Listen, Aimes, I'm coming in. Okay? I'm not armed, I just want to talk." Johnston stays with his back to the wall, grabbing the door handle with his right hand and slowly opening the door. When it is open a few inches, he pushes it quickly with his hand, to fully open it. He darts his head around the door and back to the wall again, to see where Aimes is. Johnston can see him, sitting at the table, profile to the door, facing the wall. He darts his head around again.

"Aimes, can I come in?" No reply. Johnston looks again. Aimes has a revolver in his right hand, resting it on the table. Johnston steps out behind the wall, into the doorway. Aimes raises the gun.

#

The black government SUV slows to a crawl.

"Five hundred yards on the right, Mam."

"Disembark here," Peterson replies. They pull over on the dirt track. All three draw their weapons, holding them two-handed in front of them, as they skirt their way up to the cabin, using the brush as cover. Peterson leads. Before the corner of the cabin, they stop and crouch down. Using hand signals, she indicates for one operative to circle around to cover the back. She signals for the other to get into position behind the sedan parked at the front to give her cover fire. She will go in the front. She moves forward, crouching below the cabin window, then stands with her back to the log wall, next to the door, her weapon raised in front of her, as she prepares to kick the door in. She nods to the operative behind the vehicle, indicating she is ready. She quickly turns, faces the door, and kicks it in.

#

Paul Johnston stands in the open doorway of Bernard Aimes's quarters. Aimes raises his weapon. Johnston instinctively goes for his gun, feeling the area where it should be. He is not armed.

"Wait," Johnston shouts as Aimes puts the barrel of the gun under his chin, tilting his head back. Johnston moves forward toward Aimes. The shot rings out, echoing through the long corridors. Johnston stops, his ears ringing, as bits of flesh, brain and bloody spatter cover the opposite wall, Aimes bed, and Johnston's face. The force of the shot knocks Aimes off the chair onto his back, a pool of blood forming on the green carpet from the missing back of his head.

#

The cabin door cracks and buckles with the force of Petersons kick. She quickly steps into the cabin with arms locked straight, her weapon pointing in all directions, looking for its target. The second operative bursts through the rear door. Inside, Brennan jumps up from his bed, searching the room for his weapon, which is on the bedside stand. He reaches for it.

"Don't to it, Brennan," Peterson calls out. The third operative comes in behind Peterson. Brennan raises his hands. Peterson holds her weapon out in front of her, taking aim at his chest. Brennan's mind races, working out his options. Decision made. He dives to his right for his weapon. He grabs it just as Peterson opens fire. He returns a shot, before slumping to the ground. Peterson makes the kill shot. Her two operatives finish Brennan at close range with several shots for good measure. They turn to see Peterson holding her stomach, blood trickling through her fingers. She looks at them with a look of horror. She knows it's bad. She knows the nearest medical help is an hour away. One of the operatives guides her to a chair. He applies pressure to the wound, holding a kitchen towel over it. She looks pale, the color leaving her face. She knew she hadn't got long. She thought of all the things she could have achieved, all the things she had done and then, all the things she should have done. Her eyesight is clouding over, her breathing heavy and strained. The operative holds her hand. She liked it. She didn't feel so alone. She let out a final rattling breath. The operative checked her pulse, then closed her eyes.

#

Johnston stands in Aimes's room, looking down at what remains of Aimes's head. Marine guards come running along the corridor, weapons pointing forward. They get to the doorway and call Johnston out. He backs out, hands raised. The President's aides come next. They peer into the room at the devastation.

"I guess that answers that," one of them directs to Johnston. Johnston just nods and drops his hands. He walks slowly past the marines and aides, head down, heading back to the command center. He didn't like Aimes much, and he felt he was a traitor to his country. But he didn't want or expect him to take his own life. It was not the result he had hoped for, but it was done. There was nothing he could do about it. He had to concentrate on the bigger picture.

Johnston's cell phone rang.

"Johnston, it's Hunter. Got some updates for you. How's it going at your end?"

"Humphries is under arrest. Aimes is dead."

"Wow, things are moving fast there. The government needs to arm and reposition its military satellites. The Nezulli command craft is heading our way. You have to ensure they are ready to defend. Don't allow the main Nezulli fleet to land. They are coming in full force. This is the big one. I'm sending you the coordinates."

"I got it. The President is putting new people in place, people he can trust, people close to him. They will take charge of the satellites. I'll contact them now, get things moving." He hangs up. Hunter turns to Jaii and Jo.

"Right, let's get back in the air, see if we can take these nasties down," he tells them.

Chapter 36.

Nezulli Command Craft

The Nezulli command craft heads towards Earth, followed closely by the bulk of their attack craft. The fleet has thousands of craft, ready to go into battle.

"We will be in position shortly, Commander," Taur informs him. Vok just nods, knowing his plan is still on track. Once he stations the command craft, the second phase of the attack can begin. Once they take full control of humans, he can switch to a landing vessel and command his soldiers from a base on Earth. His command craft will remain in Earth's orbit, prepared to move on to the next mission once they had drained Earth of the resources they required.

The command craft begins to slow as it comes close to its optimal position. From this position, it can communicate effectively with its fleet and remain ready to leave in a hurry if required. Vok's crew check communications with the remaining first phase Earth fleet and with the second wave of craft following the command craft.

Communications through human satellite links could be intercepted by Earth's military. They need to use their own system again.

"Have our engineers found the issue with our systems, I need a progress report," Vok tells Taur.

"No, Commander, the system is still affected. It will take much longer than we anticipated."

"As soon as it is safe to do so, reconnect and carry out facilities checks." The command craft moves into its final position.

#

Hunter, Jo and Jaii join the Anunnaki crew as they prepare to take to the air again. They take their positions in the craft and check their communications and instruments. Within minutes, they join the long stream of Anunnaki fighter craft, as they flow along the tunnel and out of the mountainside, shooting upwards at speed. Jaii's fleet has under a thousand craft, much smaller numbers than the Nezulli, but they are prepared to fight to the death. They are outnumbered and outgunned. But they have the backing now of the military forces on Earth.

"Take us to thirty-five thousand feet, Jo, then stop. I will try to locate the exact position of Vok's craft," Jaii tells her. Jo does as requested, leveling off and remaining stationary, whilst Jaii operates some complicated-looking instruments on the panel in front of him. The other Anunnaki craft disperse to cover a wider area, heading in all directions, ready for conflict.

"Okay, I have a lock on the command fleet. Hunter, make a note of these coordinates and pass them to Johnston. Your military will need them for the missile attacks. Hunter calls Johnston and gives him the coordinates.

"Now what?" Jo asks.

"We wait," Jaii replies.

Chapter 37.

The command room in the Pentagon bunker is a flurry of activity. Operators are busy repositioning their missile satellites. The large video wall at the end of the room shows activity and data for satellite positions. The coordinates for the Nezulli command craft are sent to other national leaders and their military. Any armed satellites are to set the coordinates for a joint missile strike. Johnston watches the activity and checks his signal feeds.

The Nezulli has not used the US satellites for some time. They are going quiet. This could be the sign of an imminent final attack. Hunter's code had only been partly successful. The Nezulli must have cleaned their system and were preparing to reinstate it for the big push.

The President is led into the command room, along with his new General and staff members. President Murray will give the order to fire the US missiles, at the same time as the other world leaders. It was a concerted effort.

#

Vok is ready. His craft is in position, but he still couldn't use his supercomputer. His only choice is to use satellite communications.

#

President Murray watches a clock with a ten-second countdown in the corner of the video wall. The same digital clock is synchronized in all the other world leader's command centers.

Beijing, Moscow, London, Tokyo. They all had missiles in space. The countdown begins, nine, eight, seven. The room falls silent. Everyone knew what was resting on this, what the option was if they failed, six, five, four. Johnston stands up at his work station, watching the seconds tick away. Three, two, one. President Murray presses the button. Thin red lines grow out of a digital image of satellites on the video wall. The lines head away from Earth to a single point in space.

#

Vok gives the order for the second phase to begin. Thousands of his craft head towards Earth.

"Commander. We have incoming missiles on a trajectory with our command craft," Taur reports.

"Defenses?" Vok asks.

"We have engaged the outer shield, but we do not know the magnitude of the incoming missiles. They appear to have been launched from space. Satellites I suspect."

"Time to impact?"

"Estimated in ten Earth seconds, Commander." Vok looks at the screen showing lines moving in their direction.

"Take evasive action."

"It won't be enough, Commander, they are coming from a number of directions."

"Prepare to board the secondary craft in the event of defenses breached. Essential crew only." A few seconds later and the command craft is violently rocked by an explosion, then another. There are a few seconds before another series of blasts rocks the craft, knocking Vok and some of his crew to the floor.

"Damage report," Vok asks his crew.

"Defenses are breached, Commander, we are vulnerable to further missile strikes." Outside the craft, Vok's defense craft are weaving in and out in the distance, attempting to take a strike by the missiles to save the command craft. Several are successful, but more missiles get through. The craft is rocked again. In the distance, his fleet is beginning to explode, one after another, sending debris into space.

"We will take the secondary craft and command the attack from there," Vok announces. He, Taur and two crew leave the command control room and head along a corridor and down steps to a smaller craft. They enter the craft and the doors beneath it open. They release a docking arm and the craft leaves the command craft from underneath. The pilot heads out into space, away from the incoming missiles. Vok is at a console, with monitors and instruments, watching the attack on his command craft. He didn't expect these primitive humans to have such firepower. He thinks he may have underestimated them. His second wave of craft are on their way to Earth, but beginning to self-destruct. Vok watches as missiles continue to breach the command craft shield. Then, the craft blows up in a series of nuclear explosions. The craft blasts into millions of pieces of debris, along with the remaining crew members.

#

A cheer goes up in the Pentagon bunker control room, as reports come in of a huge nuclear explosion in space. Monitoring instruments on satellites pick up the vibration from the explosion. People congratulate each other. The President sits at the end of the conference table, smiling. On the video wall, other world leaders are celebrating. Paul Johnston stands, pleased that the mission was successful. But his and other's fears soon return. Satellite observers report a huge fleet of incoming craft still approaching. The attack is still proceeding.

#

Jaii watches his screens as data comes in.

"The Nezulli command craft has been breached," he tells the others, "but the invasion is still coming."

"Do you think Vok was destroyed," Hunter asks.

"We should assume he has escaped and is orchestrating the invasion from another craft."

"Should we go after him?" Hunter asks.

"He will come to us," Jaii tells him. "He will want to find me and kill me. He doesn't have natural feelings, but he does like to kill in person when he can. He will want to see my face as he kills me."

"Great, so we just sit here and wait," Jo adds impatiently.

"No, when the Nezulli's second wave of fighters gets here, we take out as many as we can," Jaii replies.

"That's more like it," Jo tells him. Hunter checks his weapons and controls, making sure everything is working. He scans the monitors, looking for any sign of enemy fighters. Before long, Jaii's instruments pick up a wave of activity heading inbound from space.

"This is it," he tells Jo and Hunter, "get ready."

#

Vok tells his pilot to follow the invading craft.

"With respect, Commander, we should remain at a safe distance," Taur tells him. "We must command from safety to ensure our fighters carry out their duties and to monitor losses. Going to the battle could endanger our plans."

"I want to see Jaii die. He is behind much of this planet's defenses. He has brought them together to fight us. Our allies on Earth are weak and useless. I want to take away Jaii's life myself. Take us down there. Find out where he is and head to him. That's an order." The crew follow orders and turn around and head towards Earth.

#

Jo takes control of the craft and gives chase to a group of Nezulli craft. She tries to get below them, to give Hunter the shot at the belly of the craft, it's the weakest point. She struggles to keep up with them. Other Anunnaki craft join the chase, trying to herd the Nezulli towards Anunnaki craft. Laser weapons shoot across the skies as the dog-fights continue. Several Anunnaki craft are shot down or blown up. The Nezulli lose a few of theirs to the Anunnaki weapons. Hunter chooses his targets carefully, waiting as long as possible to get them in close range, for less chance of missing. His aim wasn't the best, but he was tactical.

#

Vok's craft enters the atmosphere and his navigator reports the location of Jaii. They turn and head towards his location, somewhere over Arizona. They are to the rear of the attack fleet. Watching the entry into Earth's atmosphere, Vok sees some of his fleet falls from the sky, seemingly powerless to do anything about it. Others ahead of them explode into a ball of flames. He knows it is the computer virus, but all he can do is hope his team can solve the problem before he lost many more. His team are experts in quantum computing, but they would have to reverse engineer the code to find a solution. Something they didn't have time for. The craft Vok and his small team from the command craft are in, had remained isolated from the supercomputer as soon as the issue was reported. They are safe from the effects of the virus. Vok watches the craft around him destruct. His pilot skillfully navigates around the debris left behind. They follow the coordinates towards Jaii's location.

Chapter 38.

Jo is very much at home behind the controls of an aircraft. The Anunnaki craft is the easiest aircraft she has ever flown. She didn't want to admit it to herself, but she was quite enjoying the excitement of it all. Her job did have some excitement occasionally. But for the most part, it was mundane. Routine. Catch up on paperwork, check gun licenses, drive the set routes to check on people and property, enforce any laws that needed enforcing and very rarely, lock someone up for a crime. She enjoyed the travel around the reservation and particularly if they needed to use the Cessna. Her involvement with Hunter has given her a new outlook, even in the face of adversity, she feels she is invincible, stronger. She is learning new things, finding new purpose, evolving. She doesn't know what the future held, if they had one after this, but she did know she would make some changes, prioritize her life and her work differently.

Hunter holds the weapons controls tightly, waiting to engage. They couldn't see any enemy fighters within range. The sky is clear all around them. Jo remains above cloud cover, where visibility is best. She circles an area of about sixty square miles, staying close to the Anunnaki base, just in case they need to return quickly. She feels more confident knowing there was somewhere to hide. Jaii scans the tracker system.

"Incoming at great speed, northwest at an altitude of seventy-five thousand feet and closing fast," he tells them.

Hunter and Jo check their monitors. They see the dot heading down the screen toward them.

"Take evasive action when within range," Jaii tells Jo, "try to get Hunter a good shot." Jo slows with the incoming craft approaching from the rear.

Vok watches his screens as the tracker indicator shows they are closing in on Jaii's craft.

"Open satellite comms and patch me through to the target craft," Vok tells his pilot. Vok puts a comms unit in his ear.

"Jaii. You just don't know when to quit, do you? You should be dead many times over. This time, it will happen." Jaii listens to the comms.

"I wiped out most of your civilization, you had a lucky escape, unlike your family. They suffered greatly." Jaii is visibly disturbed.

"Don't reply, Jaii," Jo tells him, "don't give him the satisfaction of upsetting you. It's a ploy. He's trying to mess with your head so you make the wrong decisions. Ignore him."

"I know, but it still makes me feel something I have only felt when he took my family. I want revenge."

"Then let's try to take this bastard down," Hunter adds. Vok continues to taunt Jaii on comms as they approach the craft. Vok's pilot sees Jaii's craft and heads directly for it. Jo speeds up with the craft behind her. Vok's craft fires lasers as Jo swings left, right, up and down, avoiding the beams. Jaii deploys the shield to protect against heat seekers and sonic blasters. He knows his craft is inferior to the Nezulli's, but they have to try to defend themselves. Jaii calls some of his support craft back to his location, to help defend against Vok. Every member of his team wants to come, to get the chance to destroy Vok, but Jaii tells the others their missions are just as important and to continue. Within twenty seconds, four of the Anunnaki craft can be seen pursuing Vok's craft on the monitors. Jo continues on, dropping into cloud cover, to allow her to go slow and low, get Vok in front of her so Hunter can take a shot as they pass over. But with a tracker, she knows the Nezulli will be able to see her maneuvers. The Nezulli support craft fall in behind the Anunnaki and begin to open fire. Two Anunnaki craft crash to the ground in flames. The others manage to evade the fire and enter the clouds. They carry out the same maneuver as Jo has planned, letting the support craft fly over them, then they open fire, taking out two straight away. Several miles further ahead, Jo slows as Voks craft approaches at speed and flying over before it can adjust its trajectory. Hunter has watched it on his screen, unable to see it through the clouds, but he takes his best guess and opens fire at the belly of the craft. He hits it with at least one shot. The craft has smoke billowing from it, but it is still mobile and shoots off past them at great speed.

"I think that was a hit," Jo tells him.

"Maybe, but she's still flying and likely to be heading back our way." Jaii checks his screens.

"Yes, they are turning back, prepare."

"Is there anything else we can do?" Jo asks Jaii. "These guys can outrun and outgun us."

"Keep a calm head and be ready. They are artificial intelligence, you have human emotion. Whilst this can hinder you, I believe it also gives you an advantage."

"Advantage," Hunter adds, "what advantage?"

"You, like I, feel things. We understand emotions. The adrenalin and electrical pulses running through your body right now are what gives you that advantage. The Nezulli are programmed to follow a pattern or sequence of events. They can only respond with programmed scenarios. You can make judgments based on emotion, feelings, a sense, a hunch, things that you can't explain, but just makes sense. You will feel when it is right to evade or chase, when to fire or to hold on until it feels right."

"I sure hope you know what you're talking about, Jaii. Otherwise, we are eating dust," Hunter replies. Jaii continues to watch the screens. Vok's craft comes into vision on the screen, lasers firing. Jo makes a steep climb, the Nezulli craft follows, then she stops and drops backward towards earth in reverse. As she drops past Vok's craft she spins the craft one hundred and eighty degrees on the horizontal to allow Hunter to take another shot. He opens fire into the underneath of the craft. Another hit. Vok's craft continues to climb. Jo slows down and levels off above the clouds.

Vok's pilot reports.

"Two direct hits, Commander. Our craft is showing signs of damage. Our proton particle accelerator computer is malfunctioning, as is our defensive shield."

"Okay. Take us to this planet's outer atmosphere so we can assess the situation." The pilot hits the hyper-drive and they shoot up to the outer layer.

"Where are they," Jo asks, exhilarated.

"They are not in our locale. They may be regrouping," Jaii replies. "I must confirm the situation with my crew, they will give me a report on the situation at ground level." Jaii gets on his communications system and talks to his team of fighters. He writes down information, gathering data from his crew.

"My team report Nezulli craft are exploding or falling to the ground by the thousands, without being shot down. They are self-destructing. Vok will not have the capacity to carry out his invasion without the ground teams to orchestrate it. He is still out there, but he has a much smaller fleet than he started with, and that is diminishing by the minute."

"What do we do," Jo asks, "go after him or what?"

"No. As much as I want to see him destroyed, it is not worth your lives for my satisfaction. You have done enough. You have defended your people, but Vok is my problem for another time."

"He's all our problem if he comes back," Hunter adds.

"Let us return to our base and take stock of the situation. We can confirm the numbers of casualties from the virus. If the governments have moved quickly, they should begin to control the effects of the virus." Jo sets a course for the Anunnaki base in the mountains to the north end of the Arizona reservation. They follow returning fighters as they all make their way back to base.

#

Vok and his craft crew assess the damage.

"We are not able to continue, Commander. We should return to the moon base for repairs," the pilot confirms.

"Very well. Take us back. We must analyze the data regarding the invasion. The computer virus has taken out most of our fleet. I want to know how and why."

"Yes, Commander," Taur replies. "We will gather the data and report our losses. Should we resume a rebuild program on return to the supply base? We are low on personnel?"

"It will depend on the data. It will also take time. I will let you know in due course. I want to get Jaii. He is the reason for our failure. I will choose the time and place, but we must lure him to us, to our domain. We will destroy him on our terms. We will return to this planet in due course." The Nezulli craft and its few remaining support fighters set a course for the dark side of the moon.

#

Jaii, Hunter, and Jo return to Jaii's office. Jaii sits at the screens on the sidewall, looking at data. Hunter and Jo sit on the seats in front of Jaii's desk. They are both exhausted.

They didn't realize how tired they were due to the adrenalin, but now, as they relax, they both sit low and heavy, dazed by the amount of information they have processed, the amount of action and firefights they encountered.

Like soldiers returning from front line action, they just sit, quietly, looking into space. Looking at nothing, seeing nothing, just glad to have survived, to be there, nothing else.

"We have taken quite a lot of losses. My team is greatly reduced," Jaii tells them, still looking at the screens. "But the Nezulli have had a greater loss, in percentage terms. I do not believe they will continue with their invasion with such low numbers. This is one fight that the Nezulli underestimated. They may return, but they would have to rebuild their resources and personnel to enable another invasion. This is just my assessment, you understand, based on my data. I could be wrong and they could strike again immediately."

"Great," Hunter replies, jolted out of his trance by the sound of Jaii's voice. "Sounded good there for a few seconds. Do you think he would attempt another attack straight away, with much lower numbers, based on his history and based on his current knowledge of our military resources and resilience?"

"In that context, no. I believe he will want to build a stronger, bigger fighting force. But when he does, when they return in the future, be very aware, they will not come to enslave, they will kill the population outright. They will learn from this battle. They are learning machines. The next time, they will destroy all human life, then take what they want. This is just the beginning." Jo and Hunter sit on the seats, looking at each other, thinking about what might be to come for them and the people of Earth. The outlook didn't look too promising.

Jaii finishes checking his data and turns and looks at Jo and Hunter. He smiles.

"One more thing, Hunter. I believe the time is right. I'm sorry for having taken your daughter from you that night, but it was important that she remain safe. Your daughter is a special person, very special."

"Can I see her now? What do you mean special, I know she's special, she's my daughter?"

"No, I mean, the future of your planet is reliant on her safety. You must protect her at all costs."

"I do, Jaii, she's my daughter. That's what fathers do."

"Yes, I understand, Jaii continues, "but Laura is one of a number of young humans that will lead the future of your planet and your species. We have given her, and others of her age, a gift."

"What kind of gift?" Jo asks, intrigued.

"She, like the others, will see the future. They know what is coming and what they can do to change the direction of your species. They are the ones who you must protect and who you must listen to when they tell you how to change, why to change, when to change. These are not the first we have given this knowledge to, some others were successful in their attempts to change your existence, improve your lives, move forward with technology, such as electricity and computing. Others, only long after they departed, did you realize their true genius, such as Mr. Tesla. We gave them the knowledge to move you forward. The next stage is the knowledge to help you survive. You didn't make the best use of our gifts and you have developed a destructive society."

"Maybe you should have told us that you had given us this knowledge," Hunter replies, "we might have understood and made better choices."

"We couldn't," Jaii tells him, "you were not ready to accept other living entities from outside your world. Many years back, they accepted our visitations as 'Gods'. This helped us greatly, as we could convince people to do our willing without resistance. These times were when you made some of your biggest leaps forward in beliefs, weaponry, tactical battles, mathematics and understanding of your solar system." Jaii stands and goes to the door.

"Now, you have more to learn. New ways, new ideas, new beliefs you would never have thought possible." Jaii opens the door and stands to the side. Hunter and Jo both look at the open doorway. From the side, Hunter's daughter steps into view. She stands for a few seconds, looking at her dad and the lady next to him. Laura is young, fresh-faced, no make-up. Her long dark brown hair is loose down her back. She smiles and runs to her dad. He grabs her in his arms and lifts her off her feet, swinging her around in a full circle. They hold each other for a few seconds more. He sets her down gently. They break their embrace and hold hands, just looking at each other. Hunter has tears in his eyes. Jo looks on, smiling. She has never seen Hunter look like this. His face is much different. He has lost his frown, his face looks younger, even with four days-worth of stubble. He has a new vibrancy to him. He towers over his daughter as they again hug each other. Laura is smiling, so happy to be reunited with her dad. Hunter realizes Jo is next to him and he hasn't introduced her.

"Laura, I'd like you to meet a friend of mine. This is Jo," he tells her. Laura turns to Jo and shakes her hand.

"Nice to meet you, Jo. A friend, eh? How close?" she asks Jo. Jo was a little taken back.

"Well, we have killed some bad guys together. That's quite close."

"It's lovely to meet you, Jo." Laura gave Jo a tight squeeze, hugging her around the waist. Jo is not sure what to do but cautiously hugs her back. Hunter watches, happy to see Laura safe and well. Laura releases Jo and turns and looks her dad up and down.

"Really dad. You're still wearing those awful boots," she says, looking down. Hunter looks down.

"These are a classic, sweetheart."

"Yeah right," Laura replies. "Listen, I don't know how much Jaii has told you, but there are some things you need to know. It's about the future of the planet and us. We don't have long. But we can change the path of destruction we are heading down. But we need your help." She looks at Jo and Hunter.

"It's no accident, Laura adds.

"What, sweetheart? What's no accident?"

"You two meeting." Hunter and Jo look at each other, confused. Jaii smiles and leaves the office, closing the door behind him.

"You're part of the plan. The plan for the future," Laura continues, "and it starts now. We have a lot to do and very little time." Laura walks to the screens on the wall, she brings up a map of San Francisco and points.

"And this is where it will start."

The End

Find out more

I hope you enjoy this novel. Please consider leaving a review.
Thank you. Arlo

Made in United States
Troutdale, OR
05/06/2025